U0077371

BEST
BOOKS

Simply Learning, Simply Best!

Simply Learning, Simply Best!

倍斯特出版事業有限公司
Best Publishing Ltd.

B咖日記

Smart俚語讓你英文B咖變A咖

有故事情節又聰明的英文學習方式
好用的英語俚語融入每天的情境

讓你按個讚 👍

第 **1** 個讚　蒐集現在最in的英語**熱門字彙**!

第 **2** 個讚　連貫情節的**對話日記**有趣好吸收!

第 **3** 個讚　**文化與用語**的歷史淵源大搜密!

He is a Zip!
他是一個拉鍊?

I don't want to be an Eye
Broccoli. 不想當眼球青花菜?

The team had Hard
Cheese yesterday.
團隊昨天硬起司?

• I can Kill Two Pigs
with One Bird this time!
這次可以一鳥二豬了?

♥ Know Your Onions.
知道你的洋蔥?

♥ She is an
Apple of my mind.
她是小蘋果?

對話 → 上班族必遇情節
單字 → 簡單實用小意思
日記 → 把心中的OS 寫出來
換句話說 → 更多道地表達方式
文化盒子 → 俚語的親朋好友與歷史精華串聯

▶ 答案請看後面。

Chris H. Radford ◎著

作者序
WORDS
FROM AUTHOR

僅以此書獻給我的好友及所有對英文俚語有興趣的朋友！

在對話當中使用英文俚語的時候，我之前從來沒有認真想過這些俚語的由來，或是其背後是否有怎樣的故事。一直到我念大學的時候，我有一位好友問了我為什麼這一個俚語在英文中是這樣說的。他還告訴我就像是成語多半都有其典故，那英文中俚語的特殊用法也應該會有其來源或是一些故事吧。當時的我只以搞笑、胡謅的解釋應對了過去，之後找了資料，我才發現真的像成語故事一般，許多俚語都有一些故事或是特殊的起源。

就跟成語故事一樣，了解俚語所發生的背景，或是故事，對於其應用及記憶是有相當大的幫助。然而俚語又是不斷的跟著時間在變化，一旦有一段時間沒有接觸，往往就會有跟不上的感覺。所以我在寫這一本書的時候，也學到了不少新的用法。我衷心的希望本書能對讀者有幫助，也感謝您和我一起學英文俚語！

Chris H. Radford

編者序
WORDS
FROM EDITOR

俚語拉近我們的距離

　　俚語是一個非正式的語言，通常用在一般的對話。每個俚語細探究竟都是一個文化的微縮歷史，有它的淵源的考察，與發展的興衰。每了解一個俚語就對文化多一分認識。通俗易懂、順口有生活化是它的特色。硬梆梆的正式用法有時比不上俚語親切可愛有個性。

一頭霧水嗎？不說你不知道

　　Dog my cats??? 狗我的貓，狗怎麼了我的貓貓?，這些字面上都是會的英文，組合一下後變成一個猜不出來的字。就是俚語有趣的地方，字面上的意思不是字面上的意思，真正的意思是它暗喻的意思或是因為時間而轉變成一個有點莫名其妙的意思。

俚語的今身與前身

　　配合菜鳥上班族Allen的職場與感情的奮鬥故事，讓俚語自然的出現在日常的對談中，讓使用更加熟悉。另外Allen's Murmur 告訴你這個俚語的前世今生、過往雲煙與至親好友。

　　那各位親愛的讀者，請一起跟著Allen烙俚語囉！

倍斯特編輯部

目錄
CONTENTS

02 Chapter

Summer 夏天

目錄
CONTENTS

03 Chapter
Fall 秋天

04 Chapter
Winter 冬天

01 Chapter

Spring 春天

Diary 3 月 05 日

Talk Turkey

打開天窗說亮
話及有話直
說。

Allen wants to talk about "turkey" with Vince, and now

they are in Vince's office.

Allen 要跟 Vince 談一下有關「火雞」的事,而現在他們正在

Vince 的辦公室裡。

對話 Dialogue

Allen: Hi, **chief**, you want to see me?

Vince: Yes, please come on in and have a seat.

Allen: Thanks, chief.

Vince: I want to talk about your **probation**. You have been doing a great job during this period and I am very satisfied with your work. I would like to inform you that you will be **transferred** to the regular **employee** starting from next month.

Allen: Wow, that's great. So, will I get a 5 percent raise that you promised before the probation?

Vince: Well, you know. Under at present **economical** whole worn out **environment**, every company tries to cut down the cost. Besides, I think you really like this job and…

Allen: Come on, chief. Let's talk turkey, okay?

Vince: Well, you'll get a 2 percent pay raise from the next month.

Allen: Well, that's better than nothing.

∷ 單字 Vocabulary

1. **chief** [tʃif] n 【口】老闆、老大；長官、領袖
   → Our new chief summoned me downstairs.
   我們的新長官把我叫到樓下去。

2. **probation** [pro`beʃən] n 試用期。
   → After an extension of three months probation period, he was sacked.
   再延長 3 個月的試用期之後，他被解雇了。

3. **transfer** [træns`fɚ] v 調動、轉換
   → Anthony was transferred from London to New York.
   Anthony 被從倫敦調職到紐約。

4. **employee** [ˌɛmplɔɪ`i] n 受雇者、雇員、員工
   → She is a temporary employee.
   她是一位臨時雇員。

5. **economical** [ˌikə`namɪkl] adj 實惠的；節約的
   → My new car is economical of fuel.
   我的新車耗油量小。

6. **environment** [ɪn`vaɪrənmənt] n 環境
   → We need a congenial working environment to increase production.
   我們需要一個舒適的工作環境來提高生產力。

✦✧ 翻譯 Translation

Allen: 嗨，老大，你找我嗎？

Vince: 沒錯，請進來坐。

Allen: 謝了，老大。

Vince: 我要談一下有關你的試用期的事。你在這一段期間表現很好，我對你的工作表現非常滿意。我要告訴你從下個月開始你將被轉成正式員工。

Allen: 哇，這太好了。所以我將獲得你在試用期之前答應我的百分之五的加薪嗎？

Vince: 嗯，你知道的。在整個經濟不景氣的大環境之下，每一家公司都試著減縮支出。除此之外，我認為你真的很喜歡這一份工作……

Allen: 拜託，老大。直接了當地說吧，可以嗎？

Vince: 嗯，你下個月開始會加薪百分之二。

Allen: 好吧，這總比沒加來得好。

心情小日記 Dear Diary

March 5th

Dear Diary,

Time flies, and now I am a regular employee. Unfortunately, I didn't get a 5 percent raise as I expected. Chief gave me loads of excuses; he talked about the recession, company policy and blah blah blah... Sigh, anyway, life is going on, at least I've got a 2 percent raise. If I want to earn my first pot of gold, maybe I'll have to make a financial plan. Talking about the financial plan, it's suddenly hit me that I haven't seen Garth for so long! Shane told me that Garth has profited greatly from his investment. I should ask him out, and pick his brains, and incidentally let him buy me dinner "LOL."

3月5日

親愛的日記，

時光飛逝，我現在已經是個正式員工了。不幸的是，我並沒有得到我預期的百分之五的加薪。老大給了我一大堆的理由，他談到經濟衰退，公司政策一堆有的沒的。唉，不管如何，日子總是要過下去，至少我有加到百分之2的薪。如果我要賺到我的第一桶金的話，也許我要規劃一下財務了。說到財務規劃，我突然想到我好久沒見到 Garth 了！Shane 告訴我 Garth 在投資上賺了不少。我應該要約他出來見面，和他討教一番，順便讓他請我吃飯（大笑）。

還可以怎麼說 In Other Words

❶ Please come on in and have a seat.
請進來坐。

- **Come in please, and grab a seat.**
  請進，隨便找個地方坐。

- **Come in and make yourself at home.**
  請進，別客氣。

❷ You have been doing a great job during this period.
你在這一段期間表現很好。

- **You did very well during the probation period.**
  你在這一段試用期間做得非常好。

- **I had my doubts when you started, but you've done very well.**
  在你剛開始時，我心存疑慮，但你真的做得很好。

13

❸ Shane told me that Garth has profited greatly from his investment.
Shane 告訴我 Garth 在投資上賺了不少。

- Shane said that Garth is so good at investing as if he's got the Midas touch.
Shane 說 Garth 十分善於投資，就像是擁有點石成金的力量一般。

- Shane told me that Garth's pulling in quite a bit in his investment.
Shane 說 Garth 在投資上獲利不少。

 這句怎麼說？ *How to Say That?*

直言不諱 → Mince no words

英釋 To say what you mean clearly and directly, even if you upset people by doing this.

中釋 直接了當地說清楚，儘管有可能會因此讓人感到不快。mince 是「絞碎，剁碎」的意思，有再加工的含意在。將 mince no words 中的 no 改成 one's，則變成有「閃爍其辭，支支吾吾」的意思。

A: If people ask you about what you think of tham, what would you say?
（如果人們問起你對他們的看法時，你會怎麼回答？）

B: I never mince my words and always tell people what I think of them.
（我總是會告訴人們我對他們的看法，絕不會閃爍其辭。）

 文化小盒子 *Culture Box*

　　火雞是一種原產於北美洲的家禽，體型大，可達到 10 公斤以上。一般談到火雞，便會令人想到美國人在感恩節及聖誕節時火雞大餐的傳統。而 "talk turkey" 這一句俚語則的確與這一個傳統有一些關連。據說在北美殖民時期，有一個白人，和一個印地安人一起去打獵，他們一共獵到了 3 隻鳥及兩隻火雞，在分配的時候，白人說 "You have three birds, and I have only two."（你分到了 3 隻鳥，而我只拿兩隻。）但因為鳥和火雞的體型相差十分懸殊，所以印地安人開口說了 "Stop talking birds, let's talk turkey."（別談什麼鳥了，讓我們來談談火雞吧。） "talk turkey" 因此成了有「打開天窗說亮話」及「有話直說，坦率說出心中想法」的含意。在商業的談判或是討論薪資時，也常能聽到有人說 "let's talk turkey" 或是 "let's say turkey"。

阿倫碎碎念 Allen's Murmur

　　據說飼養火雞的人會在給火雞的飼料當中放入彩色的彈珠，要不然火雞就會找不到飼料在哪兒，所以在英文當中，火雞被引用來罵人是愚蠢笨拙的飯桶，而一直到了 20 世紀初，則開始被用來形容劇情很爛的電影、戲劇或是文學作品等。例如我們看了一部爛片，當別人問你好不好看的時候，就可以說 "It was a real turkey."（這是一隻真的火雞＝這部片真的很爛。）而當別人問你對某人的評價時，你也可以說 "He's a real turkey, he didn't even know what he's talking about."（他真的很蠢，他連他自己在說什麼都不知道。）

　　Turkey 也跟毒品或是菸酒等的上癮扯上關係，例如常會聽到的是 "He's got turkey on his back."，這裡說的不是有一隻火雞在他的背上，而是指他喝酒或是吸毒等的成癮。而還有一種則是 "cold turkey"，猜猜看，是什麼呢？我是這樣記的，因為是冷的火雞，所以是不能吃的，而 turkey 又與某物的成癮有關，所以就是戒除某種癮，但是採取的是完全不碰的方法，而這種說法，據說是因為在戒毒、或是戒煙時會有冒冷汗及起雞皮疙瘩的情形出現，這時候跟在退冰火雞時很像，你記住了嗎？

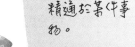
精通於某件事
物。

Diary 3 月 10 日

Know Your Onions

After using the restroom, Allen went back to the table. Now he
is discussing "candies" and "onions" with Paul in the restaurant.

上完洗手間之後，Allen 回到餐廳的座位上和

Paul 討論「糖果」及「洋蔥」。

 對話 *Dialogue*

Allen: What are you playing?

Paul: Sorry, I didn't **notice** that you're back. Did I **phub** you?

Allen: Nope. I'm just back. There are millions people in the **lavatory**.

Paul: Ha, even the Gents?

Allen: Yep. What game were you playing? Candy Crush?

Paul: Yes. I have already completed all levels, and been trying to get
all three stars.

Allen: Wow, you really know your onions.

Paul: Yes, I am a pro. Do you play candy crush saga?

Allen: Of course, it's one of the most popular mobile games with half a
billion downloads. I'm stuck on level 347, can you give me
hints?

Paul: Sure, no problem. First, you have to create as many of the **wrapped** candies as you can.

單字 Vocabulary

1. **notice** [`notɪs] ⓥ 注意、注意到
   → Did you notice her diamond ring?
   你有注意到她的鑽戒了嗎？

2. **phub** [`fʌb] ⓥ 因低頭玩手機而冷落了周遭的朋友
   → I went out for a date with Harry yesterday. And he didn't stop phubbing the whole time.
   我昨天跟 Harry 出去約會。約會時他不斷的玩手機，都沒有停過。

3. **lavatory** [`lævə,torɪ] ⓝ 廁所，洗手間
   → May I use your lavatory, please? I'm bursting.
   我可以借用一下你的廁所嗎？我快要爆炸了。

4. **billion** [`bɪljən] ⓝ 十億
   → Don't you know that my film has grossed more than 1.2 $billion?
   你難道不知道我的電影票房已經超過 12 億了？

5. **hint** [hɪnt] ⓝ 建議，指點；提示，暗示
   → She gave me some useful hints on how to make a nice decent apple pie.
   她給了我一些如何做出一個超好吃蘋果派的訣竅。

6. **wrap** [ræp] ⓥ 包，裹
   → Wrap the foil over the fish and baked in the oven for an hour.
   將魚用鋁箔紙包起來並放入烤箱裡烤 1 個鐘頭。

翻譯 Translation

Allen: 你在滑什麼？

Paul: 對不起，我沒注意到你回來了。我有沒有因為玩手機而忽略你了？

Allen: 沒。我才剛回到座位上。有超多人在等洗手間。

Paul: 哈，男廁也是嗎？

Allen: 對。你在玩什麼遊戲啊？Candy Crush 嗎？

Paul: 對，我已經全部破關了，試著要在每關都拿到 3 顆星。

Allen: 哇，你很厲害喔。

Paul: 沒錯，我可是職業級的。你有玩 Candy crush 嗎？

Allen: 當然，這可是有超過 5 億的下載人次最流行的手機遊戲之一。我卡在 347 關，可以告訴我秘訣嗎？

Paul: 當然，沒問題。首先你必須要盡可能的製造包裝糖果越多越好。

心情小日記 Dear Diary

March 10th

Dear Diary,

Yes! I just cleared level 347. I did as Paul taught me yesterday, and tried several times. Finally I achieved the objective and beat the level. Oh, yeah! This game is good for killing time, and always can find people playing candy crush everywhere. I went to the dentist this evening. When I was in the waiting room and suddenly heard the familiar melody, I looked around and found almost everyone was playing that game. Gee, it has a very wide age range. I really hand it to the game company, and they really know their onions in capturing players' hearts.

3 月 10 日

親愛的日記，

Yes！我剛破了 347 關。我照著 Paul 昨天教我的做，還試了好幾次。終於我達成目標破關。喔，耶！這個遊戲非常適合來打發時間，還有總能到處看到有人在玩 *candy crush*。我今天晚上去看牙醫。當我在候診室時突然聽到熟悉的旋律，我看了一下四周發現幾乎每個人都在玩這一個遊戲。哇，年齡層十分廣泛。我不得不佩服這一家遊戲公司，他們非常了解怎麼抓住玩家的心。

還可以怎麼說 In Other Words

❶ There are millions people in the lavatory.
有超多人在等洗手間。

- There was a long queue for the toilets.
  廁所前大排長龍。
- There are tons of people waiting for the washroom.
  一大堆人在等著上廁所。

❷ This game is good for killing time.
這個遊戲非常適合來打發時間。

- It's a terrific game to pass the time.
  這是一個用來打發時間很棒的遊戲。
- It is a wonderful game to play when waiting for a bus or in MRT.
  這是一個適合在等公車或是在捷運上時玩的遊戲。

❸ I really hand it to the game company.
我不得不佩服這一家遊戲公司。

- I want to give this game company two thumbs-up.
  我要給這一家遊戲公司滿分。
- I'll give this game company 100 "Likes."

我要給這一間遊戲公司 100 個「讚」。

 ## 這句怎麼說？ How to Say That?

瞭如指掌 ⟶ Know something like the back of my hand

英釋 to have very good and detailed knowledge of something

中釋 對某件事物非常瞭解或是清楚到就像是自己的手背一般。

A: Oh, god. Something wrong with my GPS navigation system, it is not working. （喔，我的天啊。我的衛星導航系統壞了，它不動了。）

B: Let me show you the way. I know that district just like the back of my hand. （讓我告訴你怎麼走吧。我對那一區瞭如指掌。）

 ## 文化小盒子 Culture Box

　　Know your onions 中的 onions 一般認為所指的是 onions 這一個姓氏，而不是指洋蔥。而有名的 Mr. Onions 有兩位，一位是 S.G. Onions，他所發明的錢幣教具，從 1843 年開始，便被廣泛的使用在英國的學校，教導孩童如何分辨及計算英鎊，先令和便士。而另一位 Mr. Onions 是 Charles Talbut Onions，他是一位文法學家及辭典編纂者，從 1895 年時便開始擔任牛津英語辭典的編輯一直到 1965 年，他的最後一本著作是牛津詞源字典，於他過世之後同一年出版。Know your onions 最早出現在文獻上是在 20 世紀初，而在那一段時期的美國發展出各式各樣無厘頭，奇特的俚語，例如 bee's knees，而 know your onions 也被歸類為此類俚語之一。我在記這一句話時，直覺是想洋蔥有非常多層，如歌詞中所唱的「如果你願意一層一層一層的剝開我的心」剝到最後就了解透徹，精通了。這樣是不是很好記了？

阿倫碎碎念 Allen's Murmur

洋蔥原產於中亞或是西亞，其營養價值極高，富含維生素，還有鐵、鈣、磷等多種礦物質。除此之外，洋蔥還是目前所知唯一一種含有前列腺素 A 的可食用植物，具有降血壓，及預防血栓形成的功效。

雖說洋蔥對於人類的身體健康有許多的好處，但是好像還是有許多人不喜歡洋蔥的味道，我還曾經聽過我表哥說 "An onion a day keeps everyone away."（每日一洋蔥，嚇跑身邊所有的人。）用來成為他拒吃洋蔥的理由。在英文的一些俚語當中，會發現洋蔥大多扮演著正面的印象，例如在美國的俚語中就會稱討人喜歡的小伙子為 "good onion"，而會稱硬漢為 "tough onion"。不過罵人是 "onion"（笨蛋、討厭的傢伙）等的用法也不少，所以只能說請用說話者的語氣或是表情來判定。不果，我可以確定的是，如果說一個人的屁股是 "onion butt" 或是 "onion bun" 的時候，那絕對是在稱讚這一個人的屁股很漂亮，甚至有漂亮到令人想要哭泣的感覺。

還有一個一定要學，罵人吵架兩相宜的說法，那就是 "off one's onion"，這是用來說一個人笨笨的或是有點遲鈍，也可以說是精神錯亂等。好了，先說到這了，我剛起床就說了這麼一大堆，還好你們聞不到我的 "onion breath"，我先去刷牙了！附註一下，onion breath 除了形容吃過洋蔥後的口氣之外，還可以說是早上起床時的口臭喔！

Diary 3 月 14 日

Bee's Knees

用來形容出類拔萃的人或事物。

Johnny sees Allen in the company's garden.

Now they are talking about the "biz niz."

Johnny 在公司的花園中遇見 Allen，

還討論有關 "biz niz"（註：business 商業）的事

對話 Dialogue

Johnny: Hello! Anybody home?

Allen: Move aside, please. I can't see through you.

Johnny: What are you looking at with all eyes?

Allen: Did you see that girl over there? I think I've been shot by a **Cupid's arrow**! I'm in love.

Johnny: Who? Oh, that girl with brown hair and white dress? Her name is Charlene. Please allow me to **remind** you that you're <u>**drooling**</u> all over the table. You don't want to scare her, do you?

Allen: Of course not!

Johnny: Okay, now let me give you some information. And if you want to date her, you must be quick, because she's the bee's knees of the new employees and <u>lots of people have **crushes**</u> on her.

22

Allen: Oh, what's wrong with her **knees**?

Johnny: Allen!!! I said she's the bee's knees!! Nothing wrong with her knees!!

Allen: Oh, you are right; she's the best girl that I've ever seen.

單字 Vocabulary

1. **Cupid** [`kjupɪd] n 愛神邱比特
   → Cupid fired an arrow at her today.
   今天愛神的箭射中了她。

2. **arrow** [`æro] n 箭
   → The arrow flew off and split the apple in half.
   這隻箭飛射出去並將蘋果分做兩半。

3. **remind** [rɪ`maɪnd] v 提醒、使想起
   → I have to pay the phone bill, please put it here to remind me.
   我必須得付電話帳單,請將它放在這裡來提醒我。

4. **drool** [drul] v 流口水
   → I started drooling at the sight of the delicacies.
   我再看到這些美食時就開始流口水。

5. **crush** [krʌʃ] n 【口】迷戀、迷戀的對象
   → I used to have a crush on my English teacher.
   我以前暗戀我的英文老師。

6. **knee** [ni] n 膝蓋
   → All the volunteers got down on their knees and scrubbed floors and walls.
   所有的志工都跪著刷洗地板及牆壁。

翻譯 Translation

Johnny: 哈囉!有人在家嗎?

Allen: 請讓開。你擋住我的視線了。

Johnny: 你在看什麼看得目不轉睛的?

Allen: 你有看到那邊的女孩嗎?我想我被愛神邱比特的箭射中了!我戀愛了。

Johnny: 誰?喔,那一個棕髮,白色連身裙的?她的名字叫 Charlene。請允

許我提醒你一下，你的口水已經流滿地了（你已經口水流滿桌了。）你不想要嚇到她，對吧？

Allen: 當然不想！

Johnny: Ok，現在讓我給你一些資訊。而且如果你要跟她約會的話，你動作得快一點，因為她可是新進員工中的翹楚，一大堆人都被她給電到了。

Allen: 喔，她的「腳」怎麼了？

Johnny: Allen！！！我說的是她是「箇中翹楚」！！她的「腳」沒事！！

Allen: 喔，你說的對，她是我所看過的最棒的女生。

心情小日記 Dear Diary

March 14th

Dear Diary,

Today's my lucky day. I met my dream girl twice. Once was in the elevator, and the other was in front of my office. More fortunately, Charlene spoke to me. All right, I admit, she was not exactly speaking to me. The thing was, when I saw her in front of my office, I got the jitters and I thought my heart would pound right out of my chest. At that time, I accidently dropped my ID card, and she picked it up and asked me "Is this yours?" Her voice is sooooo sweet, just like the sound from the heaven. I also noticed that she got a very cute dimple in her right cheek. Oh, no, I forgot to thank her.

3月14日

親愛的日記，

今天是我的幸運日。我遇見我心目中的女神兩次。一次在電梯裡，一次是在我辦公室前面。更幸運的是，Charlene 跟我說話了。好吧，我承認，不算是真的跟我說話。事情是這樣的，當我在辦公室前看到她，我超緊張的，我覺得我的心臟都快從我的胸腔跳出來了。就在那時候，我不小心弄掉了我的ID 卡，然後她把它撿起來問我說「這是你的嗎？"她的聲音超好聽的，就像是天籟之音一般。我還注意到她右邊的臉頰有一個超可愛的酒窩。喔，不，我忘了謝謝她。

還可以怎麼說 In Other Words

❶ You're drooling all over the table.
你的口水已經流滿地了。（你已經口水流滿桌了。）

- I saw so many ants drown in your saliva.
  我看到好多的螞蟻淹死在你的口水中。

- Please stop looking at her with calf's eyes.
  請不要再色瞇瞇的看著她了。

❷ Lots of people have crushes on her.
一大堆人都在暗戀她。

- She has many secret admirers.
  她有許多的秘密仰慕者。

- She's everyone's dream girl.
  她是每個人心中的女神。

❸ I got the jitters.
我超緊張的。

- I was so nervous.
  我很緊張。

- I was all wound up.
  我感到十分緊張。

 這句怎麼說？ How to Say That?

箇中翹楚 ➞ Cat's whiskers

英釋 the best thing, person or idea

中釋 最好的人、事或物。由 cat's pajamas 延伸而出，另外還有 cat's meow 的說法。除了用來稱出類拔萃，不同凡響的人事物之外，還暗含有「領導潮流」及「前衛時尚」的意思。

A: Does Jackie know how to fight? He looks so weak.

（Jackie 真的不知道怎麼打架嗎？他看起來一副弱不禁風的。）

B: Jackie sure knows how to fight; he's the cat's whiskers.

（Jackie 當然知道怎麼打架，他可是箇中翹楚呢。）

 文化小盒子 Culture Box

　　Bee's knees 字面上的意思是蜜蜂的膝蓋，而延伸為用以指稱「出類拔萃的人或事物」以及「無論在什麼方面都相當出色的人或事物」。一般認為這一個俚語的來源是因為蜜蜂在採蜜的時候，在膝蓋部位沾染上的花粉數量最多，於是被認為是最精華的部位，藉以延伸形容出色的人事物。Bee's knees 這一個詞最早出現在 20 世紀初，本來是用來形容沒有存在意義的事物，但在 20 年代之後，開始有了新的解釋，用來形容出色的，最好的。並流行用一些押韻但不具意義的俚語，如 snake's hips, monkey's eyebrows, cat's pajamas/whiskers 來形容優異的。時至今日，僅有 cat's whiskers/pajamas 和 bee's knees 還在使用，另外還有一個較新的害羞說法，那就是 dog's bollocks（狗的蛋蛋），用中文來說的話，就是周董常說的「屌」，是不是有異曲同工之妙呢？

阿倫碎碎念 Allen's Murmur

　　不知道大家有沒有看過一部動畫片 *Bee Movie*，在片中，蜜蜂為了對抗人類的無理剝削，於是就不再替花朵授粉，停止生產蜂蜜。於是這個世界便開始陷入了花朵愈來愈少，農作物及植物數量也日益減少。

　　而在現實生活中，其實在歐洲就有面臨到類似問題，根據調查，整個歐洲的蜂群大約不足 1/3，因為缺乏替作物授粉的蜜蜂，所以造成了作物的收成量減少，作物的價格因此而提高，這個時候就讓我想起了另一部電影 "Butterfly Effect"（蝴蝶效應），Butterfly effect 這是 1979 年時由一位美國的氣象學家 Lorenz 所提出的，他根據他在 1963 年時所提出的理論，在演講中提到一隻蝴蝶在巴西揮動著翅膀，極有可能會因此造成在德州的一場龍捲風。由於這一場演講，而讓那一個有著一長串名字的氣象學理論從此有了 butterfly effect 這一個響亮的名號，而除了在科學界的影響之外，也被廣泛的運用在社會學、政治等當中。用中文來說，應該可以用「失之毫釐，差之千里」來比喻。另外，跟大家分享一個我最近聽到的 bee 的俚語 "bee arbs"，其實跟蜜蜂沒有關係，是 "be right back" 的縮寫 BRB，被用在對話上的說法，例如現在我急著去廁所，我就可以說 "Bee arbs, need the toilet!"

Flogging a Dead Horse

鞭打已經死掉
的馬,用來比
喻白費力氣。

Allen is in Vince's office and arguing something about

the "dead horse" with Vince.

Allen 在 Vince 的辦公室中

與他爭論著有關「死馬」的事。

對話 Dialogue

Vince: It's not gonna work.

Allen: Why? Chief, I thought you like my idea.

Vince: Yes, I do **appreciate** your idea, and in fact I think it's brilliant. But as I mentioned our **client** is a **conservative**, centuries-old company, they want something, um, not too **avant-garde**.

Allen: So you think I'm just flogging a dead horse, right?

Vince: Not exactly. Here's the profile of another firm. It's a new company, and according to their **representative**, they want something creative and never follow **conventions**. I have already showed them your idea, and they seemed quite satisfy with that.

Allen: Thank you, chief. I'll do my best.

Vince: I'm sure you will. And don't forget you still have to follow the first case. I want to see the new project on my desk by Friday.

Allen: Sure, no problem.

單字 Vocabulary

1. **appreciate** [əˈpriʃɪˌet]
   Ⓥ 欣賞、賞識
   → Anyone is welcomed to appreciate our music.
   我們歡迎任何人欣賞我們的音樂。

2. **client** [ˈklaɪənt]
   Ⓝ 客戶；委託人
   → I will have a meeting with my client this afternoon.
   我今天下午和客戶有個會要開。

3. **conservative** [kənˈsɚvətɪv] adj
   保守的、守舊的
   → That young man is very conservative.
   那個年輕人十分地保守。

4. **avant-garde** [avaŋˈgard] adj 前衛的
   → Their music combined elements of pop and avant-garde.
   他們的音樂結合了流行及前衛的元素。

5. **representative** [rɛprɪˈzɛntətɪv] Ⓝ 代表
   → I attended that meeting as the representative of my company.
   我以公司代表的身份參加會議。

6. **conventions** [kənˈvɛnʃən] Ⓝ 常規、慣例
   → They broke away from conventions.
   他們打破了常規。

翻譯 Translation

Vince: 這樣是行不通的。

Allen: 為什麼？老大，我以為你喜歡我這一個建議。

Vince: 對，我還蠻喜歡你這一個意見的，而且事實上我覺得很棒。但就像我說過的，我們的客戶是一家保守，擁有幾百年歷史的公司，他們要的是，嗯……不要這麼前衛的。

Allen: 所以你覺得我白忙一場了，是嗎？

Vince: 並不盡然。這裡是另一家企業的資料。這是一家新公司，而且根據

他們的代表說，他們要的是創新並且不落於俗套的東西。我已經讓他們看過你的提案了，他們看起來非常滿意。

Allen: 謝謝你，老大，我會盡全力的。

Vince: 我確定你會。還有不要忘記你還是必須跟進第一個案子。我要在星期五之前看到新的提案在我的桌子上。

Allen: 當然，沒問題。

心情小日記 Dear diary

April 3rd

Dear Diary,

I met our new client this afternoon. He is a very attractive man. As soon as he stepped into our company, he was the cynosure of all eyes. He wore a simple white shirt and jeans today, but I have to admit that he's a real clothes horse even I didn't like his attitude. He got on his high horse during the meeting and caviled at everything. Just at the time I was about to explode with anger, Mary and Jane both advised me to hold my horses, because there's no captious client, but faulty product and service. All I have to do is to meet his requirement and perfect this project.

4月3日

親愛的日記，

我在今天下午與新客戶碰面了。他是一個很有魅力的男士。當他踏進我們公司的一瞬間，他便成了所有人的焦點。他今天穿著簡單的白襯衫及牛仔褲，雖然我不喜歡他的態度但我還是必須承認他的確是一個衣架子。他在會議中一直非常的趾高氣昂，還挑剔所有的事情。就在我將要發火的時候，Mary和 Jane 都勸我要沉住氣，因為沒有挑剔的客戶，只有不對的產品及服務。我所要做的是滿足他的要求，完美地完成這一個項目。

還可以怎麼說 In Other Words

❶ It's not gonna work.
這樣是行不通的。

- **We can't do that.**
  我們不能這樣做。

- **I don't think that our client will accept this proposal.**
  我不認為我們的客戶會接受這一項提案。

❷ I'm just flogging a dead horse.
我白忙一場了。

- **I'm just beating a dead dog.**
  我在「打死狗」。＝我白忙一場。

- **I'm wasting my time.**
  我在浪費我的時間。

❸ He was the cynosure of all eyes.
他成了所有人的焦點。

- **He was in the limelight.**
  他是眾人注目的焦點。

- Everyone in the lobby was attracted by his handsome looking.
  每個在大廳的人都被他的帥臉給吸引了。

這句怎麼說？ How to Say That?

竹簍打水一場空 → Carrying water in a sieve

英釋 to exert efforts but fruitless; a waste of time

中釋 投入努力但卻沒有收到任何成效；浪費時間。

A: I've done everything to dissuade him from smoking, but he just wouldn't listen. （我已經試過所有方法勸他不要抽煙，但他就是不聽。）

B: If I were you, I won't waste my time. It's just like carrying water in a sieve. （如果我是你的話，我不會浪費我的時間。這是在白費功夫。）

文化小盒子 Culture Box

　　Flogging a dead horse 亦可說是 beating a dead horse 或是 whipping a dead horse，其含意都是指付出努力都卻卻未能收到成效，徒勞無功的意思。而 flogging，beating 及 whipping 都是指鞭打之意，只是在打法上有稍稍的不同。Flogging a dead horse 中的 dead horse 字面上的意思為死馬，一般認為是因為死馬無法奔跑，所以鞭打死馬無法達到任何效果。但有趣的是，根據文獻及學者的研究顯示這一句在 17 世紀時就出現的話，之中的 dead horse，其實在當時是指工人在完成工作之前，雇主事先預付的工資，而這一句話的由來則是因為工人已經收到了預付的工資，所以在未完成的工作上便不是那麼的盡力，甚至是在雇主鞭策之下也絲毫達不到任何成效。

說到與馬相關的俚語，我認真的想了一下，似乎還不少。我想也許是因為在以前，不管是在東方、還是西方國家，馬都算得上是重要的交通工具之一。不知道在幾百年後，跟車子相關的俚語是不是也會這麼多呢？

言歸正傳，當說到馬的時候，不知道大家第一個想到的是什麼呢？我第一個想到的會是白馬王子，大家應該知道 Allen 我正朝著 Charlene 心目中的白馬王子方向而努力著。但其實白馬王子在英文中的正確說法，應該是 Prince Charming，而有時也會聽到有人以 "white horse" 來稱英雄救美的人，或是女性心目中的白馬王子。但我比較常聽到的 "white horse" 卻是指一種威士忌，因為那是一種威士忌的廠牌。

而另外常聽到的有關 horse 的片語，例如有指能將衣服穿出流行感，及凸顯其價值的人，我們稱之為衣架子的 "clothes horse"，其原意是曬衣架，有四腳站立的那一種。這有時候也會被引用來比喻大量添購新衣的人，有嘲諷之意。For example: My little sister is a real clothes horse. 別誤會，我可是真心的稱讚我妹，而不是暗指她買太多衣服喔！還有我在跟阿祐少爺談公事時，常會處在一種瀕臨爆發的狀態，這時候，同事們最常對我說的就是 "Hold your horses." 叫我要沉住氣，忍著點。這個在字面上的意思為要拉住馬的韁繩，而特別要注意的是，這句片語中是用複數的 horses，不能用單數的 horse。

除了這幾個之外，大家不妨找找看，我在日記裡還寫了另一個我常聽到的有關 horse 的片語，下次再聊囉！

Eye Broccoli

其貌不揚，不是很有吸引力。

Allen sees Sean on his way to the office in the morning. They are greeting each other and then starting the topic of "broccoli."

Allen 今天早上進辦公室前遇見 Sean。

他們向彼此打招呼並開始討論有關「青花菜」的話題。

對話 Dialogue

Allen: Good morning, Sean.

Sean: Argh, it's you, what's wrong with you? <u>Don't tell me it's the new sexy.</u> You look um⋯ very eye **broccoli**.

Allen: Oh, it's all right, I've never been the eye candy.

Sean: I was just being **polite**. Telling the truth, <u>I thought you were beaten with the ugly stick.</u>

Allen: Ouch, that hurts me a little. I have been working late for over a week, and I didn't have time to pick up my **laundry**. And this is the only one clean shirt that I have in the **wardrobe** and I know it's not a good **match** with my paints.

Sean: Do you need a hand?

Allen: In which way?

34

Sean: Whatever you need, just let me know.

Allen: It's very nice of you. In fact, I need some **information** about the ABC Company.

Sean: We can talk while walking.

單字 Vocabulary

1. **broccoli** [ˋbrɑkəlɪ]
   n 青花菜、球花甘藍
   → Eat up your broccoli; it's good for your health.
   將你的青花菜吃完,這對你的健康很有幫助。

2. **polite** [pəˋlaɪt]
   adj 有禮貌的、客氣的
   → Please be polite and consider toward our guests.
   請對我們的客人要有禮貌並關心體諒。

3. **laundry** [ˋlɔndrɪ] n 待洗[洗過]的衣物;洗衣店;洗衣房
   → Please hang out the laundry in the backyard.
   請將洗好的衣服曬在後院。

4. **wardrobe** [ˋwɔrd͵rob]
   n 衣櫥、衣櫃
   → I stuffed all my clothes in the wardrobe.
   我將我所有的衣物都塞進衣櫃。

5. **match** [mætʃ]
   v 相配、相適合
   → The wallpaper and furnishings match pretty well.
   壁紙和傢俱搭配得很好。

6. **information**
   [͵ɪnfɚˋmeʃən]
   n 情報資料、資訊;消息
   → I got a piece of information from an unnamed resource.
   我從一位不願具名的人士那裡得到一條情報。

翻譯 Translation

Allen: 早安,Sean。

Sean: 啊,是你啊,你怎麼搞的?不要告訴我這是最新的性感造型。你看起來,嗯…非常地其貌不揚。

Allen: 喔,無所謂,我本來就不是能讓人眼睛為之一亮的那一種人。

Sean: 我只是說客氣話。老實說,我還以為你被醜人杖給打到了。

Allen: 喔，這有一點傷到我了。我這一個多星期以來都在加班，沒有時間去取回我送洗的衣服。還有這是我衣櫃中唯一剩下的乾淨襯衫了，我知道看起來非常不搭我的褲子。

Sean: 你需要幫忙嗎？

Allen: 哪一方面？

Sean: 都可以，跟我說一聲就行了。

Allen: 你人真好。事實上，我需要一些 ABC 公司相關的資訊。

Sean: 我們可以邊走邊談。

心情小日記 Dear Diary

April 7th

Dear Diary,

Sean told me loads of useful information about the ABC Company this morning, and he even mailed me a list of dos and don'ts. I believe that with Sean's information, leaving work on the dot is in the not too distant future. Hooray! A little crow of triumph for myself. Allen, you can make it! And one more thing, I want to thank my roommate, Jason, he picked up all my laundry this evening. He said he can't stand my "arty clothes" any more. I think I'm a lucky guy with so many good and helpful friends around.

4 月 7 日

愛的日記，

Sean 今天早上告訴我一大堆有關 ABC 公司的資訊，他甚至還寄給我一份需注意事項的清單。我相信有了 Sean 給的情報，準時下班是指日可待的事了。喔耶！給我自己小小的勝利歡呼。Allen，你一定可以做到的！還有一件事，我要謝謝我的室友 Jason，他今天晚上取回了我所有送洗的衣物。他說他再也受不了我的奇裝異服了。我有這麼多樂於助人的好朋友讓我覺得我真是一個幸運的人。

還可以怎麼說 In Other Words

❶ Don't tell me it's the new sexy.
不要告訴我這是最新的性感造型。

- I don't think your style will be popular in the near future.
  我不認為你的造型能在近期之內造成流行。

- Are you wearing your mother's paints?
  你是穿你媽媽的褲子嗎？

❷ I thought you were beaten with the ugly stick.
我還以為你被醜人杖給打到了。

- I don't think your mama can recognize you!
  我不認為你媽能認得出你來。

- Oh, my, your style is so fugly.
  喔，我的天啊，你的造型醜爆了。（fugly 是由一個 f 開頭的字加上 ugly 所組成的。）

❸ Leaving work on the dot is in the not too distant future.
準時下班是指日可待的事了。

- Maybe I can punch out on time tomorrow.
  或許我明天可以準時下班。

- I'll move back to my apartment from the office recently.
  我最近會從辦公室搬回我的公寓住。

 這句怎麼說？ *How to Say That?*

可遠觀不可近看 ➔ Monet

英釋 A person who is attractive from a distance, but unattractive on closer in-
spection.

中釋 某人在一段距離外看似非常有吸引力，但在近距離接觸後便魅力全失。

A: He is such a Monet. （他就像是莫內的畫一樣可遠觀，但不能近看。）

B: What does that mean? （這是什麼意思？）

A: He looks great from afar, but up close he's a mess with terrible body
odor. （從遠的地方看，他看起來還不錯，但接近後會發現他長的有點糟還有
可怕的體臭。）

文化小盒子 *Culture Box*

　　Eye broccoli 是 eye candy 的反義詞，是指長相普通，沒有什麼吸引力
的人。最早出現的是 eye candy，是在 20 世紀的 80 年代，用以指稱漂亮，
足以吸引目光的人或是事物。而 eye broccoli 則是出現在 2005 年開演的一
齣美國電視劇 "*How I met Your Mother*" 中，用來形容劇中男主角的長相平凡
的已婚女助理。而至於為什麼是用 candy 和 broccoli 呢？Eye candy 通常指
的是養眼，秀色可餐，但卻也帶點華而不實的感覺，因為糖吃多了是會蛀牙
的。而 eye broccoli，我個人覺得大概是青花菜是西餐餐點中常見的配菜之
一，所以給了編劇靈感用來形容平凡普通，其貌不揚的感覺。

阿倫碎碎念 Allen's Murmur

相信許多人跟 Allen 一樣不喜歡吃青花菜,所以小時候總是會聽到媽媽大吼地說 "Can't leave the table until you finish your broccoli." 而長大之後,我發現其實青花菜是一種對健康相當有益的蔬菜屬於十字花科的青花菜,含有數種強力抗癌效果化合物。根據醫學研究顯示,食用青花菜可以降低得到大腸癌、胃癌、乳癌、子宮癌等……的機率,而且還含有一種酵素能破壞破壞致癌的化學物質,吃青花菜可以說是好處多多呢。

所以第一次在美劇當中所出現的那一位 "eye broccoli" 的女秘書,對於她的老闆來說雖是一個「其貌不揚」的秘書,但卻是不可少的幫手。而在對話中所出現的 "beaten with the ugly stick",所形容的則比 eye broccoli 要慘多了,用以指長得很難看,或是醜爆了!

有趣的是,ugly stick 是一種加拿大紐芬蘭島的傳統樂器,常會使用拖把的把柄加上瓶蓋、錫罐及小型鐘或是一些可以發出聲響的東西來製作,長得不算醜,但有點,嗯……「可愛」,建議大家不妨可以去 google 一下 "ugly stick",就能瞭解了。我個人認為沒有什麼音樂細胞的我,在聽這樣的演奏會,是無法 cool as a cucumber(鎮定自若的),應該會有點忍不住地想笑,but I think I'm not going to get myself into pickle.(但我覺得我應該不會讓自己陷入這樣的困境的。)大家不知道有沒有注意到,我在這裡說了另外兩種蔬菜類的用法,有 cucumber(小黃瓜)和 pickle(酸黃瓜),還有其它很多不同的蔬果類俚語,就在其它的章節跟大家分享囉!

Diary 4 月 28 日

Out to Lunch

就是指心都沒
放在公事上，
魂都不知道飛
到哪兒了！

Allen sees angry Mary in the convention room. Mary is furious at "someone's out to lunch."

Allen在會議室中遇見Mary。

Mary對某人「外出吃午餐」感到生氣。

 對話 Dialogue

Allen: **Calm** down, Mary! What are you so mad at? I can feel your **anger** miles away.

Mary: It's Kathy, she's always out to lunch these days. I can't stand her any more.

Allen: Nope, I think she's still in her **cubicle**, I just saw her there.

Mary: Oh, darn! Allen, I am in no mood for **joking**. I know she's in the office but her mind is elsewhere.

Allen: My bad, I was just trying to **quell** your anger. Ok, tell me, what did she do this time?

Mary: I asked her to arrange a pile of unsorted papers and put them into the file cabinet. But she put them through the **shredder**.

Allen: Oh, no, that's too bad.

:: 單字 Vocabulary

1. **calm** [kɑm]
   Ⓥ 鎮定下來，平靜下來
   → She patted me on my back and tried to calm me down.
   她輕拍著我的背並試著讓我鎮定下來。

2. **anger** [`æŋgɚ]
   生氣、怒火
   → I could feel the anger welling up inside me.
   我可以感覺到我的怒火都冒上來了。

3. **cubicle** [`kjubɪkl]
   Ⓝ 小隔間
   → You can study in one of the cubicles on the second floor of the library.
   你可以在圖書館二樓的其中一個小隔間中讀書。

4. **joke** [dʒok]
   Ⓥ 開玩笑
   → You can tell he's just joking.
   你能看出來他只是在開玩笑。

5. **quell** [kwɛl]
   Ⓥ 減輕；平息
   → Soldiers were sent to quell the violence.
   士兵被派去平息暴力事件。

6. **shredder** [`ʃrɛdɚ]
   Ⓝ 碎紙機；絞碎機。
   → She tried to convince me to buy a new shredder.
   她試著勸說我買一台新的碎紙機。

翻譯 Translation

Allen: 冷靜點，Mary！妳這麼生氣是為了什麼？我在幾英里外就能感受到妳的怒火了。

Mary: 因為Kathy，她這些日子總是在狀況外。我無法再忍受她了。

Allen: 沒啊，我想她還待在她的小隔間裡，我剛還有看到她。

Mary: 喔，可惡！Allen，我現在沒有心情跟你開玩笑。我知道她人在辦公室裡，但是她的心不在。

Allen: 是我不好，我只是想要讓妳不要那麼生氣。好吧，告訴我，她這一次又做了什麼？

Mary: 我請她整理一堆還沒分類的文件，並收進檔案櫃中。但她卻將這堆文件送到碎紙機了。

Allen: 喔，不，這太糟糕了。

心情小日記 Dear Diary

April 28th

Dear Diary,

I met Mary in the pantry this morning. She looked absolutely horrible with her two gigantic dark circles. I gave her a quizzical look and she showed me the whites of her eyes. Mary told me that she spent a night and tried to mend that pile of shredded documents, and she only finished half of them. I volunteered to help, and I saw her eyes filled with tears. This incident gave me a good lesson that even we work individually, but all our works are closely related. So I'll do my best in my every work.

4月28日

愛的日記，

我今天早上在茶水間遇見Mary。她的兩個超大黑眼圈讓她看起來超恐怖的。我給了她一個詢問的眼神，而她則給了我兩個大白眼。Mary告訴我她花了一整晚的時間試著修復那堆被切碎的文件，而她只完成了一半。我自願幫忙，還看到她眼眶裡噙滿了淚水。這次的事件讓我清楚的知道儘管我們各自獨立工作，但我們的工作卻是緊緊的關聯著。所以我要盡全力去完成每一件工作。

還可以怎麼說 In Other Words

❶ What are you so mad at?
妳這麼生氣是為了什麼？

- What made you so angry?
  什麼事讓妳這麼生氣？

- Well well, I'm so curious about who can make you so furious.
  嗯，我真好奇倒底是誰有這本事讓妳這麼生氣。

❷ She's always out to lunch these days.
她這些日子總是在狀況外。

- She seems to be a bit out of it recently.
  她最近有些魂不守舍的。

- She was absent minded all the time.
  她總是心不在焉的。

❸ I volunteered to help.
我自願幫忙。

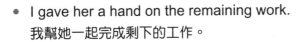

- I gave her a hand on the remaining work.
  我幫她一起完成剩下的工作。

- I help her to finish the rest of the work.
  我幫著她來完成其餘的工作。

這句怎麼說？ How to Say That?

心不在焉 → Have one's head in the clouds

英 釋 to be unaware of what is going on from fantasies or daydreams

中 釋 搞不清楚狀況，做白日夢，不切實際。

A: Bob, do you have your head in the clouds again? （Bob，你是不是又在心不在焉了？）

B: No, Annie. I've got my head out of the clouds when I heard your voice. （沒有，Annie。當我聽到妳的聲音時，我就把我的心給收回來了。）

文化小盒子 Culture Box

我曾經在部落格中看過一段商務上的對話，其中有一句 "You know my boss, he's out to lunch. I always take what he says with a grain of salt." 造成了誤解，對話的另一方誤認為對方的老闆外出用餐，並以為對方十分聽從老闆的話，因為老闆吃過的鹽比他吃過的米多。而渾然不知其實對方是在抱怨老闆總是心不在焉，對他的話只能姑且聽之。Out to lunch除了指外出吃午餐之外，還有心不在焉的意思，跟我們常說的「靈魂出竅」，「雲遊四海」相類似。相信大家多少都有發生過曾在課堂上或是工作中想著午餐要吃什麼而走神的經驗吧，人雖然還在教室或是辦公室中，但靈魂已經去吃午飯了，而這就是 "out to lunch" 的來源。如果怕造成誤解的話，外出吃午餐（我說的是真的去吃）可以說 "out for lunch"。

阿倫碎碎念 Allen's Murmur

　　Lunch在中文裡稱做午餐，也可以說是中飯、中餐、午飯等說法，一般是指在早上 11 點到下午 1 點之間所享用的餐點。營養師建議「早餐要吃好、午餐要吃飽、晚餐要吃少」，對於上班族而言，午餐不僅僅是補充早上工作時所消耗的能量，還有供應下午上班所需的能量之外，午餐時間可是重要的與同事們相處，交換情報的重要時刻。

　　在美國，有些時候除了利用早餐時間作早餐會報之外，還會有所謂的午餐會議，這時候就要注意，有些會議上是有供應午餐，但有一種被稱為是 "brown bag lunch meeting" 的，指的不是會有供應用咖啡色紙袋裝的午餐，而是要你自備午餐的意思。因為在美國，多半會以brown bag（咖啡色的紙袋）來裝午餐的三明治、果汁等，可以被認為是在台灣所稱的「便當袋」。不過因為brown bag中的brown，除了單純的指顏色之外，也有指非裔美國人膚色的含意存在，所以為了避免帶有種族歧視的意味，所以去年在美國曾經有被提出討論，而有些人建議將這一種型態的午餐會議改稱為 "bring your own lunch meeting"，而brown bag lunch改稱為 "sack lunch"。

　　另外還有一個跟lunch相關的俚語，是 "lunchbox cutie"（午餐盒小可愛），指的是有一個人可愛到讓你想要把她放在午餐盒中，和你的午餐三明治還有保溫瓶一起帶著走，這應該就跟中文裡所說的想把一個人放進口袋隨身帶著的感覺吧！唉，我好想把Charlene變成我的lunchbox cutie喔！

Diary 4 月 29 日

Elephant in the Room

意指為問題很大，但大家卻都視若無睹不去處理。

Mary and Allen are sitting in the convention room and trying to finish a pile of document jigsaws. Meanwhile, they are talking about the "elephant in the room."

Mary 和 Allen 坐在會議室中，
試著完成一大堆的文件拼圖。同時還討論著「房裡的大象」。

對話 Dialogue

Allen: Seriously, I really think that Kathy will cause big trouble one day, if she doesn't change her **attitude** towards work. Have you ever thought about reporting this condition to the manager?

Mary: Of course I have! I've been thinking about it for **million** times. But other colleagues always **dissuade** me from reporting this to our manager. Jim told me that Kathy is a **niece** of our general manager's wife. There was one such man who complained about Kathy's work attitude to the manager, and he's been **shunted** into the branch office.

Allen: Maybe it's just a **coincidence**.

Mary: Well, maybe. Anyway, it becomes the elephant in the room.

Allen: And nobody wants to mention this problem?

Mary: Nope.

單字 Vocabulary

1. **attitude** [`ætətjud]
   n 態度
   → There's need a change of attitude.
   那裡需要態度上的改變。

2. **million** [`mɪljən]
   adj 百萬的；無數的
   → The website gets about a million downloads a month.
   這個網站每個月的下載量約有上百萬次。

3. **dissuade** [dɪ`swed]
   v 勸阻
   → I tried to dissuade her from giving up her job.
   我試著勸阻她不要放棄她的工作。

4. **niece** [nis]
   n 姪女、外甥女
   → I'm going to my niece's birthday party.
   我要去參加我外甥女的生日派對。

5. **shunt** [ʃʌnt]
   v 把……轉到另一個地方
   → Kevin was shunted into a minor job.
   Kevin 被調任到一個不太重要的職位。

6. **coincidence**
   [ko`ɪnsɪdəns] n 巧合
   → We arrived at the same time by pure coincidence.
   我們同時抵達純屬巧合。

翻譯 Translation

Allen: 說正經的，我真的認為 Kathy 總有一天會搞出個大麻煩，如果她的工作態度不改變的話。妳有沒有想過要跟經理報告這個情形呢？

Mary: 當然有。我已經想過上百萬次了。但是其他同事總是勸我不要上報到經理那。Jim 跟我說 Kathy 是總經理老婆的外甥女。曾經有這麼一個人向經理抱怨過 Kathy 的工作態度，結果他被調職到分公司去了。

Allen: 也許只是巧合吧。

Mary: 嗯，也許。不管怎樣，這成了大家不想去碰觸的事實。

Allen: 那沒有人要提出這個問題嗎？

Mary: 沒有。

心情小日記 Dear Diary

April 29th

Dear Diary,

I had a brief talk with Kathy today. I found her a super nice, approachable person. Even I am not satisfied with her work performance, but I cannot dislike her. She looked like a harmless little lamb when she talked. I almost couldn't help myself to pat her on the head. I told Mary about my feeling, she totally agreed with me and said that's another reason they don't want to blame her too much. Oh, one more thing, Kathy told me due to some personal reasons, she already gave the one month's notice. I bet Mary doesn't know that yet. I can't wait to see Mary's face when she knows this news.

4 月 29 日

親愛的日記，

我今天和 Kathy 簡短的聊了一下。我發現她是個超好，超親切的人。即使我不滿意她的工作表現，但我也無法討厭她。當她說話的時候像是一隻無害的小綿羊，我差點忍不住的想要拍她的頭。我告訴 Mary 我的感覺，她完全同意我的看法還說這是他們都不想太苛責她的另一個原因。喔，還有一件事，Kathy 告訴我因為一些個人因素，所以她已經提出辭呈了。我猜 Mary 一定還不知道。我等不及要看當她知道這一件事時的表情了。

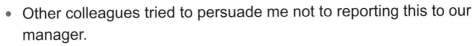
還可以怎麼說 In Other Words

❶ But other colleagues always dissuade me from reporting this to
our manager.
但是其他同事總是勸我不要上報到經理那。

- Other colleagues tried to persuade me not to reporting this to our
manager.
其他同事試著說服我不要跟經理報告這一件事。

- They told me that it's aimless to cast water into the sea.
他們告訴我「這像是將水倒入海中」。=他們告訴我這是徒勞無功的。

❷ I found her a super nice, super approachable person.
我發現她是個超好，超親切的人。

- For your information, she's a good egg.
告訴你，她是一個「好蛋」。=告訴你，她是一個好人。

- She's not as mean as I thought.
她不是我想像中的那樣自私。

❸ She already gave the one month's notice.
她已經提出辭呈了。

- She has filed her resignation.
她已經提辭呈了。

- She quit.
她辭職了。

這句怎麼說? How to Say That?

視而不見 → Turn a blind eye to something/someone

英釋 to refuse to see or recognize something

中釋 對於某人或是某件事物裝作沒看見,或是不認同。

A: Does that bitch keep bugging you? (那個賤人還有一直在找你的麻煩嗎?)

B: Of course she does. But I just turn a blind eye and a deaf ear to her. (她當然有。但我就對她保持著什麼都視而不見及充耳不聞的態度。)

 文化小盒子 Culture Box

　　相信大家都聽過國王的新衣(the emperor's new clothes)的故事,在故事中,騙人的裁縫師聲稱這一件新衣只有有智慧的人才能看見,而眾人為了自己的面子而不敢說出實話。這一個情形就像是在房間裡有一隻大象,但大家卻視而不見,閉口不談是一樣的。所以 elephant in the room 或是 gorilla in the room 也可以說 emperor's new clothes,指的都是對於一個明顯的事實,但大家都將其視為禁忌,或是為了不造成尷尬而不願意明講及說破。有時還會聽到 elephant in the corner, elephant on the dinner table 將其所在的範圍縮小,以突顯出問題的嚴重性或是 pink elephant in the room 的不同說法。其中以 pink elephant 的說法有一點不同,這大多是指家中有酗酒或是有毒癮的家人,為了家族問題而閉口不談的情況。

阿倫碎碎念 *Allen's Murmur*

Talking about the elephant, 這讓我想到我最近學到的一個新的說法 "El-ephant shoe", 請先對著鏡子, 然後說 "elephant shoe", 仔細的看著自己的嘴型, 這樣看起來, 是不是很像是在說 "I love you" 呢? 另外一個我知道的還有 "olive juice", so when someone says "elephant shoe" to you, and you can reply "olive juice, too." 不過這當然是指對對方不討厭, 甚至是喜歡或愛的時候。

言歸正傳, 說到大象, 大家第一個想到的應該大多是牠的巨大體型。所以在英文當中便常以 elephant 來比喻相當大、或是非常顯而易見的事物。所以在美國俚語中就有了 "see the elephant" 這樣的用法, 用來指「開眼界、見世面（如大都市的生活等）」, 還可以說是 "get a look at the elephant" 或是 "get a sight of the elephant"。所以有時候會在影集或是電影中聽到嚮往大都市生活的主角說 "I have to go out and get a look at the elephant."（我得出去見見世面。）

還有一個我覺得超貼切的有關大象的俚語, 大家應該都知道在英文中傾盆大雨是 "It rains cats and dogs", 而大家應該也知道陸地上最大的生物是大象, 而海中最大的生物則是鯨魚吧！所以當碰上發佈豪雨特報時那一種大到不像樣, 甚至被雨滴打到就有快瘀青的感覺的那種雨時, 就可以用 "It rains elephants and whales." 這一種誇張的說法。我曾經聽過下阿貓阿狗這樣的說法的起源之一有可能是因為在當時英國的街道, 因為設計不佳, 所以每當下大雨時總會有貓、狗淹死, 屍體漂流在街頭。哈哈, 說到這, 我就會不禁的想像當 rain elephants and whales 時的畫面⋯⋯

Diary 5 月 02 日

In the Soup

比喻麻煩大
了，深陷問題
中。

Jason is Allen's roommate, and he's just home after work. Jason and Allen are talking about the "soup" in the kitchen.

Jason 是 Allen 的室友，他剛下班回來。

Jason 和 Allen 在廚房裡談論著「湯」。

對話 Dialogue

Jason: Holy shit! I think I am in the soup this time.

Allen: Oh, what happened? Is there anything wrong with your new **project**?

Jason: Nah, nothing wrong with the project. The thing is that I left my phone in the **convention** room after a meeting this afternoon. So I went back for my phone, and then I **bumped into** an office romance.

Allen: That sounds okay for me.

Jason: No, it's not okay at all. What I found is that my married boss and his secretary are having a **torrid** affair. And the worst thing is they saw me when I tried to **slip away unobserved**.

Allen: Oh, no. You're due.

52

單字 Vocabulary

1. **project** [prə`dʒɛkt]
   n 計畫、項目、工程
   → He has the power to pull the plug on that project.
   他有權中止那一個計畫。

2. **convention** [kən`vɛnʃən]
   n 會議、大會
   → She was delegated to the convention.
   她被指派參加會議。

3. **bump into**
   ph 撞上；遇上
   → We will probably bump into him in Sally's birthday party.
   我們或許會在 Sally 的生日派對上遇見他。

4. **torrid** [`tɔrɪd]
   adj 狂熱的、熱情的
   → She began a torrid love affair with her bodyguard.
   她和她的保鏢展開了一場狂熱的戀情。

5. **slip away**
   ph 溜走、不告而別
   → They cannot afford to let the chance to slip away.
   他們承擔不起讓這一個機會溜走的後果。

6. **unobserved**
   [ˌʌnəb`zɝvd] adj 沒有觀察到的、沒有被察覺的
   → Tommy took a seat in an unobserved corner.
   Tommy 在一個不起眼的角落坐下。

翻譯 Translation

Jason: X*Z#！我想我這一次麻煩大了。

Allen: 喔，怎麼啦？你的新項目有什麼問題嗎？

Jason: 不，新項目沒事。事情是這樣的，我今天下午開完會後不小心把手機忘在會議室裡。所以我回去找手機，然後被我撞見了辦公室戀情。

Allen: 我聽起來覺得還好啊。

Jason: 不，一點也不好。我發現的是我那已婚的上司和他的秘書之間正進行著一場火辣辣的戀情。最糟糕的是，當我正想要偷偷溜走時，卻被他們給發現了。

Allen: 喔，不。你死定了。

心情小日記 Dear Diary

May 2nd

Dear Diary,

Jason looked so worried yesterday, but <u>he seemed quite delight-ed when he returned home this evening.</u> Jason told me that things took a more decisive turn. He said that his boss nodded him into his office this morning, and asked him to keep the se-cret. And even the haughty secretary was nice to him all day long. But I was worried that maybe they just pretended to be nice to Jason, but tried to kick out Jason after his services are no longer needed. I told Jason about my thought. Jason said with a cryptic smile "I have got a few ideas in my sleeve."

5月2日

親愛的日記，

Jason 昨天看一來一副憂心忡忡的樣子，但是他今晚回家時看起來卻很高興。Jason 跟我說事情發生了決定性的轉折。他說他的老闆今天早上示意他進去他的辦公室裡，並要他保守這一個秘密。甚至是那一個高傲的秘書一整天都對他超好的。但我卻擔心也許他們只是假裝對 Jason 好，但卻想在 Jason 沒有任何利用價值後解雇他。我告訴 Jason 我的想法。Jason 只是神秘地笑著說「山人自有妙計」。

還可以怎麼說 In Other Words

❶ Oh, what happened?
喔，怎麼啦？

- All right, tell me. What kind of shit you are in this time?
  好吧，告訴我。你這一次又惹上什麼樣的麻煩了？

- Are you finally going to quit?
  你終於要辭職了？

❷ That sounds okay for me.
我聽起來覺得還好啊。

- I didn't get your point.
  我不知道你的重點是什麼。

- Stop fussing.
  別大驚小怪的。

❸ He seemed quite delighted when he returned home this evening.
他今晚回家時看起來卻很高興。

- He's in a good mood when he came back.
  他回來時心情很好。

- He looked fabulous as if nothing had happened.
  他看起來神采飛揚就像什麼事都沒發生過似的。

這句怎麼說？ How to Say That?

水深火熱 → In hot water

英釋 in big trouble or disgrace

中釋 陷入困境或是不光彩的事件中。

A: What can I do now? I have been cutting too many classes this semester. （我該怎麼辦？我這個學期翹太多課了。）

B: Furthermore, you failed your mid-term exam. Now, I think that you're really in hot water. （而且，你還搞砸了你的期中考。現在，我想你的麻煩大了。）

 文化小盒子 Culture Box

　　"In the soup" 在中文裡的意思為陷入困境，或是陷入水深火熱之中，也可以是說一個人的麻煩大了。關於這一個俚語的來源有幾種說法，第一種是據說在 19 世紀的 40 年代的愛爾蘭大飢荒中，作為其主要糧食來源的馬鈴薯因疫病腐爛而欠收。而當時的愛爾蘭是在英國政府的統治之下，在都柏林有一些具有賑災用途，發放馬鈴薯湯給民眾的餐廳，但是條件是接受的民眾必須放棄天主教的信仰，並且將名字英國化。民眾不喜歡這樣的條件但因為攸關性命而妥協。而另一種說法則是較廣為大眾所接受的，發生在 19 世紀後期的紐約有一間名為 Hoffman House，一個拿著一鍋湯但卻不小心絆倒的服務生，整鍋湯都倒在他自己的身上，在場有一位政客，當朋友詢問發生什麼事時，他回答 "He's in the soup." 再加上當時服務生除了全身被燙傷，而還需收拾殘局並有可能會被解雇的情形，"in the soup" 被後人引用成為陷入水深火熱的困境。

阿倫碎碎念 Allen's Murmur

　　用來形容陷入困境或是大麻煩是除了用前面所提到的 "in the soup" 及 "in hot water" 之外，我們還可以說 "in big trouble" 或是 "in deep water"。在一般的河川或是游泳池旁，我們常會看到有關於水深的警告標示，如果不諳水性卻誤闖深水區，是有可能造成生命危險的，所以 "in deep water" 被引伸成為有大麻煩的意思。

　　「陷入大麻煩」還有另一種粗俗、但較為口語化的說法是 "in deep shit"，想想看，光是不小心踩到「黃金」，就夠讓人嘔上一天了，更何況還是陷在裡面，光用想的，就讓我感到噁心，這還真不是普通的麻煩。除了陷在「湯」、「水」、「黃金」等，在英文中還有陷在「酸黃瓜」裡的說法，也可以用來指陷入困境，我們說 "in a pickle"， pickle 指的是酸黃瓜或是醃漬過的蔬菜等，"in a pickle" 的原意為陷入生活的困境，但現在則演變成泛指陷入各種的困境。

　　其它相類似的說法還有 "up a tree"（進退兩難）。例如常會在漫畫或是電影中看到有一位白髮蒼蒼的老奶奶站在一棵樹下叫著她的貓咪的名字，這時候我們可以說 "Her cat is up a tree." 除了有指貓在樹上的意思之外，還有指這一隻貓正陷入一個進退兩難的困境。這時候常會有一個見義勇為的人會爬上樹去救貓，但多半下場會是和貓一起卡在樹上，不敢爬下來，這時候就可以說 "He is up a tree with that cat." 接下來就等著英勇的消防人員及梯子上場來救下老奶奶心愛的貓及那位仁兄。

Dead Presidents

美金的紙幣，
上面印有美國
已逝總統的肖
像。

Allen and Johnny are in the company restaurant. Allen is now standing in front of the cashier with Johnny and discussing something about the "dead presidents."

Allen 和 Johnny 在公司的餐廳。

Allen 和 Johnny 一起站在收銀台前討論著「已逝的總統們」。

對話 Dialogue

Allen: Oh, gee. I forgot my **wallet** in the office. Buddy, may I **borrow** some money from you, please.

Johnny: I am sorry, mate. Laura doesn't **allow** me to lend money to anyone. If there's anyone trying to borrow some dead presidents from me, he or she will have to be over my dead body, she said.

Allen: Can't you make an **exception** for me? I am your best friend. I was your best man in you and Laura's wedding.

Johnny: Sorry, Allen. Rule is rule.

Allen: Come on, Johnny. I just need 10 **bucks** to pay for my lunch. I'll pay you back when I **return** to the office.

Johnny: No worries, it's on me this time.

:: 單字 Vocabulary

1. **wallet** [ˋwɑlɪt]
   n 錢包、皮夾
   → I felt my wallet and keys in my inside pocket.
   我在內側的口袋裡摸索著皮夾和鑰匙。

2. **borrow** [ˋbɑro]
   v 借、借入
   → They cannot borrow anymore from the bank.
   他們無法再從銀行那借到一分一毛。

3. **allow** [əˋlaʊ]
   v 准許、允許
   → The judge allowed his claim.
   法官允許了他的請求。

4. **exception** [ɪkˋsɛpʃən] n
   例外、例外的人（或事物）
   → There's an exception for every rule.
   凡事都有例外。

5. **buck** [bʌk]
   n【美】【俚】元
   → They don't want to overlook the opportunity to make a quick buck.
   他們不想錯過任何可以賺容易錢的機會。

6. **return** [rɪˋtɝn]
   v 回、返回
   → Cedric will return to Sydney tonight.
   Cedric 今晚會回雪梨。

翻譯 Translation

Allen: 喔，天啊。我把皮夾忘在辦公室裡了。兄弟，我可以向你借一點錢嗎，拜託？

Johnny: 我很抱歉，老兄。Laura 不喜歡我借錢給任何人。她說，如果有人試著要從我這借到錢的話，就必須踩過我的屍體。

Allen: 不能為我例外一次嗎？我是你最好的朋友。我還是你和 Laura 婚禮上的伴郎耶。

Johnny: 對不起，Allen。規矩就是規矩。

Allen: 拜託，Johnny。我只需要十塊錢來付午餐的錢。回辦公室之後我就會還你了。

Johnny: 別擔心，這次我請客。

心情小日記 Dear Diary

May 9th

Dear Diary,

In fact, Johnny is the most generous person that I've ever know. It's definitely not because he bought me lunch today, but he indeed lent me money and saved my ass once. The thing was, <u>my sister Ashlee came to visit me last summer, and was involved in a serious car accident on her way to my apartment.</u> I was panic when I got the news in my office. Johnny comforted me and left me his ATM card and pin code. At that time I realized that he's not a cheapskate as everyone made it out to be. He's just doing it in the right time.

5月9日

親愛的日記，

事實上，Johnny 是我所認識最慷慨的人了。這絕不是因為他今天請我吃中飯的緣故，而是他真的借過我錢，幫了我一個大忙。事情是這樣的，我的妹妹 Ashlee 去年夏天來看我，在她到我住的公寓的路上碰到一場嚴重的車禍。我在辦公室得知這個消息的時候，我整個人都慌了。Johnny 安慰我並留給我一張他的提款卡和密碼。那個時候，我就瞭解了他並不是大家所說的小氣鬼。他只是會在對的時間才做。

還可以怎麼說 In Other Words

❶ I forgot my wallet in the office.
我把皮夾忘在辦公室裡了。

- I neglected to bring my wallet.
  我忘了帶皮夾了。

- I haven't got any money with me.
  我身上沒有半毛錢。

❷ May I borrow some money from you, please.
我可以向你借一點錢嗎，拜託？

- Would you please lend me some money?
  你可以借我一點錢嗎？

- Can you front me some hunnies?
  可以借我一點錢，頂一下先嗎？

❸ My sister Ashlee came to visit me last summer, and was involved in a serious car accident on her way to my apartment.
我的妹妹 Ashlee 去年夏天來看我，在她到我住的公寓的路上碰到一場嚴重的車禍。

- Ashlee, my sis, was injured in a terrible car accident when she came to my apartment last summer.
  Ashlee，我的妹妹，去年夏天在她到我公寓的路上因為一場可怕的車禍而受傷了。

- Ashlee was injured in a car crash when she came to visit me last summer.
  Ashlee 去年夏天來拜訪我時，因為一場車禍而受傷了。

這句怎麼說? How to Say That?

綠油油的美鈔 ➡ Long green

英釋 US, old-fashion slang, paper money, cash, especially means the US dollar.

中釋 美國,老派的俚語,以其形狀及顏色用以指稱美金紙幣或是現金。

A: I think the cops find me and it's time for me to make a getaway. Do you think you can rustle up some long green in an hour? (我想條子發現我了,我該是時候逃亡了。你覺得你在一個小時內能籌到多少現金?)

B: How much do you need? (你需要多少呢?)

A: As much as you can. (越多越好。)

文化小盒子 Culture Box

　　在 1995 年時有一部電影名為 "Dead Presidents",中文翻譯為《絕命戰場》。電影海報的設計十分特殊,電影的名稱 "Dead Presidents" 遠看是花花綠綠的一片,近看就會發現它是以美金作為背景。用 "Dead Presidents" 來表示錢,並被廣泛的使用,根據一些資料顯示應該是起源自由饒舌歌手團體 Eric B. and Rakim 在 1987 年時錄製的歌曲 "Paid in Full" 中的一句 "So I start my mission, leave my residence. Thinking how could I get some dead presidents.",而以 dead presidents 來代表錢,則是因為在美國現行的紙幣一共有七種,而除了 100 元美金及 10 元美金之外,其它五種紙幣上的肖像皆為美國歷任的總統。1 元美金上的是第一任的華盛頓總統,2 元美金上的是第三任的總統傑弗遜,5 元美金的是第十六任的林肯總統,20 元美金的是第七任的傑克遜總統,50 元美金則是第十八任的格蘭特總統。

阿倫碎碎念 Allen's Murmur

在美國，因為在紙鈔上的人頭肖像大多為歷任的總統，所以被稱為 "dead presidents"，在台灣則會稱千元大鈔為一張「小朋友」，在大陸則是稱 100 元的鈔票是「毛爺爺」，都是以鈔票上的人物來作為暱稱。

然而在美國，除了介紹過的 "dead presidents" 之外，也有類似像在台灣及大陸對於最大幣值的紙鈔暱稱，一般會稱 100 美金的大鈔為 "Benjamin"，這是因為在 100 美金上的是美國著名的政治、科學、發明家 Benjamin Franklin（班傑明·佛蘭克林）的肖像。他是美國革命時的重要領導人物之一，也曾參與起草美國獨立宣言，是美國政治史上相當重要的人物之一。除了這些暱稱之外，在英文中還有用許多不同的俚語來稱錢。Allen 我就將它大致分為兩種不同的類型來介紹，第一種，我稱它為象徵類，像是 bread, dough, clams 等，都是食物，但有些許的不同。相信大家都聽過 "Love or bread" 吧，是要選擇愛情還是麵包，自古以來都是個難解的問題，在這裡的 bread 指的是與經濟條件相關的，也就是錢，所以用 bread 或是 dough 來稱錢，而稱 clams 則是因為遠古時代是以貝殼做為貨幣。第二種，我稱它是色彩類，例如是 lettuce, cabbage, greenbacks, long green 等，說到這，大家應該都已經注意到了，都是綠色的。沒錯，因為印製美金鈔票的墨水是綠色的，所以大家也都用「綠油油」來形容這一種在全世界都能通行的貨幣。

最後請大家跟我一起來喊一句在電影 *Jerry Maguire*《臺譯：征服情海》中有名的經典台詞 "Show me the money"！

Diary 5 月 14 日

Bad Apple

害群之馬或是
鼠屎的意思,
專門扯後腿
的人物。

Miri and Allen are talking about "apples" during the lunch break.Miri 和 Allen 在中午休息時間時,討論到「蘋果」。

 對話 *Dialogue*

Miri: Hey, Allen. Long time no see! How are you doing?

Allen: Hey, Miri. Not so good…I have been working **overtime** from last week and still can't finish the sales report.

Miri: But I think there're so many people in your team, and the report can be finished in no time.

Allen: Yea, I know! But the problem is that there's a bad apple in my team.

Miri: What? An apple? What does that mean?

Allen: A bad apple means someone who always **drags** the others in the group.

Miri: Oh, I see! So you mean that one of your **colleagues** doesn't want to share the workload

Allen: Yep, and **furthermore** his behavior has shaken the team **morale.**

Miri: Alas! Poor you.

單字 Vocabulary

1. **overtime** [`ovɚ,taɪm]
   n 加班；超出的時間
   → I pull in a lot of overtime pay each month.
   我每個月掙了不少的加班費。

2. **drag** [dræg] v 拉，拖；拖著（腳等）行進
   → He hates parties so much, we need an elephant to drag him into going.
   他超討厭派對的，我們需要一頭大象才能把他拖去參加。

3. **colleague** [`kɑlig]
   n 同事
   → She's a former colleague of mine.
   她是我以前的同事。

4. **furthermore** [`fɝðɚ`mor] adv 而且、此外
   → I don't want to go to that party, furthermore, I don't have time to do so.
   我不想去參加那個聚會，而且我也沒有時間去。

5. **behavior** [bɪ`hevjɚ]
   n 行為、舉止
   → I won't stand for the behavior of that kind in my office.
   在我的辦公室裡絕不容許那樣的行為。

6. **morale** [mə`ræl]
   n 士氣，鬥志
   → Mail from home is a great morale booster for soldiers.
   家書對於士兵而言可以大大的鼓舞士氣。

翻譯 Translation

Miri: 嘿，Allen。好久不見！最近好嗎？

Allen: 嘿，Miri。不太好。我從上星期開始一直加班還沒能完成銷售報告。

Miri: 但我想你的團隊中有很多人，應該不需要多少時間就能完成那份報告吧。

Allen: 對啊，我知道。但是我的團隊中有一個「壞蘋果」。

Miri: 什麼？一顆蘋果？是什麼意思呢？

Allen: 一個「壞蘋果」代表的是在團體中總是扯大家後腿的角色。

Miri: 喔，我懂了。所以你說的是有一個同事不願意分擔工作。

Allen: 對，而且他的行為還打擊了團隊的士氣。

Miri: 唉，你真可憐。

心情小日記 Dear diary

May 14th

Dear Diary,

Mary gossiped me this morning. She said that Yo's a big fish's son. Mary got this through the grapevine, and I believe that's quite true, and that explains everything why as a green hand, Yo's so confident that he won't get any penalty from not doing his job. His behavior seriously caused morale damage in our team and brought bad influences. In fact, several colleagues refused to do the report as well, and slacked off at work. I really have to have a serious talk with our team members, after all not every-one is the member of the "lucky sperm club" !!

5月14日

親愛的日記，

Mary 今天早上報了一個八卦給我。她說阿祐是一個重要人物的兒子。Mary 是聽小道消息知道的，我相信真實度還蠻高的，而且這也解釋了為什麼就一個菜鳥而言，阿祐相當有信心他不會因為不做事而受到懲罰。他的行為嚴重的打擊了士氣，並帶來不好的影響。事實上，有幾位同事也不願意做報告，並在上班時打混。我真的必須要好好的和我們的成員談一談，畢竟不是大家都是「幸運精子俱樂部」的成員啊！！

還可以怎麼說 In Other Words

❶ I have been working overtime from last week.
我從上星期開始一直加班。

- I live in the office recently.
  我最近住在辦公室裡。 = 最近一直在加班。

- I've been burning the midnight oil all week.
  我已經點了一整個星期的「午夜油燈」。 = 我已經一個星期都在熬夜加班。

❷ Alas! Poor you.
唉，你真可憐。

- What bad luck you have!
  你真倒楣。

- Well, I guess you're shit out of luck.
  嗯，我猜你所有的好運都「屎」光了。 = 嗯，你已經陷入一個萬劫不復的境界。（shit out of luck 可以縮寫成 SOL）

❸ Mary got this through the grapevine.
Mary 是聽小道消息知道的。

- Mary heard it from a secret source.
  Mary 從一個秘密的源頭得知的。

- A little bird told Mary.
  有一隻小鳥跟 Mary 說的。 = Mary 聽別人說的。

這句怎麼說？ How to Say That?

老鼠屎 → Rotten apple

英釋 A rotten apple is a member of a group, or a single element in a set of things, that is bad and likely to corrupt the other people or things in the group.

中釋 個人做出不良的行為，甚至會帶壞團體中的其他人，及敗壞團隊名聲。rotten apple 與 bad apple 同義，但在程度上有差異，bad apple 是指壞蛋，而 rotten apple 則更壞，是壞蛋中的壞蛋，行為更令人髮指。

A: How could he do that! He's ruining our reputation. （他怎麼能這樣做呢！他敗壞了我們整體的聲譽了。）

B: This is the typical case of a rotten apple injuries its neighbors. （這就是典型的一人作惡，萬人遭殃。）

 文化小盒子 Culture Box

　　蘋果在成熟過程中會釋放出「乙烯」，這一種氣體會加速蔬果類的熟成及老化。所以如果將蘋果與其他的蔬果一同放置時，將加速其他蔬果老化及腐敗的速度。而壞掉的蘋果所釋放出的乙烯量更多，所以在英文中有 "A bad apple spoils the whole bunch/barrel."（一顆壞蘋果，敗壞了一籮筐）的說法，相當於中文裡「一顆老鼠屎，壞了一鍋粥」的說法。"bad apple" 便是由這樣的說法中所延伸出，進而被引用來稱「害群之馬」，一般是指品德上有問題的人，因本身的不良行為而影響團隊的名聲，甚至還會帶壞周遭的朋友。另外還有一個常見類似的說法 "black sheep"，不同的是 black sheep 通常是指家族中的異類，常含有形容不幸，並非完全帶有貶義，且有轉圜的餘地。"He's a black sheep in the family." 可用來形容家中的敗家子，也可用來形容一家人都很成功，但僅有這一人表現平庸。

阿倫碎碎念 *Allen's Murmur*

　　亞當與夏娃因為受到蛇的誘惑而偷吃了禁果，因此被上帝逐出了伊甸園。而在一般大眾認知中，禁果就是蘋果。但是根據查證，在聖經上並未提及禁果到底是什麼果實，在猶太教中則推測禁果可能是無花果或是葡萄等。有歷史學家認為普羅大眾認為禁果就是蘋果可能是受到復興文藝時期畫作的影響，當時的畫家會在聖經的場景中加入希臘神話的元素。而在希臘神話當中，希拉將金蘋果樹種在赫斯珀里得斯果園，並命其三姊妹看守，而且在拉丁語中蘋果（mālum），和罪惡（mălum）的拼音相似，所以當時的畫家將蘋果當作禁果，畫入作品中。

　　阿倫我想的就沒有這麼多了，我只是單純的覺得蘋果紅通通的樣子感覺是會吸引人去咬一口，而畫在畫作上，看起來的效果很棒，還有最重要的是，畫家應該都很會畫蘋果吧。大家應該在基礎的美術課上都畫過蘋果吧？畫蘋果可是訓練畫工最基本的。

　　蘋果除了我剛剛說的在視覺上有很棒的效果之外，其營養價值也很高。所以在英文諺語中有將心肝寶貝、掌上明珠稱為 "apple of one's eye"。Speaking of that, I think you guys already know who the apple of my eye is. 當然是 Charlene 囉。If she asks me to be nice to the manager, I will try my best to be an apple-polisher. 為什麼是 apple-polisher 呢？相信大家都有看過電視上的大哥身邊總是有幾個小弟，在大哥要吃蘋果時，愛拍馬屁的小弟會盡職的將蘋果在身上擦個幾下後，再遞給大哥，這樣的馬屁精，我們就稱他是 apple polisher。

02 Chapter

Summer 夏天

All Ears

就像長了很多的耳朵，用來形容全神貫注地聽，也就是洗耳恭聽。

Allen had a hard time with his colleague, and his best friend, Johnny's trying to lend him "an ear."

Allen 和他的同事關係緊張，他最好的朋友，

Johnny 正試著要借給他「一隻耳朵」。

 對話 Dialogue

Johnny: How are things?

Allen: Well, today was a **rough** day for me but everything's okay now.

Johnny: Are you sure? You sure you don't want to talk about it? Come on, Allen. I am all ears, you can trust me. I know Tim was so hard on you this morning, and he's **breathing down your neck** all the time.

Allen: How do you know that?

Johnny: I have eyes everywhere. I also know that he's likely to do something behind your back. Because there's an assistant manager **position** opening up in our department, and you and Tim are both on the list. **Apparently,** Tim already got the news.

Allen: Oh, I see, and that's why he **nags** at me all day long. Thanks, mate. <u>You are really a Jack of all trades.</u>

Johnny: Let's make some plans; we can't let him get that position, can we?

單字 Vocabulary

1. **rough** [rʌf] adj 【口】難受的，艱難的 → We had a rough time. 我們有過一段艱辛的日子。

2. **breathe down one's neck** 對某人緊迫盯人 → Please stop breathing down my neck while I work. 當我在工作的時候請不要一直緊盯著我。

3. **position** [pə`zɪʃən] n 職位、職務；工作 → She's the only female to rise to such an exalted position in our company. 在我們公司，她是唯一一位高升到這樣一個崇高職位的女性。

4. **apparently** [ə`pærəntlɪ] adv 顯然地 → It's apparently that they're getting divorced soon. 很顯然地，他們就快要離婚了。

5. **nag** [næg] v 不斷的找…的麻煩；與…糾纏不休 → Ray, how often do I have to nag at you to tidy your room? Ray，到底要我有多常來嘮叨你整理你的房間？

6. **mate** [met] n 同伴、夥伴 → Hey, mate, where are you going? 嘿，老兄，你要去哪兒？

翻譯 Translation

Johnny: 最近好嗎？

Allen: 唉，對我而言今天真難熬，但還好現在沒事了。

Johnny: 你確定嗎？你確定你不要跟我談一下？說說看啊，Ray。我洗耳恭聽，你可以信任我的。我知道 Tim 今天早上對你很過份，還有他一直都對你緊迫盯人。

Allen: 你是怎麼知道的？

Johnny: 我到處都有眼線。我還知道他極有可能會在你背後搞些小動作。因為我們部門有一個經理的空缺，你和 Tim 都在候選名單上。顯然 Tim 已經得到這一個消息了。

Allen: 喔，我懂了，這就是他整天都在挑我毛病的緣故。謝啦，兄弟。你真是一個萬事通耶。

Johnny: 讓我們來計畫一下，我們可不可以讓他得到那個職位，不是嗎？

心情小日記 Dear Diary

June 1st

Dear Diary,

To speak frankly, Tim is a very strong opponent in this campaign. I admire his outstanding performance at work, but his unfriendly behavior recently has roughened my temper. <u>Good thing I've got a caring friend</u> who's willing to listen to my complaints and that makes me feel an inexpressible relief and able to face further challenge with great courage. When Johnny said "I'm all ears." and "I have eyes everywhere." that always reminds me of two famous guardian generals known as "Thousand Miles Eye" and "With-the-Wind Ear" in Chinese mythology. Thank you, Johnny, for always listen to me and stand by my side. I'll pay you back DOUBLE when you need me!!

6月1日

親愛的日記，

老實說，*Tim* 在這一次的競爭當中是一個相當強勁的對手。我非常佩服他在工作中優異的表現，但他最近不友善的行為惹惱了我。幸好我有一個體貼的朋友總是會傾聽我的抱怨，讓我感到無法言喻的寬慰及有勇氣面對接下來的挑戰。當 *Johnny* 說「我全身上下都是耳朵」及「我的眼睛遍佈各地」時總讓我想到中國神話中兩個護衛將軍「千里眼」及「順風耳」。謝謝你，*Johnny*，總是會聽我訴苦及站在我這一邊。當你需要我的時後，我一定會「加倍」奉還的！！

▦ 還可以怎麼說 In Other Words

❶ That's why he nags at me all day long.
這就是他整天都在挑我毛病的緣故。

- Now I know why he picks on me all the time.
  現在我知道他一直找我碴的原因了。

- No wonder that he's gunning for me recently.
  難怪他最近老是針對我。

❷ You are really a Jack of all trades.
你真是一個萬事通耶。

- You are Mr. Know-it-all.
  你是包打聽先生。

- You are a walking "information bureau."
  你是一個行動「情報局」。＝ 你是一個萬事通。

❸ Good thing I've got a caring friend.
幸好我有一個體貼的朋友。

- Luckily, I have got such a considerate friend.
  幸好我有這麼一個體貼人的朋友。

- My ancestors did good things, so I've got such a caring friend.
  祖上有德,所以我才能有這樣一個體貼的朋友。

 這句怎麼說? How to Say That?

傾聽 ⟶ Lend an ear to someone

英釋 to listen carefully and with understanding to someone or something

中釋 仔細聆聽,認真傾聽。也可以說 lend someone an ear (傾聽某人所說)
或是 lend me your ears(聽我說)等不同的變化。

A: Leo, I am so sad, because I just got the air from my boyfriend. I need someone to lend me an ear. (Leo,我好難過,因為我失戀了。我需要有人聽我說話。)

B: Okay, I am all ears. (Ok,我洗耳恭聽。)

文化小盒子 Culture Box

　　All ears 洗耳恭聽,全神貫注,聚精會神的聆聽。all 代表所有的,全部的,在使用 all 的時候,其數量一定是指 3 個,或是 3 個以上的人、事或物,所以當我們在說 "I am all ears." 時,除了用自己原有的兩隻耳朵聽之外,還要在身上長出其它的耳朵來聽,是不是和我們中文中常說的「用心聆聽」,除了「兩隻耳朵聽之外,還要用『心』這個第三隻耳朵去聽」這樣的說法有異曲同工之妙呢？在英文中這樣類似的全身都是某種特定器官的說法還有兩種，一個是 "all eyes"，意思是目不轉睛，聚精會神的看或是拭目以待。另一個則是 "all thumbs"，有手忙腳亂，笨手笨腳的意思。試著想一想在看一件事物時，恨不得有無數的眼睛從各種角度全方位，無死角的看時，那該是有多麼的專注。還有當所有的手指頭都變成了大拇指，那做起事來該有多麼的不方便，看起來有多麼的笨手笨腳了。

阿倫碎碎念 Allen's Murmur

人的耳朵是一個非常奇妙的器官，除了用來接受聲波，聽聲音之外，也是維持身體的平衡以及用來識別位置（就像是 GPS 中的陀螺儀）的器官。

不知道大家有沒有注意到，我們的耳朵對於聲音是有選擇性的，會選擇放大自己想聽的聲音，而其它的聲音就會相對的較小或是被忽略。相信大家都曾有過失眠的經驗，失眠時會特別的在乎一個聲音，也許是室友的打呼聲、也或許是冰箱運作的聲音，這時候雖然極力的想忽略這個聲音，但卻會有越來越清楚的感覺。

說到這就讓我想到 earworm，也有人說是 brainworm。這可不是一種專門寄生在人的耳朵或是腦子裡的昆蟲。而是指一種在人的腦海中揮之不去，一直不斷重複在耳邊響起的音樂片段，用中文說好聽的叫「餘音繞樑」，不好聽的就是「魔音穿腦」。For me, the song of Namo Amitabha Budda is the top 1 earworm song that always gets stuck inside my head. 對我而言，南無阿彌陀佛的歌是 earworm 排行第一名，簡單的歌詞及旋律，讓人在聽過幾次後，就很容易會不斷在腦中播放，這個時候我們可以說 It's time for ear bleach. Ear bleach 指的可不是漂白你的耳朵，而是以聽其它音樂或是和別人聊天的方式來轉移注意力。What are the top ten earwarm songs stuck in your head?

Hard Cheese

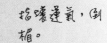

招壞運氣，倒楣。

Margot meets Allen in the canteen, and it seems that

Allen's not satisfied with what he got.

Margot 在員工餐廳裡碰到 Allen，

看起來 Allen 似乎不太滿意他得到的。

對話 Dialogue

Margot: Allen, don't play with your food, you are not a kid. It looks **disgusting**.

Allen: Ah, it's you, Margot.

Margot: What happened? Have a bad day?

Allen: Not exactly, just the **horrible** food. I strongly **recommend** you NOT to order the beef noodle; it can **ruin** your entire day.

Margot: Oh, I see. You don't like your noodle, do you? Well, it's hard cheese.

Allen: Hard cheese? What does that mean?

Margot: It means "bad luck" or "**misfortune**" in British English. I think most people prefer soft cheese instead of hard cheese. So "hard cheese" becomes the slang term for "bad luck."

" It's now becoming rather **archaic**, only old people like me still use it.

    Allen: You are not old.

  Margot: I will be 60 years old this August.

    Allen: No way!

  Margot: Oh, that pleases me! Come on, let me buy you a nice meal.

單字 Vocabulary

1. **disgusting** [dɪsˋgʌstɪŋ] adj 令人作嘔的；十分討厭的 → What a disgusting smell! 這味道真令人噁心！

2. **horrible** [ˋhɔrəbl] adj 【口】極討厭的；糟透的 → I strongly recommend that you really should go to see a doctor. 我強力推薦你應該要去看醫生。

3. **recommend** [ˌrɛkəˋmɛnd] v 推薦、介紹 → Anthony was transferred from London to New York. Anthony 被從倫敦調職到紐約。

4. **ruin** [ˋrʊɪn] v 毀壞；毀滅 → The tornado ruined all the houses here. 龍捲風將這裡所有的房屋都給毀了。

5. **misfortune** [mɪsˋfɔrtʃən] n 不幸、厄運 → I had the misfortune to lose my wallet. 我真倒楣，弄丟皮夾了。

6. **archaic** [ɑrˋkeɪk] adj 老式的 → He always swears at people by using archaic idioms. 他常用老式的片語來罵人。

翻譯 Translation

  Margot: Allen，別再玩你的食物了，你不是小孩子了。它看起來好噁心。

    Allen: 喔，是妳啊，Margot。

  Margot: 怎麼了？倒楣的一天嗎？

    Allen: 不算是，只是這食物難吃死了。我強烈的推薦妳千萬不要點牛肉麵，它會毀了妳一整天。

Margot: 喔，我懂了。你不喜歡你這碗麵，對吧？嗯，真是硬起司。

Allen: 硬起司？什麼意思？

Margot: 在英式英語中，它代表是「壞運」或是「不幸」。我想是人們大多喜歡軟的起司，而不是硬的。所以 "hard cheese" 成了代表「倒楣」的俚語。這樣的用法已經有些過時了，只有像我一樣的老人家還在用這樣的說法。

Allen: 妳才不老呢。

Margot: 我今年八月就要 60 歲了。

Allen: 不可能！

Margot: 喔，這讓我感到很高興！來吧，讓我請你吃大餐吧。

心情小日記 Dear Diary

June 4th

Dear Diary,

Today, I had lunch with Margot who's the executive assistant to our big boss. She looks like only in her mid-forties, but she said that she'll be 60 years old this year. What the f... a shock!!! (<u>No backyard language in my diary.</u>) She is a very modest person despite her position. And I think that's the reason why she's so successful in her career. Margot gave me some advice about the surviving rules in the workplace during the lunch break. I have benefited greatly from her talk. Thanks to that yucky beef noo-dle, <u>it gave me a chance to get to know Margot.</u>

6 月 4 日

親愛的日記，

今天，我和大老闆的特助 Margot 一起共進午餐。她看起來大概是 45 歲左右的年紀，但她說她今年就要 60 歲了。真他ㄇ……令人驚訝！！！（在我的日記中不說髒話）。儘管她有相當的地位，但她卻是一個謙虛的人。我想這就是她在工作上這麼成功的原因吧。在午餐休息時間時，Margot 給了我一些有關職場上生存法則的意見。我從她的言談中獲益不少。感謝那碗難吃的要命的牛肉麵，它給了我更進一步認識 Margot 的機會。

還可以怎麼說 In Other Words

❶ Allen, don't play with your food.
Allen，別再玩你的食物了。

- **Please stop playing with your food, Allen.**
  請停止玩你的食物，Allen。

- **The food is for eating, not for playing.**
  食物是用來吃的，不是用來玩的。

❷ No backyard language in my diary.
在我的日記中不說髒話。

- **I don't swear in my diary.**
  我在日記裡不罵髒話。

- **No dirty words allowed in my daily records.**
  在我的每日記錄中不允許有髒話出現。

❸ It gave me a chance to get to know Margot.
它給了我更進一步認識 Margot 的機會。

- I've got more familiar with Margot.
  我對 Margot 更熟悉了。

- I have learned a lot from the talk with Margot.
  我在和 Margot 的談話中學到了非常多。

 這句怎麼說？ How to Say That?

真倒楣！ → Just my luck!

英釋 something that you say when something bad happens to you

中釋 真倒楣，用在有不好的事發生自己身上時說。有嘲諷的意味，如同在中文中，我們會在倒楣時說「吼，真好運！」一樣。

A: Did you get the concert ticket? （你買到演唱會的票了嗎？）

B: The girl before me in the queue got the last one. Just my luck! （排在我前面的那個女生買到了最後一張。我真倒楣！）

 文化小盒子 Culture Box

　　Hard cheese 照字面上的意思為硬起司，而造成硬掉的原因有可能是因為放太久了；因保存不良而造成的乾硬，甚至有可能會在食用後造成消化不良等毛病產生。"Hard cheese" 是英式俚語，多半被使用在說英式英語國家，如英國、澳洲、紐西蘭等國家，在美國並不常聽到這樣的說法。關於用 "hard cheese" 來表示倒楣的由來有幾種說法，其中有一種認為人們喜歡口感軟嫩，綿密的起司，而吃到硬掉的起司有可能會造成消化不良，是一件倒楣的事。而也有另一種看法是 cheese 與波斯語中 chiz（=thing），因此在英文當中 cheese 也有「正確，適當的事物；頭等的人或事物」的含意存在，例如一般常見的 "big cheese"（大人物）的用法。所以 "hard cheese" = "hard thing"（壞事情），也就有了倒楣的含意及用法。一般在說 "hard cheese" 時有兩種口吻，一為表是同情「喔，真衰！」的感覺，還有一種則帶有嘲諷「只能自認倒楣」的語氣。

阿倫碎碎念 Allen's Murmur

有關 cheese 的用法在英文當中用得相當廣泛，也許是因為 cheese 是歐美人士經常食用的食品之一吧，所以總能在許多不同的情境中用到 cheese。例如，在美國俚語當中有 "cut the cheese"，猜猜看是什麼意思呢？想像一下當切一塊起士時會散發出的味道是不是會有一點像「放屁」呢？還有在比較事物時，常會說的 "chalk and cheese"，這兩種完全不一樣的東西所代表的就是「截然不同」的意思。

而最後要介紹一個相當有趣的起士說法 "cheese it"，我知道光看是找不出有趣在哪，別先急著翻白眼，請聽我解釋。這一個說法是源自於 19 世紀初的英國，"cheese it" 中的 cheese 據說是 Jesus 的委婉說法，在當時為「停下、住手；安靜一下」等的意思，例如 "Will you cheese it! I don't want to hear a single word."（拜託安靜一會兒！我一個字都不想聽。）但是演變至今則成為「快跑、快走」的意思，最常在躲警察的時候會聽到，像是警察來取締攤販時，就可以說 "Cheese it! Cops!" 照其原義為「趕快停下手邊的交易」而逐漸地變成「快跑」的意思，這種兩極化的說法應該還蠻有趣的吧？！

Golden Parachute

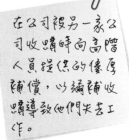

在公司被另一家公司收購時向高階人員提供的優厚補償，以彌補收購導致他們失去工作。

Johnny gets the news about a "parachute" and wants to share with Allen.

After a careful searching, he finally finds Allen alone in the conference room.

Johnny 得到有關一個「降落傘」的情報，他想告訴 Allen。

經過一番仔細的尋找，他終於發現 Allen 一個人在會議室裡。

對話 Dialogue

Johnny: Thank god, you are here. Do you know that I have been chasing up hill and down dale trying to find you?

Allen: Now you've found me. Ok, what kind of valuable information you want to give me this time, Mr. Paparazzo?

Johnny: Be serious, Allen. It is very important, it's about our future.

Allen: All right, I'll prick up my ears.

Johnny: I've just got the news that none of you and Tim got promoted, but someone's going to parachute into that position.

Allen: Oh, well, I already know it. You know our company has bought up a local firm weeks ago, right? Our new assistant manager was one of their upper executives, who has a golden parachute.

Johnny: That doesn't make sense. An **upper** executive with a golden parachute, then he should be parachuted into the executive position.

Allen: I don't understand that, either. But for your information, our new assistant manager is "she," not "he."

單字 Vocabulary

1. **chase** [tʃes] ⓥ 尋找，追蹤。chase up hill and down dale 翻山越嶺，到處
→ He made to chase Susie, who ran back laughing.
他假裝要去追一邊大笑一邊往回跑的 Susie。

2. **valuable** [ˋvæljʊəbl] adj 值錢的、貴重的
→ He let me to choose a piece of valuable jewelry for birthday present.
他讓我選一件貴重的珠寶當作是生日禮物。

3. **paparazzo** [ˌpɑpəˋratso] ⓝ【義】專門偷拍名人照片的攝影師，狗仔隊
→ Paparazzi were out in force at the restaurant.
狗仔隊們聚集在餐廳的外面。

4. **prick** [prɪk] ⓥ 豎起（耳朵）
→ We heard voices and then we stopped talking and prick our ears up.
我們聽到聲音之後便停止說話還豎起了耳朵聽。

5. **parachute** [ˋpærəˌʃut] ⓝ 降落傘
→ I was almost strangled by my parachute harness straps.
我差一點就要被我的降落傘背帶給勒死了。

6. **upper** [ˋʌpɚ] adj （地位）較高的，上層的
→ Most of them came from wealthy, upper class families.
他們大部分都是來自富裕的上流社會家庭。

翻譯 Translation

Johnny: 感謝老天，原來你在這啊。你知道我到處找你嗎？

Allen: 現在你找到我了。OK，你這一次要給我什麼樣重要的信息呢，狗仔

隊先生？

Johnny: 嚴肅點，Allen。這個非常重要，這有關我們的將來。

Allen: 好吧，我會豎起我的耳朵聽。

Johnny: 我剛得到的消息指出你和 Tim 都沒有得到升遷，但是有人會空降到那一個位置。

Allen: 喔，嗯，我已經知道這件事了。你知道我們公司在幾個星期前收購了一家公司，對吧？我們的新副理是那家公司中有簽訂黃金降落傘協議的高層之一。

Johnny: 這樣不合理啊。一個有黃金降落傘的高層，那他應該會被空降到高階管理的職位啊。

Allen: 我也不懂。但是供你參考一下，我們的新副理是「她」，不是「他」。

心情小日記 Dear diary

June 16th

Dear Diary,

Chief called me to his office yesterday afternoon, and we had a brief talk. He told me that we will have a new assistant manager, and he wanted me to help her to get into the swing of things A.S.A.P. Chief said our new assistant manager is an experienced hand in this field, he hopes that I can learn a lot from her. After the talk, I got myself into the contradiction between happiness and sadness. I am happy to be able to learn from an expert. But a little bit sad, because I didn't get promoted though I have little expectation of it.

6月 16日

親愛的日記，

老大昨天下午把我叫到他的辦公室裡，和我有一段簡短的談話。他告訴我，我們將有個新的副理，他要我幫她儘快的熟悉情況。老大說我們的新副理是這一個領域的老手，他希望我能多向她學習。談話之後，我陷入高興及難過的矛盾境界。我很高興能有機會和專家學習。但有一點點難過，因為沒有被升職，雖然我本來就不抱希望。

還可以怎麼說 In Other Words

❶ I have been chasing up hill and down dale trying to find you.
我到處找你。

- I have looked for you high and low.
  我四處地在找你。

- I've been hunting for you everywhere.
  我一直在追蹤你的蹤跡。

❷ All right, I'll prick up my ears.
好吧，我會豎起我的耳朵聽。

- Okay, I will listen very carefully.
  好的，我會仔細聽的。

- I shall be very glad to hear what you wish to say.
  你要講什麼，我都會洗耳恭聽的。

❸ Our new assistant manager is an experienced hand in this field.
我們的新副理是這一個領域的老手。

- The new assistant manager is an old hand in this industry.
  新副理是這一個產業中的相當有經驗的能手。

- Our new assistant manager is a well-known expert in this field.
  我們的新副理是這一個領域中相當有名的專家。

 這句怎麼說？ *How to Say That?*

資遣費 → Severance pay

英釋 A sum of money usually based on length of employment for which an employee is eligible upon termination. It also can be called as the change-in-control benefit.

中釋 因非自願性離職時，公司需付給離職員工一筆依其年資計算的金額，以保障員工的生活。也可以被稱為是控制權變動福利金。

A: What's the relative solution for those laid-off workers? （對於那一些被解雇的員工有什麼相關的配套措施呢？）

B: Those laid-off workers received their regular checks, plus vacation and severance pay. （那些被裁掉的員工拿到他們應得的薪資，加上假期及資遣費。）

文化小盒子 *Culture Box*

　　Golden Parachute（黃金降落傘），Golden Handcuffs（金手銬），及 Golden Ladder（金階梯）並稱三金，這個制度主要是適用於核心管理團隊，以簽訂合約的方式來提供專業經理人高額豐厚的獎勵，也一方面設限以保障公司的權利。其中 Golden Parachute 則是針對該公司在被收購的情況下，高層管理人員無論是被迫或是主動離開公司，都能獲得一筆金額相當高的安置補償費用。因為這樣的制度會使收購的成本增加，所以成為一種抵禦惡意收購的防禦措施。golden 在英文中有高額豐厚的意思，而 parachute 則有保護措施的含意，是在公司控制權變動時，高層管理人員能因這個制度而不受衝擊。除了企業當中，另外還有像是高層官員在離職或退休後，常能得到在經濟上提供保障的工作安排，這時我們也能說 He/She has a golden parachute.

阿倫碎碎念 Allen's Murmur

在最近新聞當中，因為兩起重大的嚴重氣爆事件，所以常會看到有用「肥貓」來形容一些在某個官職退休下來後在企業當中任高職，並享有高薪待遇的人，而這一些人就是我們上面所說的有 "golden parachute" 的人。而「肥貓」在英文當中，不要懷疑，就是叫 "fat cat"。"Fat cat" 在最先是指一些企圖以捐獻政治現金來操控選舉，並不管窮人死活的有錢人。之後被用來泛指些領著天價高薪但卻績效極差的主管。

既然有 golden parachute，想當然耳也有 silver parachute 及 tin parachute 的說法，其差異最只要是在於其層級，以及所給予的福利保障，其中以 golden parachute 為最高的等級。說到了 golden，相信無論是東西方，雖說是不同的文化，但是對於 gold 這一種象徵著財富的東西都應該是愛不釋手，所以都不約而同的會在覺得珍貴的東西前面冠上跟「金」有關，例如是 golden age（黃金時代）。而特別的是在英文當中會稱 60 歲以上的銀髮族為 "golden years"，有子女都長大可獨立生活，所以可以盡情享受人生的含意在。還有一個是我非常想要的，相信大家也很喜歡的 "golden goose"，在中文裡稱「金雞母」，這一個說法是從有一隻會下金蛋的鵝的故事而來的，故事中的主人因為短視近利，所以殺掉了這一隻鵝，便也因此失去穩定的財富來源，而也因此有了 "to kill the goose that lays the golden eggs"（殺雞取卵）這樣的說法。但英文是鵝，不是雞喔！

Diary 7 月 01 日

Pain in the Neck

脖子裡的痛,其意指的令人感到討厭或是麻煩的人或事,也有眼中釘、肉中刺的意思。

Ralph is Allen's colleague who works in the IT department. He's now in Allen's place and trying to fix the "pain-in-the-neck" **desktop**.

Ralph 是 Allen 公司資訊部的同事。他現在在 Allen 家裡,正試著要修理「脖子裡的痛」電腦。

 對話 *Dialogue*

Allen: Hey, Ralph. Thank you for coming. I've already tried everything on my computer, but it just doesn't work.

Ralph: So, did you **kick** it?

Allen: Not yet. Should I do that?

Ralph: No. That's great you didn't do that. Show me your computer.

Allen: Follow me, it's in my room.

About an hour later...

Ralph: Okay, it's done. But it seems like it would **crash** at anytime. To **avoid** such a pain in the neck, maybe you should **consider** buying a new one.

Allen: Yes, I will think about your suggestion, and give you my answer by this Friday.

Ralph: Okay, before that, make sure to backup your files in this **external** hard drive.

Allen: Okay, I will, and thanks!

單字 Vocabulary

1. **desktop** [ˈdɛsktɑp]
   n 桌上型電腦
   → She doesn't own a desktop or laptop computer.
   她沒有桌上型也沒有筆記型電腦。

2. **kick** [kɪk] v 踢
   → He went to kick the ball but completely missed it and pulled his back muscle.
   他跑去踢球但完全地落空而且還拉傷了背部的肌肉。

3. **crash** [kræʃ]
   v 【電腦】當機
   → Let's hope that no one's computer is crashing now.
   讓我們一起希望現在大家的電腦都沒有當機。

4. **avoid** [əˈvɔɪd]
   v 避免
   → The royal couple married in a small island to avoid the media circus.
   為了擺脫媒體瘋狂的關注，這一對皇室新人在一個小島結婚。

5. **consider** [kənˈsɪdɚ]
   v 考慮、細想
   → Please take the time to consider this problem.
   請抽空考慮一下這一個問題。

6. **external** [ɪkˈstɚnəl]
   adj 外面的、外部的
   → This medicine is for external use only.
   這種藥只能外用。

翻譯 Translation

Allen: 嘿，Ralph，謝謝你過來。我已經試過各種辦法了，但我的電腦就是不能開。

Ralph: 所以，你有踢它嗎？

Allen: 還沒耶。我應該這麼做嗎？

Ralph: 不。你沒有踢它這樣很好。帶我去看你的電腦吧。

Allen: 跟我來,在我的房間裡。

大約 1 小時候……

Ralph: 好了,修好了。但它看起來還是一副隨時會當機的樣子。為了避免這樣的麻煩事,也許你應該考慮要買一台新的。

Allen: 好,我會考慮一下你的建議,星期五之前告訴你我的答案。

Ralph: 好啊,但在這之前,你一定要將你的資料備份在這一個外接硬碟中。

Allen: 好的,我知道了,謝啦!

心情小日記 Dear Diary

July 1st

Dear Diary,

Today, Ralph came to my apartment and fixed my old desktop for me. He warned me that have to remember to back up my files every time I use it and recommended me to buy a new one. It took him around an hour on the computer repair and then we watched football together. We had a great time tonight, except for that annoying computer problem. Ralph even gave me interesting information that Joe has so many porn films on his office computer and Mimi is running an internet shop and etc. He's just like Johnny of another version.

92

7月1日

親愛的日記，

今天，Ralph 來我的公寓幫我修我的老電腦。他警告我必須在每一次使用時都一定要記得做資料備份，還建議我應該買台新的。花了他大約一個小時的時間來修電腦，之後我們就一起看足球比賽。我們今天晚上過得很愉快，除了那惱人的電腦問題之外。Ralph 甚至還給了我一些有趣的情報像是 Joe 辦公室的電腦裡有一大堆的 A 片，還有 Mimi 在經營一家網路商店等等的。他就像是另一個版本的 Johnny。

還可以怎麼說 In Other Words

❶ I will think about your suggestion.
我會考慮一下你的建議

- I will definitely take your suggestion into consideration.
  我一定會將你的建議列入考慮的。

- I'll check my account to see if I have budget to buy a new one.
  我會查一下我的帳戶看看是不是有預算可以買一台新的。

❸ Joe has so many porn films on his office computer.
Joe 辦公室的電腦裡有一大堆的 A 片。

- Joe downloaded so many adult movies on his computer.
  Joe 下載了許多的成人電影在他的電腦裡。

- Joe's computer's hard drive is filled with porn.
  Joe 的電腦硬碟裡裝滿了愛情動作片。

 這句怎麼說？ How to Say That?

惹事生非的人 → Trouble maker

英釋 A person who cause trouble; a person who creates problems or difficulties involving other people.

中釋 製造麻煩的人；某人為他人製造出問題或是困境。

A: You'd better stay away from Justin. He is such a trouble maker. （妳最好離 Justin 遠遠地。他總是惹是生非。）

B: I know, but I can't help myself, 'cause he's so charming. （我知道，但我克制不了自己，因為他實在是太迷人了。）

 文化小盒子 Culture Box

　　相信大家或多或少都有過落枕的經驗，那一種隱隱約約的痛及做什麼事都會引起的疼痛感（除非你能保持絕不轉動你的脖子）讓人感到十分不快。而 "pain in the neck" 要指的就是造成這一種的感覺的人或是事物，也就是我們一般所說的討厭鬼或是令人生厭的事情。而跟我們所提到的另一個俚語 "trouble maker" 最大的不同是在於 "trouble maker" 單指人，而 "pain in the neck" 則可以用來指稱人、事或物。這一個俚語，一般認為是起源自 19 世紀末時的美國俚語 "you give me a pain" 或是 "he's a real pain" 等這樣的說法（最早的記載是在 1884 年的文獻中），而一直到了 20 世紀初（1911 年時），則開始出現了 "pain in the neck" 這樣的說法，用來指令人感到討厭或是麻煩的人或是事物。

阿倫碎碎念 Allen's Murmur

　　除了 "pain in the neck" 之外，相信大家最熟悉的應該是 "pain in the ass"，但其實在英文中一般比較常用到的是 "pain in the butt"。其實 ass 和 butt 指的都是屁股，只是在用語上，butt 會比 ass 來得文雅一點（請注意我說的是只有一點）。所以在一般口語中，比較常說的是 "It's a big pain in my butt."（這讓我感到十分的痛苦/討厭。）

　　剛才 Allen 我有提到 butt 是比 ass 稍微文雅一點的說法，那就代表還有更文雅的說法，而其出現的時間也比較早一點，大約是在 1937 年的時候（在 "pain in the neck" 之後）有了 "pain in the rear end" 這樣的說法，the rear end 指的是後端，用在人的身上時，指的就是「臀部」，而一直到了 1951 年時，才開始有了 "pain in the ass" 這樣的說法，而傳到英國則成了 "pain in the arse"。隨著時間的演變，甚至在 1990 年時，一度流行說 "pain in the bahakas"。Actually, I have no idea about what "bahakas" means.（事實上，我不知道 bahakas 所代表的意思。）但我個人覺得（純粹為我個人的意見喔）bahakas 唸起來有點像 behind（另一種「屁股」的說法，多用在對小孩子說的時候）。

　　除了上面所說的之外，偶爾還會聽到有人說 "pain in the kiester"，這裡的 kiester（在字典上找不到）其實是 keister 的錯誤拼法，應該是因為 keister 是較新的字（1881 年開始才有）且用的並不廣泛，原意為小提包，而一直到了 1931 年才有了指「屁股」的意思。

　　介紹了這麼多，其實真正痛的部位也只有兩個，那就是脖子跟屁股。除了痛在脖子之外，我們可以發現這一個俚語的發展方向持續的朝屁股前進，也許是因為在屁股裡的痛遠比在脖子的痛讓人感到更麻煩吧。

Sweet Fanny Adams

沒有的意思。

Allen visits Mary in her cubicle. They are talking about

something about "Fanny Adams."

Allen 去 Mary 的辦公小隔間。他們正在聊著有關

"Fanny Adams" 某些事。

 對話 Dialogue

Allen: How are you doing, Mary. You look **fabulous** as usual. May I have the **handouts**, please?

Mary: What handouts?

Allen: Handouts for the **seminar** this afternoon. Yo said that he gave you the file yesterday, 'cause you wanted to check the document, and made sure every part's **perfect**, and you would get the handouts done.

Mary: Yes, I did say that, but I got sweet Fanny Adams from Yo so far. I was about to ask him.

Allen: Oh, cheese and rice! Not again. I knew I shouldn't **trust** him.

Mary: Thanks god, we still have enough time to make up for it. Do you have the **copy** of the seminar files?

單字 Vocabulary

1. **fabulous** [ˈfæbjələs]
   adj 【口】極好的
   → Tony is a fabulous cook!
   Tony 的廚藝超讚的！

2. **handout** [ˈhændaʊt]
   n 講義；課程綱要
   → Did you read the hangouts I gave you thoroughly?
   你有沒有仔細地讀過我給你的講義？

3. **seminar** [ˈsɛmə͵nɑr]
   n 研討會、專題討論會
   → The seminar went with a swing and we all learned something from it.
   這一個研討會非常順利的進行，我們大家都從中學到不少。

4. **perfect** [ˈpɝ·fɪkt]
   adj 完美的、理想的
   → I am not a paragon. I would never be perfect.
   我並不是完人。永遠都不會是十全十美的。

5. **trust** [trʌst]
   v 信任、信賴
   → You said you'll keep this secrete forever, but can I really trust you?
   你說你會永遠保守這一個秘密的，但我真的可以相信你嗎？

6. **copy** [ˈkɑpɪ]
   n 副本；複製品；拷貝
   → I sent a copy to the authority.
   我寄了一個副本給相關單位。

翻譯 Translation

Allen: Mary，妳好嗎？妳跟往常一樣的美麗動人。可以給我我的講義嗎？

Mary: 什麼講義？

Allen: 今天下午研討會要用的講義啊。阿祐說他昨天就給妳了，因為妳說妳要檢查一下，以確保每一個部分都完美無誤，還有妳會把講義給印好。

Mary: 對啊，我是說過，但是到目前為止，我並沒有從阿祐那兒拿到任何東西啊。我才正要問他說。

Allen: 喔，我的天啊！怎麼又是這樣。我就知道我不應該相信他的。

Mary: 感謝老天爺，我們還有時間來彌補。你有研討會檔案的副本嗎？

心情小日記 Dear Diary

July 18th

Dear Diary,

The afternoon seminar was excellent; many colleagues of other departments came to join the seminar, including Charlene. She waved at me when I was making the presentation. <u>My heart pounded with nervous while I was on the stage</u>, and her encouragement and support made it pounded even more wildly. I was worried about my performance, and felt relieved when Mary told me that I did a great job. Good thing, Mary did very well as always. <u>Yo's irresponsible behavior did not mar the smooth running of the seminar.</u> Yo even didn't show up in the seminar. Don't know what kind of excuse he's going to make for this time?

7月18日

親愛的日記，

今天下午的研討會棒極了；許多其它部門的同事都有過來參加，包括 Charlene。當我在做簡報的時候，她向我揮了揮手。我在台上的時候，我的心臟緊張得蹦蹦跳，她的鼓勵和支持讓我的心跳得更快了。我超擔心我的表現，當 Mary 告訴我表現得不錯時才放鬆了下來。幸好 Mary 跟往常一樣表現得很好。阿祐那不負責任的行為並沒有影響到研討會的順利進行。而阿祐甚至沒有出現在研討會上。真不知道這一次他會用什麼樣的理由？

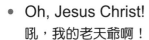 還可以怎麼說 In Other Words

❶ Oh, cheese and rice!
喔，我的天啊！

- **Oh, Jesus Christ!**
  吼，我的老天爺啊！

- **For land sakes!**
  我的媽呀！

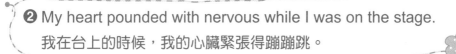 **❷ My heart pounded with nervous while I was on the stage.**
我在台上的時候，我的心臟緊張得蹦蹦跳。

- **My heart seemed to block my throat when I was on the stage.**
  我在台上的時候感覺我的心臟都快跳到喉嚨了。

- **I felt my heart beaten violently when making the presentation.**
  當我在做簡報的時候可以感覺到心臟狂暴地跳著。

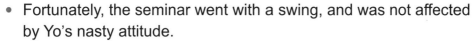 **❸ Yo's irresponsible behavior did not mar the smooth running of the seminar.**
阿祐那不負責任的行為並沒有影響到研討會的順利進行。

- **Fortunately, the seminar went with a swing, and was not affected by Yo's nasty attitude.**
  幸好，研討會進行得很順利，並沒有受到阿祐那討人厭的態度影響。

- **The seminar went very well, no one even noticed that Yo's not in.**
  研討會進行得十分順暢，甚至沒有人注意到阿祐沒有到場。

這句怎麼說？ How to Say That?

零鴨蛋 → Goose egg

英釋 Zero, especialy when written as a numeral to indicate that no points have been scored.

中釋 零，特別是指以數字表示沒有得到任何分數的時候。（中文裡以鴨蛋來表示零，而在英文當中則是以鵝蛋來形容。）

A: Mom, look! I got a goose egg. （媽，你看！我得到一個鵝蛋耶。）

B: Oh, really? Where's the goose egg? （喔，真的嗎？鵝蛋在哪兒啊？）

A: It's on my exam paper. （在我的考試卷上。）

文化小盒子 Culture Box

　　"Sweet Fanny Adams" 又可以做 "Fanny Adams"，如同我們第一眼所看到的是一個人名，但所代表的意思卻是 "nothing at all"（什麼都沒有）。這是一個在英國常用的俚語，而它的起源背後有一個悲傷的故事。Fanny Adams 是一個 8 歲大的英國女孩在 1867 年的 8 月 24 日被慘忍的殺害了，她的屍體被兇手分解，並丟棄在不同地方，而在當時供應給海軍的食物中有一種是罐頭的羊肉，其味道應該不怎麼好吃，因此產生了兩種說法，一是海軍的水手用 "Fanny Adams" 來形容這個罐頭像屍體一樣地難吃，而另一種說法則是當時兇手棄屍的地方分佈極廣，而其中包括了製作供應海軍食物的屠宰場，暗指極有可能混入供應給海軍的食物當中。"Fanny Adams" 從最早的指羊肉或是燉肉慢慢的轉變成用來指「什麼都沒有」。

阿倫碎碎念 Allen's Murmur

　　在每種不同的語言當中，或多或少都不可避免的會有一些髒話，而說髒話被認為不禮貌且會降低別人對你的看法，所以因此就會衍生出許多不同髒話的文雅說法。

　　例如在中文當中，常會將某個字說成「看」，將某個短句講成「草泥馬」，別問我是哪個字、及哪個短句喔，我這麼彬彬有禮的人是不知道的。而在英文當中也不例外，常會以一些縮寫相同的字來代表。例如我們上面所介紹的 "Fanny Adams" 的縮寫為 F.A.，與 "fuck all" 的縮寫一樣，oh, please pardon my French.（為了解釋上的需要，請原諒我說髒話），所以 Fanny Adams 也常見被用在文雅的髒話上。然而在書籍的紀錄上，在 20 世紀之前是極少會將所包含的髒話意義記載下來的，但根據推測，則應該早在 19 世紀就開始被用於代表 "fuck all" 的用法。而在第一次世界大戰時，有一位澳洲的士兵在 1919 年時寫了一本名為 "Digger Dialects" 裡面記錄的是第一次世界大戰時，士兵間常用的俚語，其中就有記載著以 "Fanny Adams" 來代替 "fuck all" 的用法。

　　這一個用法讓我想到在中文當中，有的時候，也會又因為生氣到不行，但是卻礙於場合不對，或是個人的修養不允許，所以在別人問說「那還有問題嗎？」的時候，只能惡狠狠的瞪大眼睛說「沒有」，但心中卻是有一大堆的圈圈叉叉，這是不是很像用英文說 "Fanny Adams" 時的感覺，嘴巴說著 "Nothing at all" 但其實應該是在表達 F.A.縮寫的精髓吧！

Break a Leg

祝你好運。通常用在要登台的人身上。

Johnny and Allen are chatting in the office.

Johnny wishes Allen to "break his leg."

Johnny 和 Allen 在辦公室裡閒聊。

Johnny 祝 Allen「摔斷他的腿」。

 對話 Dialogue

Allen: Hey, **buddy**, I think I need your help.

Johnny: Sure, no problem. What can I do for you? I will surely try all my best and **succeed**, **come hell or high water**. Just don't ask me to **lend** you money, you know, I'm always **hard up** at the end of the month.

Allen: No, it's not about the money, it's … Er, never mind, I think I must be losing it.

Johnny: Come on, Allen. I don't have all day. I think you want to know that did Charlene break up with her boyfriend, right?

Allen: Yes, and how do you know that?

Johnny: I am your mind reader. Since she broke up with her boyfriend, she has been **depressed**. Maybe you can start with caring for her as a friend.

Allen: That sounds good. I think I'll go for it.

Johnny: Go break a leg, my friend!

單字 Vocabulary

1. **buddy** [`bʌdɪ] ⓝ 【美】【俚】（用作稱呼）老兄，老弟；好朋友
→ He is my buddy.
他是我的好兄弟。

2. **succeed** [sək`sid] ⓥ 成功；辦妥
→ They succeeded in persuading me to stay in the haunted hotel.
他們成功的說服我待在鬧鬼的飯店裡。

3. **come hell or high water** ⓟ 赴湯蹈火，在所不辭；無論如何
→ Come hell or high water, I will want to get paid.
無論如何，我都會要回這一筆錢的。

4. **lend** [lɛnd] ⓥ 把……借給
→ I would be glad to lend a hand.
我很樂意幫忙。

5. **hard up** 【口】 ⓟ 經濟困難、缺錢
→ I was rather hard up for a time.
我有一陣子很缺錢。

6. **depressed** [dɪ`prɛst] ⓐⓓⓙ 沮喪的、消沉的、憂鬱的
→ I like to eat cakes and sweets when I feel depressed.
當我感到沮喪的時候，我喜歡吃蛋糕和甜的東西。

翻譯 Translation

Allen: 嘿，兄弟，我想我需要你的幫助。

Johnny: 好啊，當然沒問題。我可以幫你什麼呢？我一定會竭盡所能，赴湯蹈火在所不辭的。只要不要跟我借錢就行了，你知道的，我每逢月底手頭都有點緊。

Allen: 不是，不是要跟你借錢，只是……呃，算了，我想我一定是瘋了。

Johnny: 拜託，Allen。我沒有這麼多的閒工夫。我猜你想要知道 Charlene 是不是和她男朋友切了，對吧？

Allen: 對啊，你怎麼知道我要問什麼？

Johnny: 我是你肚子裡的蛔蟲。自從她和她男朋友分手後，她的情緒一直都很低落。也許你可以從朋友的關心開始。

Allen: 聽起來不錯。我想我會努力的。

Johnny: 祝好運啊，我的朋友！

心情小日記 Dear Diary

July 20th

Dear Diary,

After the news of Charlene's breakup with her boyfriend (hehehe, ex-boyfriend now!) trickled out. She's always surrounded by so many people (single and non-single males and even females), and there are always piles of gift boxes and bouquets in her cubicle. I suddenly realize that I have so many tough opponents. However, the worst is that I still haven't got the chance to talk to her since she picked up my ID card and handed it to me. Maybe I should buy some books to learn the art of talking or how to chat-up with girls.

7月20日

親愛的日記，

自從 Charlene 和她男朋友（嘿嘿嘿，已經是「前」男友了）分手的消息傳出之後。她身邊總是圍繞著一大群人（單身還有非單身的男性，甚至還有女性），在她的小隔間中總是有一大堆的禮物盒及花束。我突然瞭解到我有許多的強勁對手。然而，最糟的是自從上一次她撿到我的 ID 卡並遞給我之後我們就再也沒說過話了。也許我應該要去買一些書好好的學一學說話的藝術或是如何和女生搭訕。

還可以怎麼說 In Other Words

❶ I must be losing it.
我一定是瘋了。

- I am crazy!
  我「起肖」了！

- I think I've gone cuckoo.
  我想我一定是「阿達」了。

❷ I am your mind reader.
我是你肚子裡的蛔蟲。

- I can read your mind.
  我能讀出你的心意。

- We just clicked.
  我們心有靈犀「一點通」。

❸ She's always surrounded by so many people.
她身邊總是圍繞著一大群人

- Tons of people hit on her.
  一大堆人跟她獻殷勤。

- Many colleagues all vied in paying her attentions.
  許多同事搶著跟她獻殷勤。

 這句怎麼說？ How to Say That?

點石成金 → Midas touch

英釋 The ability to make a financial success of everything you do.

中釋 特別是指在有關金錢、財務上的運氣或是手氣很好。

A: Michael has Midas touch, everything he does would turn into gold.

（Michael 擁有點石成金的本領，所做的任何事都能變成一筆財富。）

B: Yes, indeed. Last time I asked him to buy the lottery ticket for me, and I hit the jackpot. （對啊，沒錯。上次我請他幫我買了一張樂透，然後我就中了頭獎。）

文化小盒子 Culture Box

　　"Go break a leg" 在英文中是「祝好運」的意思。在許多語言中，有類似這樣說反話來祝對方好運的方式，例如在德語中的 "Hals- und Bein-bruch"，在中文裡則是摔斷脖子和腿。而在俄語當中，在朋友出去打獵時，會說 "Ни пýха ни пера"，意為一根羽毛也沒有。這一個俚語最早是被用在表演工作者間的彼此祝福。在劇院及舞台上，一般來說有非常多的禁忌及迷信，一般據信，是以這樣的方式祝福以免遭到鬼神嫉妒而破壞。但也有人說是在舞台上接受掌聲時，屈膝致謝的方式像是摔斷一條腿後只剩一條腿的樣子，因此引用成為祝表演成功，而後延伸成為在任何事上祝好運的方式。

阿倫碎碎念 Allen's Murmur

關於 "break a leg" 的說法起源除了在 culture box 中所提到的兩種可能之外，還有許多種的說法，其中有一種，我個人覺得還蠻有道理的是在舞台兩側的布簾，在英文中稱為 side curtain，也稱為 leg，所以在表演成功時，演員會從舞台布簾中走出來謝幕，接受掌聲，所以有可能是 "break a leg" 的由來。但矛盾的是，這不是應該用複數的 legs 嗎？好吧，別理我這個人的小糾結。我接下來要談 "break a leg" 曾出現在莎士比亞的《理查三世》劇作當中，在當時具有「生下私生子」的含意，但在今日則已完全沒有這樣的用法。

英文當中與 leg 相關的說法還有許多，其中有一個我覺得應該是令所有女孩兒們羨慕的，那就是 "hollow leg"，中文裡稱為是「大胃王」或是「大酒桶」，我知道你們一定在說這有什麼好羨慕的。但請注意，當說一個人是 "hollow leg" 時，有一個先決條件，那就是那個人必定要是身材纖細的，沒錯，hollow leg 是指放縱的吃、喝，但卻不會因此而發胖的人。

還有一個我覺得很有意思的是 "shake a leg"，telling the truth，我現在已經感受到你們的大白眼了，甚至還聽到有人在問 "Are you serious or are you pulling my leg?"（你是說真的還是在開玩笑？）。大家一定覺得「抖腳」有什麼好說的，但請注意 "shake a leg" 的意思是「叫某人趕快行動」，抖腳的話，我們一般會說是 "shake one's leg"。例如是：我常聽到 Joyce 緊張地對著阿祐說 "Come on, Yo. Shake a leg, or we'll be late for the conference."（拜託，阿祐。趕緊動起來，要不然我們開會會遲到。）但我總是看到 "Yo was shaking his leg and doing nothing."（阿祐就只是抖腳而什麼事都不做。）

Round Trip Meal Ticket

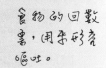

食物的回數票，用來形容嘔吐。

Allen, Ben and Johnny are sitting in canteen, and talking about the "meal ticket" that Ben got yesterday.

Allen，Ben 還有 Johnny 坐在公司的餐廳裡，談論著 Ben 昨天得到的一張「餐票」。

對話 Dialogue

Allen: Are you sure you don't want me to bring you something to eat? I heard your **stomach's growling.**

Ben: Just bring me some water, please.

Johnny: Didn't you say that you got a meal ticket yesterday? You should use it.

Allen: Nope, Johnny, you **misheard** him. Ben said that he got so drunk last night and found himself slept in the round trip meal ticket he did in his apartment this morning.

Johnny: Eww! What a **gross**-out! So… did you take a shower?

Ben: Of course, I did. I have used up a bottle of **shower gel.**

Johnny: You should use two bottles.

Allen: Johnny, what do you want for lunch?

Johnny: Nah, I have no **appetite** now, maybe some soup please.

單字 Vocabulary

1. **stomach** [ˈstʌmək] n 胃 → The stink of the rotten rat turned my stomach.
   腐爛老鼠的臭味讓我感到反胃。

2. **growl** [graʊl] v （雷、砲 → My stomach growled.
   等）轟鳴；（肚子）餓得 我的肚子餓得咕嚕叫。
   咕嚕咕嚕作響。

3. **mishear** [mɪsˈhɪr] → She must have misheard.
   v 聽錯、誤聽 她一定是聽錯了。

4. **gross** [gros] adj 【俚】令 → His behavior was so gross and made me vomit
   人噁心的；令人討厭的 up all I had just eaten.
   他的舉動實在是太令人噁心了，害我把剛吃下的
   所有東西都吐出來了。

5. **shower gel** [ˈʃaʊɚ dʒɛl] → I usually use shower gel instead of soap.
   n 沐浴乳 我通常用沐浴乳而不是肥皂。

6. **appetite** [ˈæpɪˌtaɪt] → I try to curb my appetite for food and drink.
   n 胃口、食慾 我試著克制我的食慾。

翻譯 Translation

Allen: 你確定不要我幫你帶點吃的？我聽到你的肚子餓得咕咕叫。

Ben: 請幫我帶杯水就好了。

Johnny: 你不是說你昨天拿到一張餐票嗎？你應該要用它的。

Allen: 不，Johnny，你聽錯了。Ben 是說他昨晚喝的超醉，今天早上在他
的公寓裡，發現他自己睡在他吐的嘔吐物上。

Johnny: 嘔！這真是太噁心了。所以……你有洗澡嗎？

Ben: 當然有。我甚至還用光了一整瓶的沐浴乳。

Johnny: 你應該要用兩瓶的。

Allen: Johnny，你午餐要吃什麼？

Johnny: 不了，我現在已經沒什麼胃口了，來點湯好了。

心情小日記 Dear Diary

July 27th

Dear Diary,

I was soooooo starving after work, and I ate two Big Macs, an apple pie and large fries for dinner tonight. It's all because of Ben's gross story, so I didn't have my lunch properly. During the lunch time, when I was eating my salad with Thousand Island dressing, Ben said promptly that the Thousand Island salad dressing looked like the vomit, and Johnny's spicy and sour soup also looked like it. His words almost made us throw up our food, and completely lost our appetites. I swear I will not have lunch with Ben ever again.

7月27日

親愛的日記，

我下班時都快餓死了，我今天的晚餐吃了兩個大麥克，一個蘋果派還有大份的薯條。全都是因為 Ben 那噁心的故事，害我沒有好好的吃午餐的緣故。在午餐時間，當我正在吃佐千島醬的沙拉時，Ben 突然說千島沙拉醬看起來好像嘔吐物喔，Johnny 的酸辣湯看起來也是。他的話讓我們差一點把吃下的都吐出來，還完全的失去胃口。我發誓我以後絕不再跟 Ben 一起吃午餐了。

還可以怎麼說 In Other Words

❶ I heard your stomach's growling.
我聽到你的肚子餓得咕咕叫。

- I can hear your tummy's making loud noise.
  我能聽見你的肚子正在製造噪音。

- Your stomach's rumbling at me.
  你的肚子正對著我咕嚕作響。

❷ I was s soooooo starving.
我快餓死了。

- I was famished.
  我餓扁了。

- I was so hungry and could eat a horse.

  我餓到可以吃下一匹馬了。

❸ Spicy and sour soup.
酸辣湯。

- Hot and sour soup.
  酸辣湯。

- Sweet and sour soup.
  酸辣湯 / 糖醋湯。（在美國常見的酸辣湯英譯，因為一般外籍人士偏好酸甜味的中國菜，不喜歡辣味。）

 這句怎麼說？ How to Say That?

大吐特吐 → Calling Ralph on the big white telephone

英釋 vomiting most profusely in the toilet

中釋 在廁所裡大量嘔吐。

A: Where is Lily?（Lily 在哪兒？）

B: She poured almost a bucket of red wine in her stomach. And now she's talking to Ralph on the big white telephone.（她剛剛灌了將近一桶的紅酒到她的肚子裡。現在她正在廁所裡大吐特吐。）

 文化小盒子 Culture Box

　　根據統計，「嘔吐」在英文中的說法除了一般常見的 puke，vomit，throw up 等等之外，居然有上百種以上的說法。其中有些是跟嘔吐時所發出的聲音有關，例如除了之前提到的 Ralph，還有 Earl，Jacob，Carl Earl 等人名會被用在形容嘔吐上。試著唸唸看這一些名字，是不是就像是聽到幾種不同的嘔吐聲呢？而 big white telephone 指的則是馬桶，打趣的形容對著馬桶吐就像是對著一個巨大的白色電話在說話。在對話中說的 "Round trip meal ticket" 則是另一種用食物來形容嘔吐的方法，意指為吃進去的食物買了來回票，吃進去了又吐出來。有些還會形容是 "Recycle your lunch."（回收午餐），這些說法是不是很有趣呢？但為了大家的食慾著想，就介紹到這了，其它的說法就請讀者自己去發現囉！

阿倫碎碎念 Allen's Murmur

　　Meal ticket 在英文中，照字面上的意思一般被解釋為「餐票」，是可以在指定的餐廳中用餐的憑證，或是可以換取食物等。例如我在日本的一家餐廳的櫃臺上有看過放一個標誌提醒客人 "Please buy your meal ticket first."（請先購買餐票。），必須先到餐廳門口的販賣機選定自己要的餐點，在投入足夠的錢之後，就會有一張票券掉下來，再憑著這一張票換取餐點。這一方面能減少人力在點餐、收銀上，也能減少餐點點錯而帶來的糾紛。

　　而除了字面上的意思之外，meal ticket 又可說是某人賴以維生的物品或是技能。An example of the meal ticket is that a singer's beautiful singing voice is his meal ticket. 美妙的歌聲是歌手所必備的，所以美妙的歌聲是歌手所賴以維生的技能。

　　不過說到 meal ticket，大家應該會想到我們中文裡的「飯票」，而在英文中，meal ticket 也的確帶有這樣的含意。例如說，有一個男人娶了有錢的老婆，並靠著老婆的錢來過生活，這時候，我們就可以說 His rich wife is his meal ticket. 或是有一個女人並不愛她的男友，只是因為要靠著男友的金錢支援而在一起，這時可以說 "She is a selfish woman who looks upon her boyfriend only as a meal ticket."

Diary 8 月 06 日

Chinese Whispers

以訛傳訛；不
實的傳聞，耳
語的由來。

In the lobby, Allen and Chris are whispering something about the wedding.

（在大廳，Allen 和 Chris，

他們倆私下在談論有關婚禮的事。）

 對話 Dialogue

Allen: Hey, Chris. I hear from Winston that you're getting married.
Congratulations!

Chris: Oh, no, not again. I have already explained it for a thousand
times today.

Allen: So… what's going on? Are you okay?

Chris: I'm not the one who's going to get married, it's my sister Marga-
ret, and she's getting married next month. So I applied for personal leave yesterday in advance, and suddenly I became the
groom-to-be. It's a typical result of Chinese **whispers**.

Allen: You know, the gossip always spreads at a very high speed.

Chris: You tell me!

Allen: Anyhow, good thing it's not that kind of **rumor** which can **wreck**

your **reputation.**

Chris: Yeah, just being a fake groom.

單字 Vocabulary

1. **congratulations**
   [kənˌgrætʃəˈleʃən] n 恭喜、祝賀
   → Please convey my congratulations to him.
   請代我向他致上我的祝賀之意。

2. **groom** [grum]
   n 新郎
   → Toast to the bride and groom.
   向新娘和新郎敬酒。

3. **whisper** [ˈhwɪspɚ]
   n 低語、私語、耳語
   → Their voices fell to a whisper.
   他們降低音量到成了耳語。

4. **rumor** [ˈrumɚ]
   n 謠言
   → Rumor has it that her husband is having an affair with her best friend.
   謠言指出她丈夫和她最好的朋友有一腿。

5. **wreck** [rɛk]
   v 破壞、毀滅
   → No one can wreck the friendship between them.
   沒有人能破壞他們之間的友誼。

6. **reputation** [ˌrɛpjəˈteʃən]
   n 名聲、名譽
   → This is a great chance to enhance the reputation of the company.
   這是一個提升公司聲譽的好機會。

翻譯 Translation

Allen: 嘿，Chris。我聽 Winston 說你要結婚了。恭喜啊！

Chris: 喔，拜託，不要又來一個。我今天已經解釋過上千遍了。

Allen: 所以…怎麼一回事？你還好吧？

Chris: 要結婚的不是我，是我的妹妹 Margaret，她下個月要結婚了。所以我昨天先請了事假，我卻突然成了準新郎。這是典型的以訛傳訛的結果。

Allen: 你知道的，八卦總是以非常快的速度在傳播的。

Chris: 那還用你說！

Allen: 無論如何，幸好這不是那一種會敗壞你名聲的謠言。

Chris: 對，只是成了假新郎而已。

心情小日記 Dear Diary

August 6th

Dear Diary,

Rumors of Chris' wedding were afloat, and even I became a part of it. Someone said that he or she saw Chris complained to me about his bride-to-be, and they surmised that there will be no wedding any more. When I heard the "news," the rumor has already gone through the company. Whenever people asked me about Chris' wedding, I just couldn't stop rolling my eyes. Now I do understand what he felt. I tried to find out where the rumor emanated from, but everyone said "a little bird told me." Oh, god, please tell me who's that "little bird"?

8月6日

親愛的日記，

有關 Chris 婚禮的謠言四起，而且甚至我也成了謠言的一部份。有人說他或她看到 Chris 跟我抱怨他的準新娘，他們推測將不會有婚禮。當我聽到這一個「消息」時，謠言已經傳遍整個公司了。當有人向我問起 Chris 的婚禮時，我就忍不住的翻白眼。現在我真的了解他的感覺了。我試著找出這謠言的起源，但是每個人都說「有小道消息指出」。喔，我的天啊，請告訴我「小道消息」是誰放出來的？

:: 還可以怎麼說 In Other Words

❶ I hear from Winston that you're getting married. Congratulations!
我聽 Winston 說你要結婚了。恭喜啊！

- It's about time you settled.
  也該是你定下來的時候了。

- What kind of wedding you'll have? Big, small or Vegas?
  要舉行怎樣的婚禮？大型、小型還是在拉斯維加斯結婚？

❷ I tried to find out where the rumor emanated from
我試著找出這謠言的起源。

- I tried to find out who's the rumormonger.
  我試著找出造謠者。

- I wanted to reveal the identity of the gossiper.
  我要揭露造謠者的真實身份。

❸ A little bird told me.
有小道消息指出。

- I got the information from an unnamed source.
  我從一個不願具名的人得到的消息。

- I got it straight from a horse's mouth.
  我直接從馬的口中得到的。=我從相關人士的口中得知的。（與 a little bird told me 相比，這樣的說法真實性更高。）

 這句怎麼說？ How to Say That?

道聽塗說 → Hearsay

英釋 unverified information heard or received from another; rumor

中釋 從他人處聽來的未經證實的訊息；謠言。

A: It's only hearsay that Ian has many girlfriends. （這只是道聽塗說的，有人說 Ian 有很多女朋友。）

B: That's not true, he's the most faithful man that I've ever known. He has only one boyfriend, and they have been together for more than ten years. （這不是事實，他是我所認識的人之中最專情的。他只有一個男朋友，他們已經在一起超過 10 年了。）

 文化小盒子 Culture Box

　　Chinese whispers（在美國則稱為 the telephone game）是團體遊戲的一種，由 3 人以上排成一列，自隊伍的首端將指定的句子以耳語的方式告知下一位，一直傳到最後一個人為止。在傳話的過程中，音量不得讓第三人聽到，也就是我們所說的口耳相傳或是傳話遊戲。遊戲的趣味在於所傳達的這一句話通常傳到最後一位時就會變得荒腔走板。而這就是 Chinese whispers 成為以訛傳訛；不實的傳聞，耳語的由來，亦可稱為是 Chinese whispers effect。這個遊戲的名稱原本是叫做 "Russian scandal" 或是 "Russian gossip"，在 20 世紀中才改稱為 Chinese whispers，更名的原因不詳，但推測應該是在西方國家，學習中文的人口增加，而且覺得中文遠比俄文來的更為複雜難懂的緣故，其中並不含有歧視的意味存在，但在使用上必須小心，不要涉及一語雙關的暗示。

118

阿倫碎碎念 Allen's Murmur

在英文中，有許多的詞彙和 Chinese whispers 相類似的用法，將某個國家的名稱加在某個事物上便有了其特殊的意義。

例如像是，大家都耳熟能詳的 "Go Dutch"，據說是在 16、17 世紀時，當時的荷蘭和威尼斯是海上貿易的發跡地，而四處奔波的義大利及荷蘭商人有著在聚餐時各付各的習俗。而後又因為在 17 世紀末時，荷蘭成為當時最大的殖民帝國，也成了英國的競爭對手，彼此間的利益關係，讓當時的英國人對荷蘭人產生了敵意，也因而表達在言語上，例如義大利及荷蘭商人共有的各付各的習慣，被稱為 go Dutch，用以嘲諷荷蘭人精明不吃虧的個性，甚至還有 "Dutch treat" 一被邀請的客人要自費；"Dutch concert" –各唱各調的音樂會等的說法。什麼，你問我敢不敢在我的荷蘭籍朋友面前說這些，當然不敢，我可是很有禮貌的，更何況他們可是平均身高有 185cm 的國家，個個人高馬大的，所以吃飯時，我都是說 "Let's go fifty–fifty."（平分）或是 "Separate checks."（各付各）。

在英文用語中，提到其它國家的還有 "excuse my French"（請原諒我說粗話）；"Indian giver"（送東西給人但又索回的人）；"Italian hand"（幕後操控）；"Italian athlete"（愛吹牛的人）等等。都略帶有貶意，所以在用的時候需特別小心。不過這就是文化，在不同文化中或多或少會因為歷史背景，而嘲諷另一種文化或是該國家的人，在經過一段時間後，成了常用的語言，也許不再有當時的貶低之意，但在說的時候還是需特別注意，不要傷了彼此的關係。

Goodnight, Vienna

意指完蛋了、
玩完了。

Meryl, the assistant manager, asks Allen to call all colleagues back, due to a crisis. Now they are talking something about "Vienna."

為了因應一個危機，副理 Meryl，請 Allen 打電話叫回所有的同事。現在他們正在討論有關「維也納」的事。

對話 Dialogue

Meryl: Allen, I need your help. We need to call an **emergency** meeting within 15 minutes, would you please inform everyone, and our entire department staffs are required to participate.

Allen: I **conceive** that there must be some difficulties in assembling people for the meeting within 15 minutes, since it's about half way through the lunch break already.

Meryl: I'm not thoughtful enough, please phone every single one of our team, and ask them to come back as soon as possible. 'Cause I've just got a warning from the IT department that they have **detected** some unusual activities in our system last night.

Allen: Could that be a **hacker** attack?

Meryl: Probably. If our new project gets out, it'll be goodnight Vienna for us. So some **remedies** are required.

Allen: Okay, I got it. I'll call them **immediately.**

單字 Vocabulary

1. **emergency** [ɪˈmɝdʒənsɪ]
   n 緊急情況
   → They escaped through an emergency exit.
   他們從一個緊急逃生口脫逃出來。

2. **conceive** [kənˈsiv]
   v 認為、考慮；想像
   → I cannot conceive of such a thing happening again.
   我無法想像這種事會再發生。

3. **detect** [dɪˈtɛkt]
   v 發現、察覺
   → She couldn't detect ant triumph in his eyes.
   她無法在他的眼中察覺出任何喜悅的光芒。

4. **hacker** [ˈhækɚ]
   n 駭客
   → The website was attacked by a hacker few days ago.
   這一個網站幾天前才被駭客入侵過。

5. **remedy** [ˈrɛmədɪ]
   n 補救方法
   → The only remedy for you is to appeal to law.
   對你而言唯一的補救辦法就是要訴諸於法律。

6. **immediately** [ɪˈmidɪɪtlɪ]
   adv 直接地、立即地
   → They urged vigorous action to be taken immediately.
   他們強烈要求要立即採取有力的措施。

翻譯 Translation

Meryl: Allen，我需要你的幫忙。我們必須在15分鐘之內召開一個緊急會議，你可不可以告訴大家，所有的部門同仁都必須到場。

Allen: 我覺得在15分鐘內召集大家開會可能有一點困難，因為已經過了一半的午餐休息時間了。

Meryl: 是我想的不夠周全，請打電話通知每個人，讓他們儘快趕回。因為

121

我剛收到資訊部門的警告，說他們在昨晚偵測到我們的系統中有不正常的活動。

Allen: 有沒有可能是駭客攻擊？

Meryl: 可能吧。但如果我們的新項目洩漏的話，那我們就完蛋了。所以需要一些補救措施。

Allen: 好的，我懂了。我立刻通知大家。

心情小日記 Dear Diary

August 10th

Dear Diary,

Meryl, our assistant manager, she's the ablest people that I've ever met. Throughout the crisis in this afternoon, she retained her composure and conducted us to set up some methods. Although it turned out a false alarm, we were impressed by her professionalism. Her comments always hit the nail of the head. After this incident, all colleagues and I got some inspirations to our new projects, and all thanks to Meryl's comments. I believe that we will be able to submit a sharper and more comprehensive project than the one we already had.

8月10日

親愛的日記，

Meryl，我們的副理，她是我所見過最有能力的人了。在今天下午的這一場混亂中，她始終保持著鎮定並引領著我們制訂了一些措施。雖然最後只是虛驚一場，但她的專業卻讓我們印象十分深刻。她的意見總是一針見血。在這一次的事件後，我和同事在新項目上都得到了一些靈感，全歸功於 *Meryl* 的意見。我相信我們將能交出一份比原有的更為深入及周詳的項目計畫。

還可以怎麼說 In Other Words

❶ Allen, I need your help.
Allen，我需要你的幫忙。

- Allen, could you do me a favor?
  Allen，可以幫我一個忙嗎？

- I need your assistant, Allen.
  我需要你的協助，Allen。

❷ I'm not thoughtful enough.
是我想的不夠周全。

- It was very thoughtless of me.
  我考慮的不夠周到。

- I am so thoughtless.
  是我太粗心大意了。

❸ Her comments always hit the nail of the head.
她的意見總是一針見血。

- Her analysis really strikes home.
  她的分析總能一擊即中。

- She usually gets heart of the matter.
  她通常都能一下子就擊中要害。

 這句怎麼說？ *How to Say That?*

註定失敗 → Dead duck

英釋 A person or thing that is beyond help, redemption, or hope.

中釋 註定要完蛋的人或是事物，無法可施，無論給予任何幫助都無濟於事。

A: I shall have to help her as much as I can.（我應該要盡我所能的來幫忙她。）

B: If I were you, I won't put any more money into her business. In my opinion, it's already a dead duck, there's no point to save it.（如果我是你的話，我不會再投資任何錢在她的生意上了。依我看，她的生意已經完蛋了，再挽救已經沒有任何意義了。）

 文化小盒子 *Culture Box*

　　在十九世紀時，出現一種取材於現實生活，偏重於諷刺揭露時事的歌劇，被稱為operetta（輕歌劇），除了保留歌劇的音樂型態之外還會結合當時的流行歌曲，其風格輕鬆活潑，結構時間也較歌劇來得短，在當時相當受到歡迎。而Goodnight, Vienna就是在1932年時推出的一部輕歌劇的名稱。故事背景是在維也納，描述一個貴族軍官愛上了賣花的女孩，因家庭阻力及戰爭而分開，戰爭結束後，物換星移，男主角成了鞋店工作的小助理，而女孩成了有名的歌手，之後解開誤會，再譜戀曲。而 "Goodnight, Vienna"，這一句英式俚語被解釋成為 it's all over, nothing more can be done 的原因並不可考，只知道是出自於這一部電影當中。如果有看英國足球比賽的話，就常能聽到評論員說 "Goodnight, Vienna"，用中文來說的話就是「玩完了」、「完蛋」。

阿倫碎碎念 Allen's Murmur

　　有著世界音樂之都美稱的維也納，是奧地利的首都，是目前第二大的德語城市。當提到維也納的時候，應該有許多人的耳邊就會響起 Vienna Boys' Choir（維也納少年合唱團）的美妙歌聲。

　　但是一提到維也納的時候，我就會不禁的想起一位我大學時的同學，她來自於匈牙利，為人隨和（除了非常要求我們要好好地發音，不要把她的國家Hungary發成hungry之外），非常受到同學的歡迎。有一天我聽她嘟囔了一句，好奇的問她是什麼意思，她告訴我用英文說就是 "An ox remains an ox, even if driven to Vienna."（牛趕到維也納也還是牛。）我聽到之後，心想：「天啊！這不就是中文裡牛牽到北京還是牛的匈牙利版本嘛！"我仔細問了意思之後，發現除了說法相似之外，所代表的意思也是一模一樣。我好奇的問她，那為什麼是趕到維也納呢？她說可能是因為就算趕到維也納，牛也不可能因為環境改變，而就開始唱歌、拉小提琴吧！我還記得，我們倆就因為那一句話笑了一整個下午，還差點被教授趕出教室，我還差點笑出我的 six-pack abs（六塊肌）和Apollo's belt（人魚線）。好吧，我是在用誇飾法。言歸正傳，在英文俚語中，有許多會用到城市或是國家，像是在唸書時候，我最害怕的是經濟學，每次讀的時候，都覺得 "It's all Greek to me."（對我而言全是希臘文＝完全看不懂。）相信應該有許多人跟我有一樣的感覺吧！

Up in Annie's Room

鬼才知道他在哪兒咧!

Harry is searching for Yo everywhere in the company. He sees Allen in the men's room, and Allen tells him that Yo's "up in Annie's room."

Harry 在公司裡到處找阿祐。

他在男廁遇到 Allen，Allen 告訴他阿祐在 "Annie 的房裡"。

對話 Dialogue

Harry: Do you know where Yo is? I have been looking for him **high and low** for almost an hour.

Allen: Up in Annie's room, **behind** the clock.

Harry: Annie? Annie who?

Allen: Relax, Harry. I was saying "I dunno." I hadn't seen him since the lunchtime. May I ask what happened?

Harry: We are going to have a video conference with our client at 3:30 p.m. But I want to have a **rehearsal** with Yo before the meeting.

Allen: So did you make an **appointment** with him?

Harry: Yes, I did. I told him that we'll meet in the conference room after lunch.

Allen: Oh, I see. Yo usually takes an **extremely** long lunch break. I'll **cross** my fingers for you!

單字 Vocabulary

1. **high and low** ph 到處 → Cindy searched high and low for the lost watch.
   Cindy 到處找遺失的手錶。

2. **behind** [bɪ`haɪnd] prep → She's necking with her best friend's husband
   在……的背後；在……的 behind the door.
   後面 她在門的後面和她最好朋友的先生擁吻。

3. **rehearsal** [rɪ`hɝsl̩] → The cheerleading team is in rehearsal now.
   v 排練、試演；練習 這個啦啦隊現在正在排演。

4. **appointment** → I have an appointment with Mr. President this
   [ə`pɔɪntmənt] n （尤指正式 afternoon.
   的）約會 我今天下午和總統先生有約。

5. **extremely** [ɪk`strimlɪ] → I am extremely sorry.
   adv 非常；極端地 我感到非常地抱歉。

6. **cross** [krɔs] → Sit up straight and please do not cross your
   v 使交叉；與……相交 legs or arms.
   坐直，請不要翹二郎腿或是抱臂。

翻譯 Translation

Harry: 你知道阿祐在哪兒嗎？我到處找他找了快一個小時了。

Allen: 在 Annie 的房間，鐘的後面。（鬼才知道咧。）

Harry: Annie？哪一個 Annie？

Allen: 放鬆點，Harry。我剛剛是說「我不知道」的意思。我從午餐時間就沒看到過他了。我可以問一下怎麼了嗎？

Harry: 我們下午 3 點半和客戶有一個視訊會議。但我想要在會議之前先排練一下。

Allen: 那你有跟他約好嗎？

Harry: 有啊。我告訴他午餐後在會議室見啊。

Allen: 喔，我懂了。阿祐通常中午休息時間都會休超……久的。我會默默地祝你好運的！

✏ 心情小日記 Dear Diary

August 20th

Dear Diary,

Poor Harry, another victim of careless Yo. Sophie said that Yo returned to the company at a quarter past three. Harry's face contorted with anger, and Yo just ignored him. Even I didn't see that, but I could imagine that picture. Fortunately, Harry did a great job in that conference and got the contract. I met Harry in the elevator after work. Harry said that he foamed at the mouth with anger when Yo's bluffing his well performance in that meeting. I patted him gently on his back and gave him a sympathetic look.

8 月 20 日

親愛的日記，

可憐的 Harry，又是一個被漫不經心的阿祐殘害的對象。Sophie 說阿祐在 3 點 15 分左右回到公司。Harry 的臉都給氣歪了，阿祐自動的屏蔽他的怒氣。儘管我沒看到那一幕，但我還是能想像的到那幅畫面，幸運的是，Harry 在會議中表現得極好，而且還拿到了合約。我下班時在電梯裡遇到 Harry。Harry 說當阿祐在吹噓他自己在會議中的優良表現時，他氣得火冒三丈。我輕輕的拍了他的背還給了他一個同情的眼神。

:: 還可以怎麼說 In Other Words

❶ Did you make an appointment with him?
那你有跟他約好嗎？

- Did he know about the rehearsal thing?
  那他知道要排演的事嗎？

- Did you tell him that you want to have a rehearsal before the meeting?
  你有告知他你要在會議前先排練嗎？

❷ Harry's face contorted with anger.
Harry 的臉都給氣歪了。

- Harry's face had redden with rage.
  Harry 都氣得脹紅了臉。

- He was so angry, and his face contorted, and turned purple with anger.
  他超生氣的，他的臉氣得都扭曲變形了，還氣得臉都發青了。

❸ He foamed at the mouth with anger.
他氣得火冒三丈。

- He hit the ceiling.
  他撞到天花板。= 他氣得暴跳如雷。

- He shit a brick.
  他大出一塊磚頭。= 他氣得發狂。

這句怎麼說? *How to Say That?*

一無所知 → Search me

英釋 inf. I don't know; you can search my clothing and my person, but you won't find the answer to your question anywhere near me.

中釋 【口】我不知道；你可以搜遍我的全身，但你無法從我身上得到答案。

A: Which dress should I wear for today's party?（今天的派對，我應該穿哪一件洋裝呢？）

B: Search me!（我不知道！）

文化小盒子 *Culture Box*

　　和 "Tom Atkins" 一樣，"up in Annie's room" 也是一句出自於英國軍營的俚語。起源的時間也大致相近，是在第一次的世界大戰期間。這一句俚語在當時通常是用在同袍之間，當對方詢問另一個人在哪裡？用以搪塞對方的說法。除了有我們之前所提到的 "I don't know" 的意思之外，也有 "don't ask" 的意味。那為什麼會用 Annie 呢？有一種說法是，當時在軍營中是沒有女性的，而 Annie 是一個相當普遍的女子名，所以在隨便回答時，順口說出「在 Annie 的房裡」，模糊焦點地帶過。而 "behind the clock" 也有人說是 "behind the wallpaper"，則是在第一次世界大戰結束後才加上去的，而起源更不可考。有學者猜測因為在戰爭時期的背景之下，在軍隊中回答某人在一名女子的房裡，是不太可能，有戲謔的意味，而之後所加入的在鐘或是壁紙的後面，更是不可能，讓聽的人更能清楚的知道說話的人想要表達「別問我」或是「我才不知道」的意思。

阿倫碎碎念 Allen's Murmur

說到 Annie，我就會想到 Michael Jackson 的 Smooth Criminal 這一首歌，裡面有一段歌詞提到 "Annie are you ok? So, Annie are you ok? Are you ok, Annie?" 這一段在歌曲中至少重複過十次以上，而這裡面所提到的 Annie 其實是起源自 CPR 中必備的模擬人偶（simman）Annie，在施行 CPR 前的第一步驟，必須試著先喚醒對方 "Annie, are you ok?"，所以就有了這一段歌詞的出現。

而我在這裡想要談一下這一個 Annie 的由來。據說在 20 世紀初的巴黎有一個投河自盡的少女，被打撈上來的時候，儘管她的臉部浮腫，但卻始終帶著笑容，而經由穿鑿附會之後，少女被一般大眾認定是為了要到天上去會情郎，而且還有了 Annie 這個名字。這個故事經由 word of mouth（口耳相傳）的方式，傳遍了整個歐洲。而一直到了 1958 年時，有醫生發表了 CPR 的急救技術，但因為正常人的肺部是充滿空氣，和停止呼吸的人是不同的，所以苦於沒有可以供大眾練習的對象。而這時候有一個玩具商人，因為他的兒子兩歲時曾有溺水的經驗，雖然沒事，但卻讓商人始終耿耿於懷，所以在他聽到這個消息時，便發明了可供練習 CPR 的假人，再加上當時那個已流傳半世紀溺斃在塞納河少女的浪漫傳說，所以這個假人被命名為 Annie。

而一直演變到今日，Annie 的功能不僅僅限於在練習 CPR 上面，而是精細到有心跳、血管等，身上有感應器，只要經由電腦的設定，便能呈現出將近 30 種的不同病症。難怪我有一個醫生朋友，總是稱這個人偶為體弱多病的 Annie，但也都不忘稱讚這個人偶可是近代醫學史上的大功臣，幫助許多醫學院的學生累積了診斷經驗。

Chapter

Fall 秋天

3S Lady

意指到了過婚
年齡卻沒有結
婚的女性。

Joycelyn is viewing a photo on her seat and talking

about "3S lady" with Allen.

Joycelyn 在她的座位上一邊看著照片，

一邊和 Allen 討論著 "3S 女士"。

對話 Dialogue

Allen: Who is the man in this photo?

Joycelyn: He's the one I'm going to meet in an **arranged** date tonight.

Allen: You mean like the **nearsighted** date?

Joycelyn: Yep. My parents are worried about me as a 3S lady who will be left on the **shelf** forever. This man is my last chance before the **upcoming** Moon Festival. Maybe he can accompany me home during the vacation if he's ok.

Allen: You are not a 3S lady, you are SAS.

Joycelyn: Oh, you're so sweet. But I'm sorry, I'm not a **cougar**.

Allen: Haha, it's a great **loss** for me.

Joycelyn: But no worries, I'll put in a good word for you to Charlene.

單字 Vocabulary

1. **arranged** [ə`rendʒd]
   adj 安排的
   → Her room is small but neatly-arranged.
   她的房間雖小但卻佈置的很整潔。

2. **nearsighted** [`nɪr`saɪtɪd]
   adj 近視的；近視眼的
   → Are you nearsighted or farsighted?
   你是近視還是遠視呢？

3. **shelf** [ʃɛlf] n （書櫥、櫃等）的架子、擱板
   → The books sat unread on the shelf for many years.
   這些書在書架上放了許多年了都沒有人讀過。

4. **upcoming** [`ʌp͵kʌmɪŋ]
   adj 即將來臨的
   → Everyone's looking forward to the upcoming spring out.
   每個人都非常期待著即將來臨的春遊。

5. **cougar** [`kugɚ]
   n 美洲獅
   → Have you ever seen a cougar?
   你有看過美洲獅嗎？

6. **loss** [lɔs] n 損失
   → His death was a great loss to the country.
   他的逝世對國家而言是一大損失。

翻譯 Translation

Allen: 照片裡的人是誰？

Joycelyn: 他是我今晚相親的對象。

Allen: 妳是指像是近視相親？

Joycelyn: 對。我的父母總是擔心身為剩女的我會一輩子嫁不出去。這個男的是我在即將到來的中秋節前的最後一個機會。如果他還可以的話，也許他能在這個假期中陪我回家。

Allen: 妳才不是剩女，妳是黃金剩女。

Joycelyn: 喔，你嘴真甜。但抱歉，我不搞姊弟戀的。

Allen: 哈哈，那真是我的損失。

Joycelyn: 但別擔心，我會在 Charlene 面前幫你說好話的。

135

心情小日記 Dear Diary

September 1st

Dear Diary,

Joycelyn has already been my mentor since I first joined the company. To me, she's a very attractive woman not only because of her physical beauty, but also her wisdom. I really enjoy talking to her. Her witty remarks always add a little salt to every conversation. She has a date with a good-looking stranger tonight, because she wants to find a boyfriend to make her parents happy. I cross my fingers for her, hope she can find her Mr. Right this time. If not, I believe that she'll find the right person, and all she needs is to wait for the right time.

9月01日

親愛的日記，

從我剛進公司開始，Joycelyn 一直都是我的良師益友。對我來說，她是一個非常有魅力的女人，不只是她美麗的外表還有她的智慧。我非常喜歡和她聊天。她風趣的言談總能為談話增色不少。她今天晚上要和一個陌生的英俊男子約會，因為她想要找個男朋友讓她父母高興。我祝她好運希望她這一次能找到她的理想對象。如果沒有的話，我相信她會找到對的人，她所需要的只是等待對的時機。

還可以怎麼說 In Other Words

❶ He's the one I'm going to meet in an arranged date tonight.
他是我今晚相親的對象。

- I'm going on a blind date dinner with him.
  我今天晚餐時間要跟他相親。

- He's one of my scheduled nearsighted dates.
  他是我近視相親行程中的對象之一。（nearsighted date 專指有看過相片或是在網路上聊過天等的相親。）

❷ I'm not a cougar.
我不搞姊弟戀的。

- You are not my dish.
  你不是我的菜。= 我對你沒興趣。

- You are not my prey.
  你不是我的獵物。= 我對年紀小的男生沒興趣。（英文中將姊弟戀形容成美洲獅 cougar 和獵物 prey 的關係。）

❸ I cross my fingers for her.
我祝她好運。

- I keep my fingers crossed and wish her luck.
  我交叉著手指祝她好運。

- Good luck to her.
  我祝她好運。

必「剩」客 → Doomed single

英釋 to describe those who are above the normal marriage age but still single, and need to keep struggling to find their other half

中釋 用來形容超過平均結婚年齡的單身男女，並仍繼續的在為了找到另一半而奮鬥。

A: Do you want me to arrange a blind date for you? （你要不要我幫你安排一場相親？）

B: Nah, thanks. I quite enjoy my life of being a doomed single. （不，謝了。我還蠻享受必剩客的生活。）

文化小盒子 Culture Box

　　根據一項在 2010 年時的調查顯示，在北京超過適婚年齡的未婚女性超過 50 萬人以上，而據推測到了 2020 年的時候，在大陸地區，每五個成年男性就有一個人會娶不到老婆。於是剩男剩女（Leftover man and woman）現象成了大陸普遍關注的話題之一。而在西方國家之中，這一股單身的熱潮則比亞洲國家早了約 10 年左右，所以在英文中稱這些未婚的女性為 3S ladies，意即 single，seventies（大多出生於 70 年代），和 stuck。這個族群的特徵通常為高教育程度，高薪及高獨立性，因此也有人稱其為 SAS- single, attractive and successful，中文稱為黃金剩女，如果用在男性身上則是指黃金單身漢。

阿倫碎碎念 *Allen's Murmur*

　　3S Lady 這個說法是在 21 世紀後才開始出現的，原本是指在出生於 70 年代的未婚女子，而現在則泛指年過 30 仍未婚的單身女性。但其實在英文當中，早在伊莉莎白女皇（女皇陛下可以被認為是西洋史中最有名及權勢的 3S Lady 代表，但原本表示 70 年代出生的 S，要更改成 Sixteenth—16 世紀出生）時期就已經有了對剩女的稱呼，叫做 spinster。

　　Spinster 原意其實是指在中古世紀時少數的幾種女子可賴以維生的職業—紡紗工。說到紡紗工，也許大家還不太清楚是怎樣的職業，但相信大家都看過「睡美人」這一個故事，故事當中有一個壞心的巫婆，對公主下了詛咒，詛咒公主會被紡綞刺傷而一睡不醒。而在公主陷入昏睡之前遇見的那一位由巫婆扮成的老婦人，手中不停的轉著一個有著大輪子的機器（spinning wheels 紡紗機），我們可以稱那位老婦人是 spinster，也可以說是古時候的職業婦女。而後在 16 世紀中期的英國衍生出專指未出嫁且已過適婚年齡的女子的意思，但其認定比較接近我們現在所說的剩女最高級—「齊天大剩」，會結婚的機會已經相當渺茫。

　　其他可以用來稱呼剩女的還有 Catherinette（法文）和 old maid 這兩種說法。Catherinette 是源自於在法國傳統中，聖凱薩琳（St. Catherine）是女孩的保護神，在 11 月 25 日的聖凱薩琳節中，25 歲或以上的未婚女子要配戴漂亮的頭飾以表彰其未婚的身份。也因此用 Catherinette 來稱呼 25 歲以上的剩女，在法文中這是屬於比較老式的說法，但還是偶而會聽到有人這麼說。Old maid 照字面上可解釋成老女傭，女傭和紡紗工一樣，都是古時少數幾種女人可以從事的職業。就像在清宮劇中的宮女，稍有姿色的會被王孫大臣看上，而比較不解風情且工作能力強的通常會被留下成為宮女們的領班「姑姑」，或是「嬤嬤」，終身單身。說到這，我不禁的想，單身算不算是職業婦女所要承擔的可能性「職業傷害」？

A Few Cans Short of a Six-pack

6 瓶裝的包裝少了幾瓶，意即少根筋。

After the meeting, Riley seems to complain with Allen

about the 40-watt "bulb" isn't "bright" enough.

在會議之後，Riley 似乎是在向 Allen 抱怨

40 瓦的「電燈泡」不夠「亮」。

 對話 Dialogue

Riley: Come on, Ray. I really don't want to work with Hank.

Allen: Sorry, man. I can't help you. I'm afraid the matter is out of my hands. I just do what the manager told me.

Riley: I-I-I-I-I!

Allen: Maybe I'm a bit **nosy**, but do you mind to tell me why you don't want to work with Hank?

Riley: Because he is the member of the 40-**watt** club.

Allen: What? You mean he's **bald**?

Riley: No, I mean he's not "bright" enough.

Allen: Aha! That's a very interesting **metaphor**. But I think Hank's just a few cans short of a six-pack.

Riley: As for me, they are the same. I always **notice** that he's not quite all there during the office hours! And I find it very hard to work with him.

Allen: Yeah, I also notice that. Good luck to you, anyway.

單字 Vocabulary

1. **bulb** [bʌlb] n 電燈泡 → Edison invented the light bulb.
   愛迪生發明了電燈泡。

2. **nosy** [`nozɪ] adj 【口】好 → Don't be so nosy; it's none of your business.
   管閒事的; 愛追問的　別那麼愛管閒事，這不關你的事。

3. **watt** [wɑt] n 瓦特 → The unit of power is watt.
   功率的單位是瓦特。

4. **bald** [bɔld] adj 禿頭的 → He started going bald in his early twenties.
   他在 20 出頭時就開始禿頭了。

5. **metaphor** [`mɛtəfɚ] → This metaphor is not appropriate at all.
   n 隱喻　這個隱喻一點都不恰當。

6. **notice** [`notɪs] v 注意到 → Timmy didn't notice her because he was too engrossed in his work.
   Timmy 沒有注意到她，因為他太專注工作上了。

翻譯 Translation

Riley: 拜託，Allen。我真的不想和 Hank 一起工作。

Allen: 對不起了，老兄。我幫不上忙。我恐怕這件事不是我所能控制的，我只是照經理所說的做。

Riley: 啊⋯⋯！

Allen: 也許我這樣有點八卦，但你介不介意跟我說說看你為什麼不想和 Hank 一起工作呢？

Riley: 因為他是 40 瓦俱樂部的成員。

Allen: 什麼？你的意思是他禿頭嗎？

Riley: 不，我說的是他不夠「聰明」。

Allen: 啊哈！這真是個有趣的比喻。但我覺得 Hank 只是少根筋。

Riley: 對我而言，這兩者是一樣的。我總是發現他在上班時間時心不在焉的。而且我覺得很難和他一起工作。

Allen: 對，我也注意到這一點了。不管如何，祝好運囉。

心情小日記 Dear Diary

September 3rd

Dear Diary,

After several times of talk, a compromise was reached between Riley and our manager. Riley has decided to carry out the project with Hank, and the manager must assign an extra hand for that project. Not surprisingly, Riley chose me. During these days of working in close collaboration with Hank, I found out that Hank actually can do pretty good job as long as someone urged him on. And Riley always calls me the "spiritualist" who's able to call up Hank's spirit. I had an after work drink with Hank just now, and I told him that we are all in the sink or swim situation, he has to change his attitude toward work. I hope him has eaten up what I said.

9月3日

親愛的日記，

在幾次的談話之後，Riley 和經理之間達成了妥協。Riley 已經決定要和 Hank

共同執行這一個項目，而經理必須多指派一個人手。不出意料之外，*Riley*
選了我。在經過幾天與 *Hank* 的密切合作之後，我發現 *Hank* 其實能做得很
好，只要有人督促他。而 *Riley* 則總是叫我為能將 *Hank* 的魂魄召喚回來的
「招魂大師」。我剛下班後跟 *Hank* 去喝了一杯，我告訴他我們現在是在勝負
的關鍵上了，他必須改變他對工作的態度。我希望他有將我的話聽進去。

還可以怎麼說 In Other Words

❶ I really don't want to work with Hank.
我真的不想和 Hank 一起工作。

- In fact, Hank is not an ideal teammate for me.
  事實上，Hank 不是我理想中的工作夥伴。

- I refuse to babysit Hank.
  我拒絕做 Hank 的「保母」。＝我不願意一邊工作還要一邊「照顧」Hank。

❷ They are the same.
這兩者是一樣的。

- There's no difference.
  這沒有什麼不同。

- There is not a pin to choose between.
  沒有多大的差別。

❸ I always notice that he's not quite all there during the office hours!
我總是發現他在上班時間時心不在焉的。

- I find him always out to lunch.
  我發現他總是「出外用午餐」。＝我發現他總是心不在焉。

143

- In my point of view, he switches automatically into the "day dream" mode during the office hours
在我看來，他在上班時會自動切換到「白日夢」模式。

 這句怎麼說？ *How to Say That?*

腦袋少根筋 ⟶ One sandwich short of a picnic

英釋 not very smart, lacking intelligence

中釋 不太聰明，缺少聰明才智。

A: How's the vacation?（假期過得如何？）

B: Ah, I don't want to mention it any more. Joe is one sandwich short of a picnic.（啊，我真不想提這件事。Joe 真是腦子少根筋。）

A: What's wrong?（怎麼了？）

B: When we arrived at our hotel in Hawaii, all he had in his luggage is his new leather coat.（在我們抵達夏威夷的飯店時，他的行李裡面只放了一件他的新的皮外套。）

 文化小盒子 *Culture Box*

　　six-pack 指的是可以裝 6 個，並方便於用一隻手提起的厚紙板包裝，一般是用在包裝飲料，啤酒等，也就是我們中文裡所說的「一手」。而 A few cans short of a six-pack，照字面上的意思來說就是在這個 6 罐裝的包裝中少了幾罐，用於比喻這個人做事不合常理，少根筋。在英文中的解釋為 not bright, smart enough. 但我覺得中文中的少根筋卻比英文更貼切於這樣的說法。而類似的說法還有很多，例如 a few keys short of a keyboard（鍵盤少了幾個鍵），a few fries short of a happy meal（快樂兒童餐中少了些薯條）

等。另外在對話當中，還有提到一個 40-watt club（40 瓦俱樂部），與少根筋相似，也是用於指這個人不夠聰明，因為在英文中的 bright 除了當作明亮的解釋之外，還可當作是聰明的。而因為科技的進步，燈泡的瓦數不再絕對代表亮度，所以這句話在使用上的頻率也逐漸減少。

阿倫碎碎念 *Allen's murmur*

Six-pack 一般是指以厚紙板包裝六瓶或是六罐飲料為一個販售的單位，通常會有提把或是兩個孔可供人一手拿起。也可用來形容數量為「六」，且為相同事物的集合，說到這，就讓我想到在炎炎夏日時，讓海灘上所有比基尼美女都流口水，而所有在場男士都恨的牙癢癢的 six-pack—六塊肌。Six-pack abs 在英文中的正式稱法應該為 an array of six bulges of human abdomen, rectus abdominis muscle. 中文應譯為人體腹部腹直肌的 6 塊凸起，腹直肌又可稱做腹肌，在英文中一般人都說 abs（abdominals 的簡稱）。

在 six-pack 的用法中，我覺得有一個相當的有趣。稱呼某人為 Joe Six-pack，這是一個美國的俚語，通常是指一般的美國男性，沒有什麼不良嗜好，也沒有什麼過人之處，平常就是喝喝啤酒，看看新聞。為什麼是 Joe 呢，那是因為在英文中稱普通人就叫做是 average Joe，我個人認為因為 Joe 是單音節發音，好叫又好記，所以應該有非常多的普通人叫 Joe，看到這裡，不知道你是不是也跟我一樣在腦海裡快速搜尋是否有叫做 Joe 的名人呢？而如同我剛剛提到的，集合 6 個相同的事物也可稱是 6-pack，所以也可被認為是普通的，Joe 冠上了 Six-pack 這一個姓，便成了超普通男士的代名詞。但隨著六塊肌、人魚線的流行，Joe Six-pack 又被賦予了一個新的意義，那就是「有六塊肌的男性」。

Diary 9 月 14 日

Dog My Cats

見鬼啦！輕微
地咒罵時的用
語。

Allen is looking for something high and low in his

cubicle. Mary wants to know what he has lost.

Allen 在他的小隔間裡到處找某樣東西。

Mary 想知道他到底弄丟了什麼。

對話 Dialogue

Mary: **Hurry up**, Allen. Stop **dawdling**, we don't have all day. The meeting will begin within twenty minutes. And we still have a lot of things to do.

Allen: I know, but I cannot find my **USB drive**. I need that for my presentation.

Mary: Did you check your **desktop**?

Allen: Yes, I did. Dog my cats! I put the drive on my desk before I went to the men's room.

Mary: Come on, we have only eighteen minutes now, do something.

Allen: Okay, okay, I'm thinking.

Mary: What is that? I mean in your **shirt** pocket!

Allen: Oh, my USB drive. Thanks, Mary, you **save my day**! I love you.

Mary: Keep that to Charlene, there are seventeen minutes to go.

146

單字 Vocabulary

1. **hurry up** ⓟⓗ 快一點
→ She hurried up the stage, and feeling a little bit nervous.
她快步走上台,心裡有一些緊張。

2. **dawdle** [`dɔdl]
ⓥ 浪費(時間等);閒混
→ Don't dawdle, the young head is soon white.
莫等閒,白了少年頭。

3. **USB drive** ⓟⓗ 隨身碟
→ Please do remember unplug the USB drive before you leave.
請記得在離開前要先將你的隨身碟拔出來。

4. **desktop** [`dɛsktɑp]
ⓝ 桌上型電腦
→ You can download this material to you desktop.
你可以將這一個資料下載到你的桌上型電腦中。

5. **shirt** [ʃɝt] ⓝ 襯衫
→ You look fabulous in that shirt.
你穿那一件襯衫看起來帥極了。

6. **save my day** ⓟⓗ 幫了我個大忙
→ I have been rushed off my feet at the office this morning; his presence really saved my day.
我今天早上在辦公室裡忙得不可開交,他的出現幫了個我大忙。

翻譯 Translation

Mary: 快一點,Allen。不要在拖拖拉拉的,我們可沒有一整天的時間耗在這兒。會議在 20 分鐘以內就要開始了。我們還有一大堆的事要做。

Allen: 我知道,可是我找不到我的隨身碟啊。我報告時要用的。

Mary: 你有沒有檢查你的電腦呢?

Allen: 有啊,我看過了。見鬼了!我在去廁所之前是把隨身碟放在桌上的啊。

Mary: 拜託,我們只剩下 18 分鐘了,想想辦法。

Allen: 好啦,好啦,我正在想。

Mary: 那是什麼?我是說在你襯衫口袋裡的!

Allen: 喔，是我的隨身碟。謝啦，Mary，你救了我！愛死你了。

Mary: 把那句話去跟 Charlene 說，現在只剩下 17 分鐘了。

心情小日記 Dear Diary

September 14th

Dear Diary,

We had only fifteen minutes left when we arrived the meeting room. Fortunately, Johnny already set up everything for us. How lucky I am to have a friend like him. Sometimes I joke with him and say if I were a girl, I will definitely want to marry him. And he refuses to continue this topic any further and gives me a disparaging gaze. I know he loves his wife very much, and he's the most perfect husband that I've ever known. I have a yearning for the life they have and I wish I can find my Miss Right soon!

9 月 14 日

親愛的日記，

當我們抵達會議室時只剩下 15 分鐘的時間。幸運地是 Johnny 早就已經為我們準備好所有的事了。我真是幸運有這樣一個朋友。有時候我還會開玩笑的對它說，如果我是女生的話，我一定會想要嫁給他。但他總是拒絕繼續這一個話題，還給了我一個鄙視的眼神。我知道他非常愛他的太太，他是我所認識的人當中最完美的丈夫。我很響往他們夫妻倆的生活，我希望很快能找到我的 Miss Right！

還可以怎麼說 In Other Words

❶ Stop dawdling, we don't have all day.
不要在拖拖拉拉的,我們可沒有一整天的時間耗在這兒。

- Stop dragging your legs, you are wasting my time.
  不要一直拖拖拉拉的,你在浪費我的時間。

- Think it all out before you act, and do it right now!
  在你行動之前先想清楚,還有現在馬上立刻做!

❷ Thanks, Mary, you save my day!
謝啦,Mary,你救了我!

- Many thanks for finding my USB drive for me.
  非常感謝幫我找到我的隨身碟。

- I appreciate it, Mary, you are my savior.
  我很感謝,Mary,你是我的大救星。

❸ I wish I can find my Miss Right soon!
我希望很快能找到我的 Miss Right!

- God, please send my rib back to me, please!
  老天爺啊,請將我的肋骨送回到我身邊吧。＝老天爺啊,請將我命中注定的另一半送回到我身邊吧。(據說夏娃是由亞當的一根肋骨造成的。)

- I need my soul mate desperately.
  我迫切的需要我靈魂的另一半。

這句怎麼說？ *How to Say That?*

我的媽呀 → For pity's sake

英釋 a mild exclamation of surprise or shock

中釋 驚訝或是受到驚嚇時所說的溫和的感嘆詞。

A: Mom, look at me! I am going to fly like the superman.（媽，你看我！我要跟超人一樣地飛囉。）

B: Oh, my! Zack, for pity's sake. Take off that panty immediately. That's the most expensive one.（喔，我的天啊！Zack，我的媽呀。立刻脫掉那一件內褲。那可是最貴的一件。）

文化小盒子 *Culture Box*

　　有關於 "dog my cats" 的說法來源，我所聽過的有兩種。一種是從曾祖父母輩那兒聽來的，我記得是 "Turn your dog loose on my cats." 的省略說法，意思是「讓你的狗放開我的貓」，用在鄰里之間有時不小心上演的貓狗大戰中，之後被沿用成為自己的小小咒罵時的用語。而另外一種說法則是說，是由 "doggone" 這一個字演變而來。基於信仰的關係，在西方國家中，直稱 "God" 被視為是不禮貌的。所以有時在罵人或是罵自己的時候會「禮貌性」用變體，而 dog 是 god 反過來的拼法，因此以 "doggone" 來代表 "God damn"，而 "dog my cats" 則是 "doggone" 的變體，在咒罵的程度上較有「禮貌」，算是不帶髒字，輕微用以抒發情緒的用法。

阿倫碎碎念 Allen's Murmur

　　我曾經在一些英文教學的網站上看到 "dog my cats" 的中文翻譯，很多都翻的很有趣，而且也很貼切。像是「喵了個咪」，以這一句俚語的主角之一「貓」來帶出這一句話的精髓。當我看到這一句時，心中不禁浮出一個畫面，畫面中有一名女子手中抱了隻貓，說出了 "dog my cats" 時還順便翻了個大白眼。

　　其它的除了我介紹過的「見鬼了！」還有粗獷版的「他奶奶的」、鄉土版的「哭夭／爸」、家常版的「喔，拜託」，其它族繁不及備載。讓我不禁讚嘆起中國文化的博大精深，連這一種小小的抒發情緒詞也能有這麼多的版本。"Dog my cats" 這一句話其起源是在 19 世紀的美國，大多被使用在美國的南方，一般據信是從美國黑人文化中發展出來的。而在大文豪 Mark Twain（馬克·吐溫）的書 *Adventure of Huckleberry Finn*"（頑童歷險記－又稱哈克貝利費恩歷險記，是湯姆歷險記的續集）中就有不止一次的提到 "dog my cats"。

　　言歸正傳，我就來介紹一下在英文當中與貓有關的小常識，一般我們會稱公的貓為 "Tom"，母貓為 "Queen" 也有人稱 "Molly"，而閹過的貓為 "gib"。大家應該知道在卡通 "Tom and Jerry"（貓與老鼠）中的湯姆貓吧！湯姆貓在英文中可說 "Tomcat"，是指一直不停在追求母貓的公貓，也可以用來形容人。而稱公貓為 Tom 的起源為在 18 世紀中期的一本暢銷童書 "The Life and Adventure of A Cat"，書中的主角貓就叫做 Tom。Okay，就先說到這了，my boss was "a bag of cats" yesterday（我的老闆昨天「發飆」了，所以我今天皮得繃緊一點！）

Casting Couch

檯面下的潛規則。(與性有關的那種)

Phoebe, Peter and Allen are sitting on a couch and talking about the casting.

Phoebe，Peter 還有 Allen 正坐在長沙發上討論角色分配。

 對話 *Dialogue*

Phoebe: Allen, you come just at the right time. Peter and I are talking about the **casting** of the new **advertisement**. Both of us are not quite satisfy with the leading actress.

Peter: We simply don't think she's famous enough for this new ad.

Allen: So, what can I do for you?

Peter: We know you have some connections with the **ad-agency**, and we want to know is that possible to change the **actress**?

Allen: Hoho, I don't think that's easy. To tell the truth, that girl's father is one of our company's big guns.

Phoebe: So is it kind of casting couch?

Allen: Nope, I wouldn't say it's the casting couch, but the unspoken **rule**.

152

Peter: I'm really **curious** about who that big gun is?

Allen: Sorry about that, I have no idea.

單字 Vocabulary

1. **casting** [ˋkæstɪŋ]
   n 挑選演員、分配角色
   → The casting of this movie received excellent reviews.
   這部電影的演員陣容受到極高的評價。

2. **advertisement**
   [ˏædvəˋtaɪzmənt] n 廣告
   → This is not a science-base study, but a commercial advertisement.
   這不是一項科學研究，而是一則商業廣告。

3. **ad-agency** [æd ˋedʒənsɪ]
   n 廣告公司
   → It is one of the biggest ad-agencies in the US.
   這是美國最大的廣告公司之一。

4. **actress** [ˋæktrɪs]
   n 女演員
   → The actress exited in an elegant way.
   這名女演員以優雅的姿勢退場。

5. **rule** [rul]
   n 規則
   → We need new rules before we start looking for more members.
   在我們開始找更多新會員前，我們需要新的規則。

6. **curious** [ˋkjʊrɪəs]
   adj 好奇的
   → She is a curious student.
   她是一個有好奇心的學生。

翻譯 Translation

Phobe: Allen，你來的正是時候。我和 Peter 正在談新廣告的演員部分。我們都不太滿意女主角的部份。

Peter: 我們就是覺得就新廣告而言，她不夠有名氣。

Allen: 所以，我能幫到你們什麼呢？

Peter: 我們知道你和廣告公司有一些關係，我們想知道是不是有可能換掉女主角？

Allen: 呵呵，我覺得這不太容易。說老實話，那女孩的爸爸是我們公司的

　　　　　　某位重要人士。

Phobe: 所以那算是潛規則的一種嗎？

　Allen: 不是，不算是那一種的潛規則，而是另一種潛規則。

Peter: 我真的很好奇那一個重要人士是誰？

　Allen: 抱歉，這我可就不知道了。

心情小日記 Dear Diary

September 16th

Dear Diary,

I saw our new ad on TV today. I think it's quite nice, and Lilian (the leading lady) acted very well in the ad. A few days ago, I read Lilian's interview in the newspaper, as a new star, she has a great beginning, and I think all credit should go to her big gun dad. Speaking of that, Yo told us that Lilian's father is a shareholder of our company, furthermore, he's a very important government official. And he didn't let the cat out of the bag and kept us dangling as usual. But I'm sure Johnny got the name, and I'll ask him tomorrow.

9月16日

親愛的日記，

我今天在電視上看到我們的新廣告了。我覺得還不錯，還有 Lilian（女主角）在廣告中的表現很好。就在幾天前，我在報上看到 *Lilian* 的專訪，就一位新起之秀而言，她有一個好的開始，我想這一切得歸功於她那一位大人物爸爸。說到這，阿祐跟我們說 *Lilian* 的父親是我們公司的股東，而且他還是一位重要的政府官員。他如同往常一般沒有將秘密說出來，吊著大家的胃口。但我確定 *Johnny* 一定知道是誰，我明天就去問他。

還可以怎麼說 In Other Words

❶ We know you have some connections with the advertising agency
我們知道你和廣告公司有一些關係。

- You have a friend works in that company, don't you?
  你有一個朋友在那家公司工作，對吧？

- You know someone in that company, right?
  你在那家公司有認識的人，對吧？

❷ That girl's father is one of our company's big gun.
那女孩的爸爸是我們公司的某位重要人士。

- She is CEO's daughter.
  她是執行長的女兒。

- She's a big wig's daughter.
  她是某個大「假髮」的女兒。＝她是某個大人物的女兒。

❸ He didn't let the cat out of the bag.
他沒有將秘密說出來。

- He kept the secret from us.
  他瞞著我們大家。

- He said nothing at all.
  他什麼都沒說。

 這句怎麼說？ *How to Say That?*

不成文規定 ➜ Hidden rules

英釋 The rule is understood or accepted by everyone, although it's not formally or officially established.

中釋 未經正式規範，但大家都知道或是接受的規則。

A: Should I send gifts or give kickbacks to him? （我應不應該送禮或是回扣給他？）

B: No, you shouldn't. I know it's the hidden rule, but it's also a kind of bribery. （不，你不該這樣做。我知道這是不成文規定，但這也是一種賄賂。）

文化小盒子 *Culture Box*

　　Casting couch，casting 是選角，物色演員人選的意思，couch 則是長沙發、躺椅，以選角的長沙發來比喻在娛樂圈中導演以戲中的角色為釣餌，引誘演員以性關係來換取角色。而延伸成為形容在各行業之中，與手中握有某件事決定的權力的人發生性關係，用來換取想要達成的目標，也就是我們所說的潛規則。但要特別注意的是 casting couch 指的是與性交易有關連的潛規則，而其他例如是送禮，給回扣等與金錢有關的潛規則，則是稱為 hidden rules，或是 unspoken rules，unwritten rules 等。如同在對話中提到的女主角是因為父親的關係所以出演這一次的廣告，所以用 hidden rules 或是 unspoken rules 等比較恰當。

阿倫碎碎念 Allen's Murmur

這一次公司新廣告的女主角是 Lilian，據說她是某個股東的女兒。這就又讓我想到了阿祐，這兩個人可以說是屬於 "Lucky Sperm Club"（幸運精子俱樂部）的會員啊，也就是「靠爸族」。但是這兩個人的表現實在差太多了，根據和 Lilian 共事的同仁說，Lilian 超敬業的，而且也不會擺架子，跟某人比起來，唉，我就不說了，相信大家都知道我心中的 OOXX 了。

這一次討論的 casting couch，讓我想到一些有關 couch 的有趣俚語，像是夫妻之間的吵架，並且是那一種到了睡覺時間，其中一方（大多是男性啦）淪落到要去沙發上睡一晚的那種，我們就可以說那是 "couch argument"。For example, Johnny told me that he and his wife had an intense argument last night, and it became a couch argument. （舉例來說，Johnny 告訴我他和他太太昨晚大吵了一架，最後就演變成有人昨晚睡在沙發上。）雖然他沒說是誰睡在沙發上，但是相信我，那絕對是他啦！不過他家的沙發上有超多的 "couch beef" 的，我猜他為了要空出位置來睡一覺，一定花了不少的功夫。猜到 "couch beef" 是什麼了嗎？那就是放在沙發上的靠枕，有大有小，各式各樣的形狀，只要是放在沙發上的都可以說是 "couch beef"。而他太太超愛買這類型的靠枕，而且還總是說 "I cannot stand a couch without tons of couch beef."（我無法忍受沙發上沒有很多的靠枕。）

但其實我對於 couch beef 這樣的說法是怎麼來的十分的好奇，如果有人知道的話，請告訴 Allen 我喔！

Tommy Atkins

湯姆·阿特金
司一泛指一般
的英國士兵。

Joycelyn is talking to Allen in front of his office. Allen wants to introduce his new colleague "Tommy Atkins" to Joycelyn.

Joycelyn 和 Allen 在他辦公室前聊天。Allen 要將他的新同事 "Tommy Atkins" 介紹給 Joycelyn 認識。

 對話 Dialogue

Joycelyn: Who's that good looking guy?

Allen: Oh, he's our new colleague. He was the Tommy Atkins.

Joycelyn: Tommy Atkins? Is that his name?

Allen: No, Tommy is not his name. I mean that he used to be a **soldier**.

Joycelyn: Oh, I see. But he is **indeed** a Tommy.

Allen: What Tommy?

Joycelyn: Look at his **stalwart figure**, and his handsome face. He's just like the prince **charming** that every teenage girl wants to have.

Allen: Come on, you are not a teenage girl anymore. Besides, didn't you say that you're not a cougar?

Joycelyn: No, I'm not, but I think I can make an **exception** for him.

Allen: All right, let me introduce him to you!

單字 Vocabulary

1. **soldier** [`soldʒɚ]
   n 士兵、軍人
   → He was shot by an unseen soldier.
   他被一位埋伏的士兵給槍殺了。

2. **indeed** [ɪn`did]
   adv 確實
   → She's indeed a remarkable writer.
   她確實是一位傑出的作家。

3. **stalwart** [`stɔlwɚt]
   adj 結實的、健壯的
   → The captain of the school football team is tall and stalwart.
   足球校隊的隊長長的高大魁梧。

4. **figure** [`fɪgjɚ]
   n 體型、外型
   → She has an attractive figure.
   她有著迷人的身材。

5. **charming** [`tʃɑrmɪŋ]
   adj 迷人的、有魅力的
   → I was smitten by her charming smile.
   我被她迷人的微笑給迷住了。

6. **exception** [ɪk`sɛpʃən]
   n 例外；例外的人、事、物
   → Please kindly make an exception for us this time.
   請您好心的通融這一次。

翻譯 Translation

Joycelyn: 那位帥哥是誰啊？

Allen: 喔，那是我們的新同事。他曾經是一位 Tommy Atkins。

Joycelyn: Tommy Atkins？是他的名字嗎？

Allen: Tommy 不，他不叫 Tommy。我的意思是他曾經是軍人。

Joycelyn: 喔，我懂了。但他確實是一個 Tommy。

Allen: 什麼Tommy？

Joycelyn: 看看他那高大健壯的身材，還有他的帥臉。他就像是所有年輕女孩心目中的白馬王子啊。

Allen: 拜託，妳又不是十幾歲的小女生了。除此之外，妳不是說妳不要姊弟戀嗎？

Joycelyn: 是啊，我不要，但我想我可以為他開個先例。

Allen: 好吧，那我來為你們介紹一下。

心情小日記 Dear Diary

September 22nd

Dear Diary,

We have a new colleague today, and his shining smile attracts so many of our female colleagues. And of course, some of our gay colleagues also fancy him so much. According to their claims, our new colleague is their dream type. Fortunately, the muscleman is not Charlene's cup of tea, or I really should worry about our blooming love. By the way, Charlene and I already had lunch to-gether for several times (alright, I was just near her at the table). Next time, I'll muster my courage up to ask her out, hmm… one day, maybe.

9 月 22 日

親愛的日記，

我們今天來了一位新同事，他那耀眼的笑容迷倒了我們許多的女同事。還有當然，我們那一些同性戀的同事們也被他迷得團團轉。根據他們的說法，我們的新同事可是他們的天菜。還好，肌肉男不是 Charlene 喜歡的類型，要不我就得擔心我們那剛剛萌芽的愛情。說到這，我和 Charlene 已經一起用過幾次午餐了（好吧，我只是坐在他的附近）。下一次，我將會鼓起勇氣約她出去，嗯…某一天，也許。

還可以怎麼說 In Other Words

❶ Who's that good looking guy?
那位帥哥是誰啊？

- Where comes the gorgeous?
  哪裡來的大帥哥啊？

- You've got to tell me the name of that metrosexual guy.
  你一定要告訴我那一個花美男的名字。

❷ Besides, didn't you say that you're not a cougar?
除此之外，妳不是說妳不要姊弟戀嗎？

- I remember that you say you don't date with a man who's younger than you are.
  我記得妳不是說過妳不會跟年紀比妳小的男生約會嗎？

- Besides, didn't you say that you're not a cradle rubber?
  除此之外，你不是說你不會跟太年輕的妹約會嗎？（換成是男生的角色說法。）

❸ I'll muster my courage up to ask her out.
我將會鼓起勇氣約她出去。

- I will brace myself up and try to ask her out.
  我將會鼓起勇氣試著約她出去。

- I'll gonna date her, if I can summon up my courage.
  如果我能鼓起勇氣的話，我將能跟她去約會了。

這句怎麼說？How to Say That?

二等兵 → Squaddie

英釋 （military）brit a private solder

中釋 在英式英文中用來稱呼陸軍二等兵的說法。是由 squad（軍隊中的班）
而衍生出的。

A: What is your military rank?（你的軍階是多大呢？）

B: I am just a squaddie.（我只是一個二等兵。）

文化小盒子 Culture Box

　　有關 Tommy Atkins 被用來統稱英國陸軍一般士兵的起源有許多種說
法。最早的說法起源據說是在 1743 年時，從牙買加寄回的一封敘述部隊中
叛亂事件的信件當中，曾提起 Tommy Atkins 的名字，並讚揚其在事件中的
優異表現。而一般普遍相信則是在 1794 年的弗蘭德斯戰役，當時威靈頓公
爵率領著第 33 陸軍團，經過激烈的戰爭後，公爵看到團裡最好的重騎兵
Tommy Atkins 受了重傷。而這一位士兵則是回答 "It's all right, sir. It's all in a
day's work." 隨後就因為傷重不治身亡。但在牛津辭典中指出這一個說法的
起源是在 1815 年時，官方所給的表格範例中的名字。現在已經比較少用
Tommy Atkins 來稱英國士兵，大多會以 Tommy 或是 Tommies。而有趣的是
在美國會稱讓無數少女傾心的、受家長信賴及擅長某種體育項目的青少年白
馬王子為 Tommy。

阿倫碎碎念 Allen's Murmur

　　根據一項 2013 年在美國的調查中指出，Jackson 和 Sophia 是 2013 年出生的寶寶中最多人取的名字，也就是我們說的年度菜市場名冠軍。而在台灣的調查中，2013 年則是由「宥翔」及「語桐」這兩個詩情畫意的名字奪冠。據命理專家指出，這些熱門名字都是吉祥的筆畫，應該是在取名之前有請命理師算過。

　　為什麼我要提起人名呢？那是因為在英文中常會用到一些與人名相關的俚語，跟中文一樣。例如我們常說的「張三李四」，在英文中，我們就可以說是 "every/any Tom, Dick and Harry"。就像是上次我們英明的副理就曾經冷冷的對經理說 "I want a qualified person to do the job, not just any Tom, Dick and Harry."（我要的是一個夠資格的人來做這工作，而不是隨便一個阿狗阿貓；張三李四都行。）她說這一句話的時候超酷的，我都想要起立幫她鼓掌叫好，真不愧為曾是某公司高層出身的人！

　　而 2013 年的美國男寶寶菜市場名第一的 Jackson，在一些以 J 開頭的名字，例如 Jack、Jacob、Jayden 等中脫穎而出，但其實在一般英語國家中，Jack 被公認為是男性菜市場名中的佼佼者。不蓋你，我的親戚當中，隨便就可以抓出 3 個以上的 Jack，而且還不包括講法語或是講中文的 Jack。所以在英文中就有一句話 "Jack-of-all-trades"（萬事通），來稱呼什麼都會的人，像是我就常常稱 Johnny 是 Jack-of-all-trades。但要注意的是，如果在後面加上一句 "master of none"，這時候則是有貶低的意思，說這一個人好像什麼都會，但是卻沒有一樣精通。

Zip

本意為拉錬，
用來暗指某人
腦袋的拉錬沒
拉上，乃笨蛋是
也。

Allen sees Paul in front of the corner Café, and now they are talking to each other.

Allen在街角的咖啡店遇見Paul，現在他們正在交談中。

對話 Dialogue

Allen: Hey, Paul. What's wrong? You look so **desperate**.

Paul: Hi, Allen. I'm in big trouble. What should I do?

Allen: Hey, take easy. You have to tell me what happened, and then maybe I can help.

Paul: I had an important presentation this morning, so I sat up far into the night and **rehearsed**. John gave me a bottle of Whisbih, he said it is also a kind of **energy** drink just like Red Bull…

Allen: And you got drunk, right?

Paul: Yep, how do you know?

Allen: Actually Whisbih is an **alcoholic** drink. So how's the presentation?

Paul: I think I did okay, but my breath smelled of alcohol which **irritated** my boss. He **threatened** me that he's going to fail me in the performance review.

Ray: Oh, well, John is a nice guy, but sometime he's such a zip. Maybe you could explain the whole situation to your boss.

單字 Vocabulary

1. **desperate** ['dɛspərɪt]
   adj 絕望的；極度渴望
   → She is desperate to pursue her vocation as an actress.
   她不顧一切地要成為女演員。

2. **rehearse** [rɪ'hɝs]
   v 排練，排演
   → We were given one week to rehearse.
   我們只被給了一個星期排演的時間。

3. **energy** ['ɛnɚdʒɪ]
   n 活力，精力
   → Chris could not even raise the energy to smile.
   Chris 甚至連笑一下的力氣都沒有了。

4. **alcoholic** [,ælkə'hɔlɪk]
   adj 酒精的，含酒精的
   → It's a must to cut out all alcoholic drinks during the pregnancy.
   在懷孕期間滴酒不沾是必須的。

5. **irritate** ['ɪrə,tet]
   v 惹惱，使發怒
   → Don't irritate mom, she's on a short fuse today.
   別惹媽，她今天動不動就發火。

6. **threaten** ['θrɛtn]
   v 威脅，恐嚇
   → They threaten him with a law suit.
   他們恐嚇他要告他。

翻譯 Translation

Allen: 嘿，Paul。怎麼了？你看起來一副絕望的樣子。

Paul: 嗨，Allen。我麻煩大了，我該怎麼辦？

Allen: 嘿，別緊張。你得先告訴我發生了什麼事，也許我幫的上忙。

Paul: 我今天早上有一個重要的簡報，所以我花了一個晚上的時間排練。John 給了我一瓶維士比，他說是和「紅牛」一樣的能量飲料……

Allen: 然後你喝醉了，對吧？

Paul: 對，你怎麼知道？

Allen: 事實上維士比是含有酒精成分的。那你的簡報做的如何？

Paul: 我覺得我報告的還可以，但我一身的酒味惹惱了我的老闆。他威脅我他將會在績效評估中給我不及格。

Allen: 嗯，John 是個好人，但有時候他做事不經大腦。我建議或許你應該跟你的老闆解釋整個情形。

心情小日記 Dear Diary

October 11ᵗʰ

Dear Diary,

Today I met Paul in front of the corner Café, and it's the first time that I saw him in panic. His boss threatened him to fail him in the annual performance review, because he went to the meeting with a hangover. Maybe I should have a serious talk with John. He's a decent man, but he sometimes acts without regard for what will happen afterwards. This time, <u>he really made a big trouble for Paul</u>. I'll cross my fingers for Paul, hope he can solve his problem.

10月11日

親愛的日記，

今天我在街角的咖啡店前面遇見 Paul ，這是我第一次看到他驚慌失措的樣子。他的老闆威脅他要在年度績效評估中當掉他，因為他帶著宿醉去開會。也許我應該好好的跟 John 談一談。他是一個好人，但他有時候做事情沒有考慮到後果。這一次，他為 Paul 帶來了相當大的麻煩。我會為 Paul 祈求好運，希望他能解決他的問題。

還可以怎麼說 In Other Words

❶ You have to tell me what happened, and then maybe I can help.
你得先告訴我發生了什麼事，也許我幫的上忙。

- I need to know the whole situation to give you a hand.
  我需要了解整個情況才能幫你。

- Please tell me what happened and I'll see what I can do.
  請告訴我發生了什麼事，或許我可以幫你想想辦法。

❷ I sat up far into the night.
我熬夜了。

- I stayed up late last night.
  我昨天晚上熬夜了。

- I didn't sleep for all night long.
  我一整個晚上都沒有睡。

❸ He really made a big trouble for Paul.
他為 Paul 帶來了相當大的麻煩。

- Paul was in trouble because of him.
  因為他，Paul 陷入了麻煩。

- Paul's in the soup this time, and it's all his fault.
  Paul 這一次陷在湯裡，這全都是他的錯。＝Paul 這一次惹上麻煩，全都是他的錯。

167

這句怎麼說？ How to Say That?

大腦空空、花瓶 → Airhead

英釋 Term implies the person's head contains nothing but air.

中釋 指某人的頭殼裡沒有東西只有空氣，暗喻某人沒有腦子。

A: Your sister's boyfriend is very handsome.（你妹妹的男友很帥。）

B: Unfortunately, he's an airhead.（不幸的是，他是個沒腦袋的笨蛋。）

文化小盒子 Culture Box

　　zip 在英文中的原意為拉鍊，但在英文俚語當中則有許多的含意，一般最常見的則是用來指稱 "scar"（傷疤），特別是指形狀有如拉鍊一般，手術縫合的傷疤，或是 "nothing"（什麼都沒有），"zero"（零）的意思。例如 "I have zip." = "I have nothing."（我什麼都沒有。）；"The score was three-zip."（比數是三比零）。而在用 zip 形容人的時候，則是指這個人是沒腦子的笨蛋，或是沒有用，窩囊廢。在美式俚語當中，與毒品相關的單字常會被延伸引用成來形容「精力，活力」的意思，而zip也不例外。在美式俚語當中，zip 也有被用來指「一盎司的毒品／大麻」，這大多是用於在電話中與毒販接頭所使用的術語，zip 在這原本是指夾鍊袋 "ziplock bag"，毒販將毒品分裝在夾鍊袋中，每袋一盎司以方便販售。久而久之，便有用 zip 來代稱毒品或是大麻的說法。

阿倫碎碎念 *Allen's Murmur*

　　Zip 在英文俚語當中，可以稱得上是「百搭款」，除了常見的在一般英文俚語中總是不能免俗地跟毒品扯上關係，也因為毒品而衍生出有比喻精力的含意在。更因為 zip 的形狀，而有指傷疤、疤痕的含意。

　　Allen 在這裡要談一些跟 zip 的原意「拉鍊」有關的，例如 "zip crotch"（拉鍊褲襠），這裡並不只是單純的指褲襠，相信應該有廣大的男性讀者都跟我一樣在拉褲襠拉鍊的時候，總是會小心翼翼地，怕會去夾到不該夾到的東西吧。別亂想，我指的是內褲，你知道的，夾到後就無法順利的拉上拉鍊，有時還得花上很長的時間去解開……blah blah blah。有時候非常的不小心，的確是很有可能會去夾到內褲裡面的「肉」，而那一種痛是無法形容的，而zip crotch指的就是這樣子的恐懼症。另外因為男女構造不同，所以男生總是能在尿急卻找不到廁所的情況下，隨便找個地方就地解決，而拉下拉鍊，掏出來的這個動作，可以說是 "zip and whip"。

　　另外再介紹一個可愛的說法，在別人發表完長篇大論，但卻都是令人聽不下去的廢話之後，我們可以以一種極為諷刺的用語 "zip-a-dee-doo-dah" 來回應對方。而這樣的說法則是源自於美國在 1947 年時的一首歌頌人生的歌曲 "Zip-a-dee-doo-dah"，在說的時候，要記得將 zip 和 a 和在一起發音！

Tall Order

用來說明某件
事是一個艱鉅
的任務。

Joycelyn and Dylan are talking in the pantry. And

Allen comes in and join the discussion.

Joycelyn 和 Dylan 在茶水間聊天。

Allen 走進來並加入討論。

 對話 *Dialogue*

Allen: Is there anything interesting?

Joycelyn: Hi, Allen. I just told Dylan about my nearsighted date experience before the Moon Festival.

Allen: So how's it going?

Joycelyn: He's just not my cup of tea. There's something more important that I want to talk about.

Allen: Okay, **go ahead.**

Joycelyn: Are you free this weekend? Dylan and I want to **organize** a **cookout** this Saturday, wanna come?

Allen: This Saturday? Hmmm… sorry, I have lots of work to do during the weekend.

Dylan: See! Joycelyn, I told you so! It's a tall order to ask Allen- the

170

workaholic out.

Joycelyn: Come on, Allen. The work is never done. You have to **relax** and have fun during the weekend. Besides, Charlene will go with us.

Allen: Oh, I'll **definitely** attend.

單字 Vocabulary

1. **go ahead** ph 繼續下去；先走；走在前面
   → You just go ahead, and I'll catch you later.
   你先走，我隨後趕上。

2. **organize** [`ɔrgəˌnaɪz] v 組織、安排
   → I will organize the transport for you.
   我來為您安排交通方面的問題。

3. **cookout** [`ɔrgəˌnaɪz] n 野炊、戶外烤肉
   → We will have a cookout at the Mid-Autumn Festival.
   我們中秋節時會去烤肉。

4. **workaholic** [ˌwɝkə`hɔlɪk] n 工作狂、醉心於工作的人
   → If you were born on a Saturday, you are likely to be a workaholic.
   如果你是星期六出生的，那你有可能會是工作狂。

5. **relax** [rɪ`læks] v 放鬆、休息
   → I like to relax on a sofa when I'm home.
   當我在家的時候，我喜歡坐在沙發上放鬆。

6. **definitely** [`dɛfənɪtlɪ] adv 確切地、肯定地
   → She's not exactly pretty, but definitely attractive.
   她並不算漂亮，但的確很有魅力。

翻譯 Translation

Allen: 什麼事這麼有趣啊？

Joycelyn: 嗨，Allen，我剛正跟 Dylan 聊我在中秋節前相親的事。

Allen: 所以，相親相的如何？

Joycelyn: 他不是我喜歡的那一型。我有更重要的事要說。

Allen: OK，請說。

Joycelyn: 你這一個週末有空嗎？Dylan 跟我這一個星期六要辦一個烤肉聚會，要參加嗎？

Allen: 這一個星期六？嗯……不好意思，我週末時有一大堆的工作要做。

Dylan: 妳看吧！Joycelyn，我早就說了！想要約工作狂 Allen 出去可是一項艱鉅的任務。

Joycelyn: 拜託，Allen。工作是永遠做不完的。你在週末的時候需要放鬆及找點樂子。除此之外，Charlene 會跟我們去喔。

Allen: 我一定會參加的。

心情小日記 Dear Diary

October 13th

Dear Diary,

Today is the most memorable day of my life ever. Joycelyn formally introduced me to Charlene and we had the first formal talk this evening. She's super nice and charming. Most importantly, she said that she remembers our first met in front my office. Wow, it's pretty hard to believe that my goddess has an impression of me. I think it's a good start. And now I feel like I'm on top of the world. I will surely tell Johnny about this good news tomorrow and show him that I've got Charlene's number in my phone!

10 月 13 日

親愛的日記,

今天是我這一生當中最值得紀念的日子。*Joycelyn* 正式地將我介紹給 *Charlene*,還有我們今天晚上第一次正式的說了話。她人超好還超正的。最重要地是,她說她記得在我辦公室前面我們第一次的見面。哇,這真是太難以相信了,我的女神居然對我有印象。我覺得這是一個好的開始。而且我覺得我真是幸福到極點了。我明天一定會告訴 *Johnny* 這一個好消息,還要秀給他看我已經拿到 *Charlene* 的電話號碼就存在我的電話裡!

還可以怎麼說 In Other Words

❶ Is there anything interesting?
什麼事這麼有趣啊?

- Hey, what are you talking about?
  嘿,你們在聊什麼啊?

- May I join the discussion?
  我可以參與討論嗎?

❷ He's just not my cup of tea.
他不是我喜歡的那一型。

- He is not my dish.
  他不是我的菜。

- I believe that my destiny is waiting for me in somewhere.
  我相信我的真命天子(天女)正在某個地方等著我。

❸ I feel like I'm on top of the world.
我覺得我真是幸福到極點了。

● She made me feel light of foot.
她讓我整個人都感到輕飄飄的。

● It is out of this world.
這真是太棒了，超乎我的想像。

 這句怎麼說？ *How to Say That?*

不可能的任務 ⟶ Mission impossible

英 釋 an extremely dangerous or difficult mission

中 釋 一個十分艱鉅或是危險的任務。

A: Ben, what's up? Your face looks like having trouble of constipation for many days. Ben，怎麼了？你的臉看起來好像便秘了好幾天。

B: Hi, Janet. My mom said that I have to lead the class in this examination. Otherwise, I can't go to the summer camp with you. 嗨，Janet。我媽說我在這一次的考試要拿到全班第一。不然的話，我就不能和妳一起去參加夏令營了。

A: Oh, that's too bad. It sounds like a mission impossible to me. 喔，這太糟糕了。這在我聽起來就像是一項不可能的任務嘛。

文化小盒子 *Culture Box*

在 tall order 中，order 的定義為 "a direction or commission to make, provide, or furnish something"（一個指示或是委任要去做、提供或是提交某些東西）。而 tall 的意思則是一般比較少用的 "large in amount or degree"（大量或是大程度的），而 tall 的這一個用法則是源自於 19 世紀中時的一個

美國俚語 "tall time"，於是在 19 世紀末時，便開始出現了 "tall order" 用來指稱 "被視為是一項艱鉅、困難，難以達成的任務"，第一次出現在書籍中則是在 1893 年時由 F. W. L. Adams 所著的 "*The New Egypt*"。而其也延伸出使用不同的相近形容詞來形容「艱鉅的任務」，例如 big、large 和 strong。所以如果當老闆要求你將 2 個月的事在一個月內完成時，除了 tall order 之外，你還可以說 "It's a strong order to finish all the works in one month!"

阿倫碎碎念 Allen's Murmur

在英文當中，tall 和 high 所代表的意思都是高，但是在用法上確有所不同。tall 一般是用來表示具體的高度，例如是物體或是人的身高等等，指的為具體的高度。而 high 通常則是用來表示較為抽象，例如是溫度、速度或是價錢等。

在 "tall order" 中則用了少見的以 tall 來形容程度上這樣抽象的用法。而相同於這一個用法的還有一個 "tall tale"，tall tale 在英文中的解釋為 "a long and complicated story which is difficult to believe, because most of the events it contains seem unlikely or even impossible."（長且複雜的故事，通常內容聽起來不像是真實的或甚至是不可能的。）在中文裡，我們則稱這樣的故事為神話故事、或是誇張、荒誕的故事。例如有名的「聊齋誌異」、「山海經」等就可以被稱做是 tall tale。

常出現在電視或是電影劇情中會有一個老水手，或是老人坐著在吹噓年輕的時候他以寡擊眾，有著一夫當關，萬夫莫敵的氣勢，聽在大家耳裡，都知道是在吹牛，而非事實，這個時候我們也可以說這是一個 tall tale，意思為他說大話、吹牛。說好聽一點的就是這是老水手的「海外奇聞」，老人的「狂想曲」。

Kill Two Pigs with One Bird

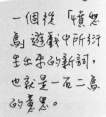

一個從「憤怒鳥」遊戲中所衍生出來的新詞，也就是一石二鳥的意思。

Allen and Johnny are waiting for the elevator, and

talking about how to "kill two pigs with one bird."

Allen 和 Johnny 正在等電梯，

他們聊著怎麼「用一隻鳥殺掉兩頭豬」。

對話 Dialogue

Johnny: Good morning, Allen. Your eyes **twinkle** with **pleasure**. I think you've got something want to **share** with me, am I right?

Allen: Yep! Can you guess what I've got yesterday?

Johnny: Umm… that's a piece of cake, you got Charlene's numbers at dinner.

Allen: Erm, you already know as usual. Damn, I thought I can surprise you this time.

Johnny: Of course, you can. Tell me more! I know you drove her home after dinner, and then…

Allen: And then? I went back to my apartment…

Johnny: So you didn't even phone her to say good night?

Allen: Nah, should I do that?

Johnny: Yeh, it's a chance of a **lifetime.** I thought you'll ask her out and **volunteer** to buy all the **grocery** for the cookout.

Allen: That's a brilliant idea, and it's killing two pigs with one bird, thank you, Johnny, gotta go.

Johnny: What pigs?! Hey, Allen, come back.

單字 Vocabulary

1. **twinkle** [ˋtwɪŋkl]
   v 閃耀、閃爍
   → Lights twinkle in distant village across the valley at night.
   夜裡，山谷那一頭遙遠的村落閃耀著點點燈光。

2. **pleasure** [ˋplɛʒɚ]
   n 愉快；樂趣
   → It has been a pleasure to attend her class.
   上她的課十分的有趣。

3. **share** [ʃɛr]
   v 分享；分擔
   → My flatmate and I share in the use of the kitchen.
   我的室友和我一同使用這一間廚房。

4. **lifetime** [ˋlaɪf͵taɪm]
   n 一生、終生
   → My grandfather wrote many books during his lifetime.
   我祖父在生前寫了非常多的書籍。

5. **volunteer** [͵vɑlənˋtɪr]
   v 自願（做）
   → Sally and I volunteer to wash all the dishes.
   Sally 和我自願洗所有的盤子。

6. **grocery** [ˋgrosərɪ]
   n 食品雜貨；南北貨
   → I went grocery shopping with my mother this afternoon.
   我今天下午跟我媽去買菜。

翻譯 Translation

Johnny: 早安，Allen。你的眼中閃耀著喜悅的光芒，我想你有事要和我分享，是吧？

Allen: 對啊！你猜猜看我昨天拿到什麼？

Johnny: 嗯……小事一件，你在晚餐時拿到了 Charlene 的電話號碼。

Allen: 嗯，跟往常一樣你已經知道囉。該死，我還以為這次能讓你感到意外。

Johnny: 當然可以啊。多跟我透露些！我知道你在晚餐後載她回家，然後呢？

Allen: 然後？我回我的公寓啦……

Johnny: 所以你甚至沒有打電話給她道晚安？

Allen: 沒啊，我應該這樣做嗎？

Johnny: 當然，這可是個千載難逢的好機會耶。我還以為你會邀她一起自願採買烤肉要用的東西。

Allen: 這真是個好主意，真是「一鳥二豬」，謝啦，Johnny，我要走囉。

Johnny: 什麼豬啊？嘿，Allen，回來啊。

心情小日記 Dear Diary

October 17th

Dear Diary,

I sent a Line message to Joycelyn this afternoon, and told her about Johnny's brilliant idea. She replied that she can't agree more and wish me luck. So I called Charlene and asked her out to do the cookout shopping on Friday evening. She said yes, and told me that she was just about to call me. She also wanted to ask me to do the shopping with her. What a coincident! We were thinking about the same thing. It seems like we are a match made in heaven. Oh, I have to look through all my clothes and select the best looking one for our first DATE!!!

10 月 17 日

親愛的日記,

我今天下午傳 Line 訊息給 Joycelyn,告訴她 Johnny 的好點子。她答覆我她再同意不過了,還祝我好運。所以我打給 Charlene 約她星期五晚上一起去買烤肉的東西。她說好,還告訴我她正想打給我。她也是要約我一起去買。這真是太巧了!我們剛剛想的是同一件事。看起來我們是天作之合。喔,我要去為我們第一次約會挑選出最帥的衣服了。

還可以怎麼說 In Other Words

❶ That's a piece of cake.
小事一件。

- It's a no-brainer.
  這不用腦子。＝太簡單了。

- It's just like a kid stuff.
  小孩子的玩意。＝易如反掌。

❷ Tell me more!
多跟我透露些!

- I want to know all the details.
  我要知道所有的細節。

- I suggest you write a report about this event.
  我建議你針對這一件事寫一份報告。

❸ She can't agree more.
她再同意不過了。

- It gets two thumbs up.
  這主意得到兩隻向上的大拇指。＝讚啦！（thumbs up 表讚許。）

- She gave it 100 "Likes!"
  她給了 100 個讚！（臉書中的 like 按鈕在中文中翻做讚。）

這句怎麼說？ How to Say That?

一石二鳥 → Kill two birds with one stone

英釋 to solve two problems at one time with a single action

中釋 丟擲一顆石頭打中兩隻鳥。用以比喻做一件事情得到兩種好處。

A: Oh, I am so hungry. Would you go to lunch with me?（喔，我好餓。要不
要跟我一起去吃午餐啊？）

B: Sorry, I have to buy a gift for my sister. Today's her birthday.（抱歉，我要
去買送我妹妹的禮物。今天是她生日。）

A: Why don't we go to SOGO? We can buy a gift there and have lunch in
the food court.（我們為什麼不去 SOGO 呢？我們可以在那裡買禮物，還可
以去美食街吃午餐。）

B: That's great, and it's killing two birds with one stone.（這太好了，真是一
石二鳥。）

文化小盒子 Culture Box

　　一定有人會感到好奇，什麼時候有了 "Kill two pigs with one bird" 這樣
的說法呢？其實這個說法無庸置疑的是從 "Kill two birds with one stone" 所
衍生而來，再加上這幾年一個相當流行的遊戲 APP "Angry Birds" 的概念。
遊戲中有各種不同的鳥，以彈弓投擲的方式去攻擊邪惡的綠豬頭，每一次的

投擲所擊中的豬頭愈多，分數就愈高。而這個說法就是從這個遊戲中所得到的靈感。不管是殺鳥還是殺豬，這在中文當中，我們都可說是「一舉兩得」、「一箭雙雕」或是「一石二鳥」等。不過，在這裡要告訴大家的是一石二鳥是由英文中的說法直接翻譯的，在中文裡，正確的成語應該用一箭雙雕。

阿倫碎碎念 Allen's Murmur

我今天下午遇到 Paul 的時候，他看起來超生氣的。我從沒看他那麼生氣過，臉漲紅的活像是憤怒鳥裡的 "Big Red Bird"。

他抱怨的跟我說 "I can't work with Yo anymore. He's a bird brain grown-up. If you expect him to do something properly at work and show some respect for his partners, it's just like killing two stones with one bird."（我沒有辦法再跟阿祐一起工作了。他是一個「小鳥腦」的成年人。如果你期望他能在工作上做些恰當的事及尊重他的伙伴的話，那真是一件「一鳥二石」的事。）在這裡，我要提醒一下大家，bird brain 是一個含有輕微嘲諷的詞，好孩子可不要學 Paul，他是太生氣了才這樣說的。bird brain 是嘲諷小孩或是不成熟的大人，當他們有幼稚的行為、舉動或是思想時，可不是說人家的腦容量跟鳥一樣的小喔。

而 Paul 所說的 "killing two stones with one bird"（一鳥二石），則聽的我一頭霧水，之後他跟我解釋，這句話是從一石二鳥延伸而得的，可以用來形容一舉完成兩種困難甚至是不太可能的任務；也可以用來形容這兩件事想要一次或是一起達成根本就不可能。所以你猜猜 Paul 在這裡指的是什麼意思呢？I am going to kill two pigs with one bird now, so talk you guys later!!

Grain of Salt

半信半疑，不
能 100% 的相
信。

Allen and some female colleagues are discussing

something with a grain of salt in the pantry.

Allen 和一些女同事在茶水間裡

正在討論要在某個東西裡「加一小撮鹽巴」。

 對話 *Dialogue*

Allen: Hey, what you girls are talking about? Why everyone's face is so **grave**?

Mary: Allen, do you ever work overtime?

Allen: Yes, sometimes.

Cathy: Archie said our office is haunted, and he heard a woman crying in that **corner** last night.

Allen: Hmm, you would better take his words with a grain of salt, Archie always **exaggerates**.

Joan: But he said he did hear the **sobs**, and he also can sense her presence.

Allen: Her? Oh, you mean that ghost. Ok, I guess that's just someone forgot to close the window last night. And ladies, if you will excuse my French. Archie likes to exaggerate a thing which is as small as the hairs on the **gnat's bollock**, just to make his story more amusing.

單字 Vocabulary

1. **grave** [grev]
   adj 嚴肅的、認真的
   → Even that grave young man could not suppress a smile.
   連那位嚴肅的年輕男子都忍不住笑了出來。

2. **corner** [`kɔrnə] n 角落
   → I found this little cat in the street corner.
   我在街角發現這隻小貓。

3. **exaggerate**
   [ɪg`zædʒəˌret] v 誇大、誇張、言過其實
   → The press exaggerated the story as usual.
   新聞媒體如同往常一般誇大了這件事。

4. **sob** [sɑb] n 嗚咽、啜泣
   → The child nodded with a sob.
   這個孩子啜泣著點了點頭。

5. **gnat** [næt] n （叮人的有翅）小昆蟲；蚋；【英】蚊子
   → You don't have to sing to me like a gnat to profound that question.
   你不必像是隻蚊子一樣在我耳邊嗡嗡叫的提出這個問題。

6. **bollock** [`bɑlək] n （also ballock）【俚】睪丸；胡說八道
   → What a load of bollocks!
   真是一派胡言！

翻譯 Translation

Allen: 嘿，女孩們，妳們正在討論什麼啊？為什麼每個人的臉色都這麼嚴肅？

Mary: Allen，你有沒有加過班啊？

Allen: 有，有時候。

Cathy: Archie 說我們的辦公室鬧鬼，他昨晚聽到有一個女人在那一個角落哭泣。

Allen: 嗯，妳們最好不要完全相信他說的話，Archie 總是會誇大事實。

Joan: 但他說他的確有聽到啜泣聲，還有他也能感覺到她的存在。

Allen: 她？喔，妳指的是那個鬼。Ok，我猜只是昨晚有人忘了把窗戶關上。還有，小姐們，請原諒我說冒犯的話。Archie 喜歡將微小如飛蟲「蛋蛋」上的毛的小事誇大，只是為了讓他的故事聽起來更有趣。

心情小日記 Dear Diary

October 31ˢᵗ

Dear Diary,

My computer crushed this morning, and it took Bryan almost 6 hours to fix it. Unfortunately, I have a report due tomorrow morning, so I worked overtime in our "haunted" office tonight. When I was alone in the office at 10 p.m., I did hear the sobbing sounds. It sounded creepy, but I ventured to go to that corner. As I thought, someone forgot to close the window. When I was trying to shut the window, suddenly, a big bang scared me. Damn it! Someone forgot to close the door.

10 月 31 日

親愛的日記，

我的電腦今天早上壞掉了，花了 Bryan 將近 6 個小時的時間才修好。不幸的是我有一份報告明天早上要交，所以我今晚在我們「鬧鬼」的辦公室裡加班。當我晚上 10 點一個人在辦公室時，我的確聽到了啜泣的聲音。聽起來有點恐怖，但我鼓起勇氣走到那一個角落。正如我想的，有人忘了關窗戶。

當我試著將窗戶關上時，突然間，一聲巨響嚇到我了。媽的，有人忘記關門

了。

還可以怎麼說 In Other Words

❶ Why everyone's face is so grave?
為什麼每個人的臉色都這麼嚴肅？

- You guys look so serious, what happened?
  你們看起來好嚴肅喔，怎麼了？

- Are you talking about a deep question?
  你們是在討論嚴肅的問題嗎？

❷ And ladies, if you will excuse my French.
小姐們，請原諒我說冒犯的話。

- Ma'ams, please excuse my bad language.
  女士們，請原諒我說髒話。

- Girls, please do ignore my swearing.
  女孩們，請忽略我所說的罵人的話。

❸ It sounded creepy, but I ventured to go to that corner.
聽起來有點恐怖，但我鼓起勇氣走到那一個角落。

- Ugh, it was so horrible, but I still walked to the corner with cautiously.
  呃，超恐怖的，但我還是小心翼翼地走到那個角落。

- Although I was very nervous, I put on a brave front and walked to

185

that corner.

雖然我很緊張，我還是強裝鎮定地走向那個角落。

 這句怎麼說？ How to Say That?

半信半疑 ➔ With skepticism

英釋 doubt about the truth of something

中釋 對某件事抱持著懷疑的態度。

A: Do you think they have any chance to get clear off this time?（你覺得他們這一次能有機會脫身嗎？）

B: No, I don't think so. That policeman listened with sympathy, but also with a slight tinge of skepticism.（不，我不這麼認為。那個警察雖是同情地聽著，但神色間也流露出一絲絲的懷疑。）

文化小盒子 Culture Box

　　Take with a grain of salt. 是指對某件事半信半疑，持保留的態度。a grain of salt 是美式的用法，而英式用法中為 a pinch of salt。pinch 是一小撮的意思，而 grain 則為顆粒。而這句話應是起源自加有一小撮鹽巴的食物能更容易的入口的事實。在西元前 77 年的一個文獻中記載，將乾核桃，無花果各兩個，20 片的芸香葉磨碎後加入一小撮鹽，如果有人能快速服下，那麼這一天將能百毒不侵。這一段文字在字面上的意思為毒性能被取用一小撮鹽所中和，但被認為是以 take a grain of salt 來隱喻事實是需要以中庸的態度來發現的。而在英文中開始被廣泛使用則是在 17 世紀中開始，而 pinch of salt 則是 grain of salt 的變體，最早出現是在 1948 年的文獻上。

阿倫碎碎念 Allen's Murmur

　　在英國童話中有一個故事描述有一天，有一位父親問他的三個女兒，想要知道他在女兒心目中的地位，大女兒說：「我愛您就像愛自己的生命一樣。」二女兒說：「我愛您超越這世上所有的事物。」但小女兒卻說父親對她而言，就像是醃肉上的鹽巴一樣是不可或缺的。父親一氣之下，將小女兒趕了出去。在若干年後，這位父親參加了一個宴會，而宴會上所有的食物都沒有加鹽巴，這個時候，這位父親哭了起來，因為他體會到小女兒當時所說的話，而也發現這個宴會是思念父親的小女兒所舉辦的，也因此一家團圓。

　　從上面的故事中，可以知道鹽巴在我們日常生活中的重要性。因此在英文中稱讚某人能勝任他的職位，做得不錯或是值得受人尊敬時，我們會說 "worth one's salt"。例如 "Any teacher worth his salt would do exactly as I did."（任何一位稱職的老師都會採取和我一樣的作法的。）還有小小抱怨一下，我認為 Yo's not worth his salt at all.（阿祐一點都算不上是稱職。）He enjoys rubbing salt in somebody's wound.（他喜歡在人家的傷口上灑鹽。）說到這，我不禁覺得英文的說法慘忍多了，中文裡只是在傷口上灑鹽，而英文裡的感覺則像是將大把大把的鹽巴放在人家的傷口上，而且還像醃韓國泡菜一樣的搓揉，聽起來就覺得好痛。

　　其他常聽到的還有 "the salt of the earth"（中堅份子），加上上面的故事，有沒有十分重要的感覺啊？另外還有老水手，因為長年在海上生活，感覺身上鹽分應該很多，所以可以用 "old salt" 來稱呼，但大多以自稱居多喔！

Diary 11 月 23 日

Conversational Blue Balls

話說到一半，
就立刻轉移話
題，令人感到
「蛋疼」的對
話。

Yo and Allen are having a conversation at the canteen. Yo gives

Allen some "blue balls" before he leave.

阿祐和 Allen 在員工餐廳談話，阿祐在走之前給了

Allen 一些「藍色的球」。

 對話 Dialogue

Yo: Did you hear about what happened in Vivienne's **baby shower** party?

Allen: No. What happened?

Yo: Erm, forget it. It's time for me to **push along**.

Allen: Wait, what happened?

Yo: Oh, don't worry about it, it's not a big deal.

Paul: Hey, what you guys are talking about?

Yo: **Gotta** go, see you then.

Paul: Bye, Yo. What's up, mate?

Allen: I **swear** that I won't talk to Yo ever again if it's not necessary. He just gave me **conversational** blue balls, and in fact, I think he enjoys doing that.

Paul: Heh heh, it's not at all **unexpected**. It's very Yo's style.

單字 Vocabulary

1. **baby shower** ph
   準媽媽派對。通常會在預產期前 30 天舉行
   → I'm going to throw her a baby shower.
   我要為她辦一個準媽媽派對。

2. **push along** ph
   【口】離開
   → It's too late, I have to push along.
   時間太晚了,我必須要離開了。

3. **gotta** [ˋɡɑtə] ph
   【口】= have got to
   → Oh, you gotta be joking!
   喔,你一定是在開玩笑吧!

4. swear [swɛr]
   v 發誓
   → I swear I've told you everything I know.
   我發誓我已經把我知道的所有事跟你說了。

5. **conversational**
   [ˏkɑnvəˋseʃənl] adj 會話的
   → The author likes to write an article in an easy, conversational style.
   這一個作者喜歡以輕鬆、口語化的方式來寫文章。

6. **unexpected**
   [ˏʌnɪkˋspɛktɪd] adj 想不到的,意外的
   → Sometimes matters proceed in the most unexpected way.
   有的時候,事情會以最出乎意料的方式進行。

翻譯 Translation

Yo: 你有沒有聽說在 Vivienne 的準媽媽派對上發生的事?

Allen: 沒有。怎麼了?

Yo: 嗯,算了。我該走了。

Allen: 等一下,到底發生了什麼事?

Yo: 喔,別擔心,不是什麼大事情。

Paul: 嘿,你們在聊什麼啊?

Yo: 得走了,再見囉。

Paul: 拜,阿祐。怎麼了,兄弟?

Allen: 我發誓如果沒有必要的話,我絕對不會再跟阿祐多說一句話了。他

剛剛吊盡了我的胃口，事實上我覺得他超喜歡這樣做的。

Paul: 呵呵，這並不令人感到意外。這非常像是阿祐的作風。

心情小日記 Dear Diary

November 23rd

Dear Diary,

I finally know what happened in Vivienne's baby shower party. Her husband's the other woman, or according to her husband, the "estranged" other woman went to the party and messed it up. Normally, I am not interested in that kind of conversation at all. The way Yo talked arouse my curiosity. Anyway, thanks to Johnny for gratifying my curiosity. Sometimes I really think he should work for CIA. And I sincerely hope that Vivienne and her unborn baby are all right.

11月23日

親愛的日記，

我終於知道在 Vivienne 的準媽媽派對上發生的事了。她先生的小三，或是照她先生的說法是「已分手」的小三，到派對上砸場。通常，我對於這一類型的話題一點都不感興趣。阿祐說話的方式激起了我的好奇心。不管如何，感謝 Johnny 滿足了我的好奇心。有時候我真的認為他應該去 CIA 工作。還有我真誠的希望 Vivienne 和她尚未出世的寶寶能一切平安。

190

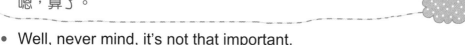 還可以怎麼說 In Other Words

❶ Erm, forget it.
嗯,算了。

- Well, never mind, it's not that important.
  嗯,別在意,不是什麼大事。

- That's no concern of your.
  這跟你沒什麼關係。

❷ What's up, mate?
怎麼了,兄弟?

- What worries you, Allen?
  Allen,你在擔心什麼嗎?

- What's going on, buddy?
  老兄,發生什麼事了?

❸ Her husband's the other woman went to the party and messed it up.
她先生的小三到派對上砸場。

- An uninvited guest, who's the mistress of Vivienne's husband, came and ruined the party.
  一個不速之客,Vivienne 她先生的外遇對象跑到派對上搞亂。

- The home wrecker of Vivienne's marriage came to bungle the party.
  Vivienne 婚姻中的第三者跑來破壞派對。

這句怎麼說? How to Say That?

吊人胃口 → Keep someone in suspense

英釋 to make someone wait anxiously for something

中釋 讓某人急於等待著某件事物,掛念著某件事物或是有懸念。也可以說 leave someone in suspense。

A: The conclusion of that movie was kind of anticlimactic.(這部電影的結局有點虎頭蛇尾。)

B: Don't keep me in suspense, tell me what happened at the end of the story?(別吊我胃口了,快告訴我故事最後到底怎麼了?)

 文化小盒子 Culture Box

　　Conversational blue balls,也有人說 conversation blue balls,照字面上翻譯成為「對話藍球」,而其正確的意思則是指一直不說清楚、講明白,吊盡胃口的對話內容。指的是某人在有意或無意之間所提起的話題,但卻在對方想進一步知道時故意轉移話題或是避而不談,而讓對方感到被吊胃口而產生心理上不舒服的感覺。conversational blue balls 其實是由 blue balls 所衍生而來的,blue balls 原本是指因充血或是精液堵塞,而呈青紫色的睾丸,被用來比喻因無法抒發,而造成難以形容的疼痛,也就是我們所說的「內傷」(心理上的),或是「蛋疼」。這一種令人感到蛋疼或是內傷的談話,常會讓人費盡千辛萬苦,想要知道談話中的訊息,但最後發現其實只是件雞毛蒜皮的小事,不知道這一種狀況,你是否有遇過呢?

阿倫碎碎念 Allen's Murmur

在英文當中，如果有人說 "I'm feeling blue, today." 這代表是「我今天心情不好」。但你知道嗎？這裡的blue雖然跟藍色相關，但其實絕大部分卻是因為美國的藍調音樂 "blues"，這一種在過去的美國，尚有黑奴制度時，由黑人奴隸所唱的讚美歌、勞動曲、聖歌等所演變過來的音樂。在藍調音樂中通常都含有濃厚的憂鬱情緒，而這一種音樂名稱的由來則是來自於 "blue devils" 有情緒低落、憂傷的含意。

除了代表憂鬱之外，還有一種常見的用法，會用「藍色月亮」或稱「藍月」來形容不常發生、難得的事，用英文來說為 "once in a blue moon"。Blue moon在天文學上來說是一種約2到3年會發生一次的現象，指的是在國曆的一個月份中出現的第二次滿月。

我還記得曾有一位朋友問我，那在 Pocahontas《風中奇緣》電影主題曲 "Colors of the wind"（風之色彩）中有提到的 "blue corn moon" 是不是指更稀有的意思？為此，Allen我認真的查了好多資料，最後發現有人也問過該曲作詞家Stephen Schwartz "blue corn moon" 的意思。Stephen表示在印地安人的語言當中並沒有這樣的說法，是他在作詞之前，讀了許多印地安作者的詩，在有一首情詩當中提到 "I will come to you in moon of the green corn."，這樣的描寫立即在他心中形成了一副美麗的圖畫。而在印地安人的語言當中，將月份以moon代替，而每一個月會有其對應的事件，例如，moon of the green corn指得就是green corn收成的那一個月份。但是在歌詞當中，如果用green corn的話，他怕會讓人聯想到綠起司（因為在英文中有一句 "The moon is made of green cheese." 的說法。），而且唱起來也怪怪的，所以改成blue corn moon，結合了英文中blue moon及印地安人所種植的一種稱為blue corn（藍玉米）的說法。這應該可以被稱做是一些美麗的錯誤吧！

Jump the Shark

過了最高峰之後，急速的走下坡。(一般多用來指連續劇)

Joycelyn and Allen just finished their client visiting in the aquarium.

Now they are still in the **aquarium** and talking about "sharks."

Joycelyn 和 Allen 剛剛結束在水族館的客戶拜訪。

現在他們還在水族館內談論著「鯊魚」。

 對話 Dialogue

Joycelyn: By the way, Allen, **seriously**, have you ever asked Charlene out?

Allen: Nope, not yet. I simply can't find a perfect timing.

Joycelyn: I knew it. That's why I ask you. This morning, I **overheard** that Charlene said she's not seeing anyone **recently**.

Allen: I meet across her very often in the canteen. And I was thinking...

Joycelyn: Yeh, yeh. Chance encounters, the fate thing, blah blah blah··· You'd better get a move on before it's too late.

Allen: But how should I do that?

Joycelyn: **Whatever**! Just go to her and ask her out when she still likes you. The love just like the **soap opera**, no one knows when it will jump the shark.

Allen: Okay, I'll go and ask her out now, wish me luck!

:: 單字 Vocabulary

1. **aquarium** [ə`kwɛrɪəm]
   n 水族館
   → The first time I saw penguins was in the Sea Life Sydney Aquarium.
   我第一次看到企鵝是在雪梨水族館。

2. **seriously** [`sɪrɪəslɪ]
   adv 認真地
   → Shall we talk seriously about your future?
   我們可不可以認真地來談一下你的未來？

3. **overhear** [ˌovɚ`hɪr]
   v 無意中聽到、偷聽到
   → She overheard a fragment of our conversation.
   她不小心聽到我們談話的一小段。

4. **recently** [`risntlɪ]
   adv 最近
   → I have recently begun to slouch over my computer.
   我最近一坐在電腦前就變得無精打采的。

5. **whatever** [hwɑt`ɛvɚ]
   pron 不管什麼
   → Whatever you tell them will be kept in confidence.
   不管你跟他們說了什麼都將會被保密的。

6. **soap opera** （以家庭問題為主要題材的）連續劇
   → In the soap opera, the old grandma rejuvenated after she smelled a bottle of Eau de toilette.
   在連續劇裡，老奶奶在聞過一瓶花露水之後就變年輕了。

✶ 翻譯 Translation

Joycelyn: 順便問一下，Allen，說真的，你到底有沒有約過 Charlene 出去啊？

Allen: 沒，還沒。我只是找不到適當的時機。

Joycelyn: 我就知道。這就是我問你的原因。今天早上，我聽到 Charlene 說她最近沒有和任何人交往。

Allen: 我在公司餐廳常遇見她。還有我是想……

Joycelyn: 對，對。偶遇嘛，緣分啊，諸如此類的……你最好動作快一點。

Allen: 但是我該怎麼做？

Joycelyn: 隨便！只要去找她，趁她還喜歡你的時候約她出去。愛情就像是八點檔一樣，沒有人知道什麼時候會走下坡。

Allen: 好啦，我現在就去約她，祝我好運吧！

心情小日記 Dear Diary

November 30th

Dear Diary,

It's more difficult than I thought. In fact, I failed today. Because I just couldn't ignore the crowd and my heart which was thumping like a drum. When I walked to Charlene in the canteen this afternoon, I felt like everyone's looking at me. Johnny told me that I walked so slow that he almost wanted to kick me to make me walk faster. Unfortunately, Char was little bit rush at that time. She asked me to keep the matter till tomorrow, which means I'll have to do it again tomorrow. God, please give me courage.

11 月 30 日

親愛的日記，

這比我想像中的難得多了。事實上，我今天失敗了。因為我無法無視圍觀的人群還有我那一顆跳得像是在擊鼓吶喊的心臟。當我在餐廳走向 *Charlene* 的時候，我感覺大家的目光似乎都投到我身上似的。*Johnny* 告訴我，我走的超慢的，他幾乎想要飛踢我讓我走快一點。不幸的是，*Char* 那時候有一點趕。她要我明天再說，這表示我明天還要再來一次。天公伯啊，請給我勇氣！

還可以怎麼說 In Other Words

❶ Have you ever asked Charlene out?
你到底有沒有約過 Charlene 出去啊？

- Did you tell Charlene that you want to date her?
  你有跟 Charlene 說過你想和她約會嗎？

- Did Charlene know that you are one of her secret admirers?
  Charlene 知不知道你是她神秘愛慕者中的一員啊？

❷ I felt like everyone's looking at me.
我感覺大家的目光似乎都投到我身上似的。

- I felt like that I was walking on the red carpet.
  我覺得好像是走在紅地毯上似的。＝受到萬眾注目。

- It made me feel like walking naked in the public.
  讓我覺得很像在大庭廣眾下沒穿衣服走著。

❸ She asked me to keep the matter till tomorrow.
她要我明天再說。

- She wanted me to tell her tomorrow.
  她要我明天再告訴她。

- "Please keep the matter till tomorrow," she said.
  她說「請將這件事留到明天再說」。

這句怎麼說？ How to Say That?

（指賣座電影系列）劇情荒謬 ➞ Nuke the Fridge

英釋 Refer to a movie reaches a point when, due to an unauthentic scene or ridiculous storyline, it loses the appreciation of the public.

中釋 指在一部電影當中出現了與前後劇情不相干的片段或是荒謬的劇情而使大眾失去興趣。

A: Have you seen the movie "Spider Man III"？（你有看過蜘蛛人三嗎？）

B: Yes, but I don't like it. The plot of Peter Parker dancing around the bar really nukes the fridge.（有啊，可是我不喜歡。那一個 Peter Parker 在酒吧跳舞的情節爛透了。）

 文化小盒子 Culture Box

　　在 1997 年時，Jon Hein 開辦了一個網站，名為 "jumptheshark"（已在 2006 年賣給 TV Guide），網站中集合了所有電視劇節目為什麼失去吸引力的原因，並且分門別類的收錄。而這一個構想則是在 1985 年時，當時的 Jon Hein 與室友 Sean J. Connolly 討論為什麼有些電視劇越來越難看的原因，Sean 提出了在 1977 年開播的影集 "Happy Days" 的第五季中有一段主角在滑水時跳過鯊魚的橋段，因為太過荒謬，所以這個影集便逐漸的走下坡。而 "jump the shark" 的用法也在 Jon 開辦網站之後被廣泛地使用，除了是用在電視劇上，也會被用在形容政治人物、政府或是公司等的形象下滑。而對於那些歷久彌新，常盛不衰的節目，我們則會用「還沒跳過鯊魚」"never jumped the shark" 來形容。

　　伴隨著傳播媒體的發達，人們的生活也漸漸的起了變化，例如俚語的流行不再像是以前一樣地緩慢，由口耳相傳的方式讓大眾接受，而是變成了例如是 bbs 上鄉民們在討論串中的一句話，突然引起熱烈的迴響，亦或像是名人在媒體上無心的一句話或是一個舉動造成討論，而這一些往往都會透過媒體的傳播而迅速的在生活中引爆，成為當代流行語或俚語。

　　就像是周杰倫常說的「瞎」或是「屌」，而在英文當中，也有不少這樣的例子，像是 Joycelyn 在提醒我要趕緊約 Charlene 出去時，她曾提到的 "jump the shark"，如果用周董的話來形容的話應該會說「這行為太瞎了」吧。類似的說法還有像是而我記得在很久以前，我在看 The Oprah Winfrey Show（歐普拉脫口秀）時，當天所邀請的來賓為 Tom Cruise。And all in a sudden, Tom Cruise jumped the couch in Oprah's show.（突然之間，Tom Cruise 在歐普拉的節目中從沙發上跳了起來。）阿湯哥的這個舉動是為了宣布他（當時）的新戀情，而奇特的是阿湯哥也不是沒談過戀愛，而且那時候他早已是離過兩次婚了，與以往的阿湯哥對於戀情的態度相比非常地大不同。而他在沙發上跳上跳下，及圍著主持人和沙發跑來跑去的行為隔天就上報了，媒體對他下了一個 "jump the couch" 的註解，相信大家一定很好奇是什麼意思，該不會是高調宣布戀情的意思吧？當然不是，如果這樣，那 Allen 我就太「瞎」了。"Jump the couch" 因為阿湯哥的行為被賦予時代新的意義成為用來描述那一些「情緒突然失控」的人，或是某人「脫軌」的行為。

04 Chapter

Winter 冬天

In a Nutshell

總而言之、概括來說。

Allen sees Charlene in the canteen. Charlene is eating crunchy nut salad for lunch.

Allen 在員工餐廳中看到 Charlene。

Charlene 正在吃脆脆的堅果沙拉當做午餐。

 對話 Dialogue

Allen: Hi, Char. Do you mind if I sit here?

Charlene: Not at all, please have a seat.

Allen: Thanks Char. Erm, Char, do you like movies?

Charlene: Yes, I do.

Allen: Um, I happen to have **complimentary** tickets. Maybe you would like to go to the movies with your friend or I can go with you if you like…

Charlene: And how about after the movie?

Allen: After the movies? Hmmm… maybe we can have dinner together. Erm, I **mean** if your friend can not go with you…

Charlene: To put it in a **nutshell**, I think you are **gonna date** me, am I right?

Allen: Hmmm… yes, if that's okay with you?

Charlene: Okay, so I'll see you in the **lobby** after work.

單字 Vocabulary

1. **complimentary**
   [ˌkɑmpləˋmɛntərɪ] adj
   【美】贈送的
   → I have got complementary tickets for the concert.
   我拿到幾張音樂會的免費入場券。

2. **mean** [min] v 表示……的意思；意思是
   → What do you mean?
   你是什麼意思啊？

3. **nutshell** [ˋnʌtˌʃɛl] n 堅果的外殼；小的東西；小容器
   → The nutshell includes the kernel.
   堅果的外殼將果仁給包裹住。

4. **gonna** [ˋgɔnə]【美】【口】= going to
   → It's gonna be great! I cannot wait anymore.
   那一定很棒！我都等不及了。

5. **date** [det] v【美】【口】約會
   → You can pin me down to a date.
   你不能強迫我答應這個約會。

6. **lobby** [ˋlɑbɪ] n 大廳
   → So many reporters were crowded into the lobby.
   許多的記者都湧進了大廳。

翻譯 Translation

Allen: 嗨，Char。妳介意我坐在這兒嗎？

Charlene: 一點也不，請坐。

Allen: 謝啦，Char。嗯，Char，妳喜歡看電影嗎？

Charlene: 嗯，喜歡啊。

Allen: 嗯，我剛好有免費的票。也許妳會想和妳的朋友一起去看電影，或是如果妳想的話我也可以和妳去看……

Charlene: 那看完電影後呢？

Allen: 看完電影後？嗯……也許我們可以一起吃晚餐。呃，我的意思是如果妳的朋友不能和妳一起去的話……

Charlene: 簡單來說，我想你是在約我，對吧？

Allen: 嗯……對，如果可以的話？

Charlene: 好啊，那下班後在大廳見囉。

心情小日記 Dear Diary

December 1st

Dear Diary,

Tonight is the most beautiful night that I ever have. Charlene and I went to a movie after work, and then had a romantic candle dinner. I drove her home after dinner, and she told me to park in the block nearby. We had a nice little stroll in the moonlight, and talked a lot. And then <u>she kissed me goodnight on the doorstep.</u> I felt my heart thumping so wildly when she kissed me on the cheek. Everything's perfect in our first date, and it's a day to remember. I'd better start preparing our first anniversary.

12 月 1 日

親愛的日記，

今晚是我有過最美麗的夜晚。Charlene 和我下班後去看電影，然後共享了一頓浪漫的燭光晚餐。晚餐後，我開車送她回家，她讓我把車停在附近的巷

子。我們在月光下小小地散了一下步，還聊了許多事。然後她在門口給了我

一個晚安吻。當她親我的臉頰時，我的心臟狂跳。我們的第一次約會非常的

完美，這是值得記住的一天。我最好開始準備我們的第一個紀念日。

還可以怎麼說 In Other Words

❶ Do you mind if I sit here?
妳介意我坐在這兒嗎？

- May I sit here?
  我可以坐在這兒嗎？

- Would you mind sharing the table with me?
  妳介意我和妳共用這一張桌子嗎？

❷ I think you are gonna date me.
我想你是在約我。

- Are you asking me out?
  你是在約我出去嗎？

- Are you gonna date me or not?
  你到底要不要約我出去？

❸ She kissed me goodnight on the doorstep.
她在門口給了我一個晚安吻。
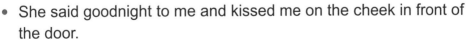

- She said goodnight to me and kissed me on the cheek in front of the door.
  她在家門前向我道晚安並親了我臉頰一下。

205

- I got a goodnight kiss from Charlene.
  我從 Charlene 那兒得到了一個晚安吻。

 這句怎麼說？How to Say That?

長話短說 → Make a long story short

英釋 get to the point, as a way to avoid a long explanation

中釋 說重點，避免有太長的解釋。

A: What's wrong with you? Your face is covered with bruises. Did you fight with others? （怎麼了？你的臉上都是淤青。你又跟別人打架啦？）

B: Nah. To make a long story short, I slipped and fell down the stairs last night. （沒有。長話短說，我昨晚從樓梯上摔下來了。）

文化小盒子 Culture Box

　　"In a nutshell" 照字面上的意思是「在堅果殼裡」，而實際上指的是「簡單來說」、「總而言之」等義。

　　做這樣比喻的用法，最早出現是在 19 世紀。在 1841 年出版的 "The Second Funeral of Napoleon"（拿破崙的第二次葬禮）中，作者 Thackeray 寫 "Here, then, in a nutshell, you have the whole matter."（在這裡，然後，總而言之，你擁有了一切。）然而，有趣的是，這句片語的起源卻可以追溯到西元 77 年時的文獻記載，書中紀錄著知名的長篇史詩《伊利亞德》被製作成超迷你的羊皮紙手抄本，小到可以放進一個核桃殼裡。說到這，大家可能還無法想像到底有多迷你。如果以 A4 大小的紙來計的話，「伊利亞德」的長度約需要 700 頁。難怪在 1601 年時，將該文獻翻譯成英文的學者會加上了「我們發現史上令人難以置信的銳利視力的例子」。

阿倫碎碎念 Allen's Murmur

　　相信大家都有過相同的經驗，當聽到台上的人正滔滔不絕的發表言論時，都會希望他能長話短說，挑重點說。但其實如果輪到自己時，就會發現其實 "in a nutshell" 並不是一件這麼簡單的事，要能去蕪存菁，用短短的幾句話精準的表示自己的意思，是需要些功力，也需要更多的準備。

　　In a nutshell，我在這裡要談一談 nuts。在植物學上的分類，堅果是指果皮堅硬的乾果類，而且成熟時，果皮不開裂，所以在植物學的分類上，開心果便不屬於堅果類。但依照英語的習慣用法，這一些有堅硬外殼，帶油脂可食用的果仁，都一律可以稱為 nuts。不知道大家有沒有看過 "Ice Age"《冰原歷險記》這一部電影。我記憶中最深刻的是片頭出現的那一隻松鼠看到堅果瘋狂的樣子。而這用英文來說，就是 "go nuts"，也就是中文裡所說的「發瘋」，或是「起肖」。而類似的英文說法還有 "go bananas"，用來比喻如同猴子看到香蕉時的瘋狂表現。要特別注意的是，這兩種食物都要是複數，數量要多，才夠瘋狂嘛！而在口語當中，還常聽到的有 "Are you nuts?" 問人家是不是瘋了？還是腦筋是不是有問題之類的。跟 "Are you crazy?" 或是 "Are you out of your mind?" 是相同的。可不要誤以為是問你是不是堅果之類的。

　　除了用來比喻瘋狂之外，nuts 也是有被用在正面的含意上的，例如是老師在課堂上會說 "We need to study the nuts and bolts of English grammar."（我們要研讀英文文法的基本細節。）在這裡的 "nuts and bolts"，原意是指螺帽和螺絲，被引用來指微不足道，但卻不可或缺的事物，而也就是我們現在常說的基本功。

Drop the Ball

失職，在工作
上犯了不該犯
的錯。

Charlene is alone in the garden. Charlene's eyes are red when Allen
finds her. Allen wants to know where to pick up "the ball" for her.

Charlene 一個人在花園裡。當 Allen 找到她時，Charlene
的眼睛紅紅的。Allen 想知道去哪裡幫她撿「球」。

 對話 *Dialogue*

Allen: Hey, Char, I get a hold of you at last. Are you okay?

Charlene: Yes, I think so, just a little bit **depressed**.

Allen: Would you like to talk about why you feel depressed? I hope it's
not because of me.

Charlene: Nah, it's nothing to do with you. It's just that I **dropped** the ball…

Allen: Where did you drop it? I can **pick** it **up** for you. What kind of ball
is it?

Charlene: I mean that I made a **mistake** in my work…

Allen: I know, baby. Joycelyn already told me. Come on! Let me give
you a **cuddle**. So you feel better now?

Charlene: Much better.

Allen: Char, you know you can always **count on** me, right? Okay, let
me buy you a good dinner.

單字 Vocabulary

1. **depressed** [dɪ`prɛst]
   [adj] 沮喪的、消沈的
   → We were all depressed to learn his illness.
   在得知他的病情之後，我們都十分沮喪。

2. **drop** [drɑp] [v] 使……掉
   下、落下
   → I dropped my cell phone and broke it.
   我不小心把我的手機掉下去摔破了。

3. **pick up** [ph]
   撿起來；學會
   → Sally quickly picked up on what I taught.
   Sally 很快就學會我所教的。

4. **mistake** [mɪ`stek]
   [n] 錯誤、過失
   → It's a beautiful mistake.
   這是一個美麗的錯誤。

5. **cuddle** [`kʌdl]
   [n] 擁抱
   → My little daughter came to me for a cuddle.
   我的小女兒向我走過來要抱抱。

6. **count on** [ph]
   依靠、依賴
   → If there's anything I can help, you can count on me!
   如果有什麼事我可以幫上忙的，你可以依靠我的！

翻譯 Translation

Allen: 嘿，Char，我終於找到妳了。妳還好吧？

Charlene: 嗯，應該吧，只是有一點點沮喪罷了。

Allen: 妳想要談談看妳為什麼感到沮喪嗎？我希望不是因為我的關係。

Charlene: 不是，跟你無關啦。只是我「把球給掉了」……

Allen: 妳在哪兒弄掉的？我可以幫妳撿起來啊。是哪一種球啊？

Charlene: 我指的是我在工作上犯錯了……

Allen: 我知道，寶貝。Joycelyn 已經告訴我了。來吧，讓我給妳一個抱抱。那妳現在有覺得好一點了嗎？

Charlene: 好多了。

Allen: Char 妳知道妳可以依靠我的，對吧？好啦，讓我請妳吃一頓豐盛的晚餐吧。

心情小日記 Dear Diary

December 20th

Dear Diary,

Char didn't have the mood to have dinner in the restaurant, so I decided to cook for her tonight. We first went to the supermarket, and then my apartment just like couples. I tried my very best to make a decent dinner for her, <u>but I guess my best just wasn't good enough as my imagination.</u> The chowder was too salty, and the steak was too chewy and so on... But luckily, we both had a good time together. Hope everything will go well and we'll live happily ever after.

12 月 20 日

親愛的日記，

Char 沒有心情去餐廳吃飯，所以我決定今天晚上要為她下廚。我們先到超市然後再回我的公寓就像是一對夫妻一樣。我使出渾身解勁來為她做一頓豐盛的晚餐，但我猜我的功夫不如我想像中的那麼好。濃湯太鹹、牛排咬不斷等等的……。但幸運的是我們在一起有了一段美好的時光。希望接下來的一切都會順利，還有我們從此能過著幸福快樂的生活。

:: 還可以怎麼說 In Other Words

❶ Come on! Let me give you a cuddle.
來吧，讓我給妳一個抱抱。

- I want to give you a big warm hug.
  我要給妳一個大大的溫暖擁抱。

- Snuggle up to me, and I'll give you some energy.
  緊靠著我，我要給妳一些能量。

❷ You can always count on me.
妳可以依靠我的。

- I am always on your side.
  我會一直都站在你這邊的。

- You can rely on me.
  妳可以依賴我的。

❸ But I guess my best just wasn't good enough as my imagination.
但我猜我的功夫不如我想像中的那麼好。

- But I couldn't make the perfect dinner as I thought.
  但我做不出我想像中的完美晚餐。

- And I screwed the dinner up.
  我把晚餐搞砸了。

 這句怎麼說？ How to Say That?

摔了個狗吃屎 ➔ Fall on one's face

英釋 to fail or to make a mistake, especially in a dramatic or particularly decisive manner

中釋 失敗或是失誤，特別是指以戲劇性的或是決定性的方式所造成的錯誤。

A: The weather man has fallen on his face today with his prediction. （氣象預報員今天在氣象預測上摔了個狗吃屎。＝預測不準）

B: Oh, really? I thought I've never seen him stand properly. （喔，是嗎？我以為我從來沒看過他好好的站著。＝一向都不準，從來沒正確過。）

 文化小盒子 Culture Box

　　一般來說，在公司裡的工作是環環相扣，必須經過眾人的合作才能完成，而這個跟在球場上的表現一樣，在球賽中完美的演出也是需要隊友之間的合作及球賽工作人員的努力才得以呈現。"Drop the ball" 這一個詞便是從球賽中衍生而後被廣泛用在生活當中的一個俚語。

　　按照字面上的意思來說，"drop the ball" 的意思是把拿在手裡的球給弄掉了，在球賽中，如果有誰失手將球弄掉了，這算的上是嚴重的失誤，除了會為所屬隊伍帶來不利分數之外，而球員本身也會因此被記上一筆失球記錄。這一個俚語是源自於美式足球，約在 1950 年左右開始被大量的應用在生活當中。最常使用在指工作上的失職，而這樣的錯誤通常是被認為不應該犯的、甚至是愚蠢的。

阿倫碎碎念 Allen's Murmur

　　常常可以在電視上或是一些職場相關的書籍中看到「職場如戰場」這一句話。而在阿兜仔的職場中，我則覺得應該是用「職場如球場」最為恰當。除了公司裡的工作之外，最常出現在辦公室中的話題大多是圍繞著球賽轉，而更是會將球場上的那一套搬來用在公事上，就像是我們這裡所介紹的"drop the ball"，在職場中有許多與"ball"相關的話語。

　　我就將從企畫到結果簡單的分為四個階段。第一個階段，在談到合作或是請人家幫忙和你一起完成時，就可以說"Please play ball with me this time."（這一次請和我一起玩球。＝這一次請和我一起完成。）而在前置作業完成後，計畫要開始動起來時，在第二個階段，就可以說"Let's get the ball rolling!"（我們開始讓球滾動吧！＝我們開始進行吧！）而在企畫進行時，最需要的是專心一致的表現，任何的不留神可能都會造成失敗，這時候是第三階段，就可以說"Please make sure you are on the ball."（請確保你是站在球上。＝請一定要用心。）在這裡要解釋一下"on the ball"，照字面來看是站在球上，但其實在運動當中，on the ball 是指"be in control of the ball"有控球、主導的意思，所以當要稱讚工作夥伴在工作上的出色表現時，可以用"You are on the ball."來說。而最後一個也是大家都不想遇到的，就是上面所介紹的 drop the ball，我個人覺得 drop the ball 不管在任何事情上，都是在所難免的，最重要的是 pick up the ball，怎麼去彌補犯下的錯，去完成計畫這才是最重要的，你說是不是呢？

Jump on the Bandwagon

本意為政治上
支持有可能獲
選的一方，後
來漸延伸成為
趨流行。

Mary and Allen are talking about Joycelyn's marriage in the pantry. Joycelyn come in and asks Allen to "jump on the bandwagon" with her.

Mary 和 Allen 在茶水間談著 Joycelyn 的婚事。

Joycelyn 進來後要 Allen 和她一起跳上「樂隊馬車」。

對話 Dialogue

Mary: Allen, did you hear the news?

Allen: What news? Are you **pregnant**?

Mary: As if!! No, it's not about me, it's about Joycelyn.

Allen: Umm-hmm, I'm listening.

Mary: She's getting married, with Dylan.

Allen: What?! I didn't even know that they are seeing each other. Speak of the devil. Hey, Joycelyn, **congrats**!

Joycelyn: Thanks! So you guys already know. Yes, I'm getting married!!!

Mary: When did you and Dylan start the **relationship**?

Joycelyn: About two months ago, after the cookout.

Allen: **Flash** marriage?

Joycelyn: Yes, I think so. Some of my friends seem very happy in their

214

flash marriage, so I am jumping on the bandwagon. My wedding will be on next month, and you and Charlene are both **invited**. I sure will toss my **bouquet** to Charlene.

:: 單字 Vocabulary

1. **pregnant** [ˋprɛgnənt] adj
   懷孕的
   → She's three months pregnant.
   她懷孕三個月了。

2. **congrats** [kənˋgræts]
   n 【口】祝賀；恭喜
   → Congrats to you and your team, well done!
   恭喜你和你的團隊，做得很好！

3. **relationship**
   [rɪˋleʃənˋʃɪp] n 戀愛關係
   → He is not ready for a new relationship yet.
   他還沒準備好要開始下一段新的戀情。

4. **flash** [flæʃ]
   adj 突如其來的
   → The area was hit by a flash storm.
   這個地區受到突如其來的暴風雨侵襲。

5. **invite** [ɪnˋvaɪt]
   v 邀請
   → Do not expect that cheapskate to invite you to dinner.
   別期待那個小氣鬼會請你吃飯。

6. **bouquet** [buˋke]
   n 花束
   → I am not really interested in doing a bouquet toss at our wedding reception.
   我不想在我們的婚禮上丟新娘捧花。

翻譯 Translation

Mary: 你有聽到消息嗎？

Allen: 什麼消息？妳懷孕啦？

Mary: 最好是啦！！不是，不是有關我的，是關於 Joycelyn 的。

Allen: 嗯哼，我正在聽。

Mary: 她要結婚了，跟 Dylan。

Allen: 什麼？！我甚至不知道他們有在約會。說曹操，曹操就到。嘿，Joycelyn，恭喜啊！

215

Joycelyn: 謝啦！所以你們已經知道了吧。是的，我要結婚了！！！

　　Mary: 你和 Dylan 是什麼時候開始的啊？

Joycelyn: 大概 2 個月之前吧，去烤肉之後的事。

　　Allen: 閃婚嗎？

Joycelyn: 對，我想是這樣的。我有些朋友閃婚看起來很幸福，所以我也就跟了流行。我的婚禮是在下個月，你和 Charlene 都會被邀請。我一定會把捧花丟給 Charlene 的。

心情小日記 Dear Diary

December 23rd

Dear Diary,

Joycelyn and I continued with the topic about her marriage after Mary left the pantry. I looked warily around and made sure no one would pop in unexpectedly, and then I asked Joycelyn if she's got pregnant. Joycelyn was rolling her eyes and then roared at me and told me "NO." From her reaction, I can see that she must have been asked about this question for many times. She said that her parents have asked her about this for million times. Sometimes she really wishes that she's already got a baby in her.

12 月 23 日

親愛的日記，

Joycelyn 和我在 Mary 離開茶水間之後繼續聊起了她的婚事。我謹慎地看了四周，並確定沒有人會突然闖進來之後，我問 Joycelyn 她是不是懷孕了。Joycelyn 翻著白眼並對著我大吼說沒有。從她的反應看來，她應該是被問到這一個問題很多次了。她說她的父母已經問過她這個問題次數多到數不清了。有時候她真的希望她肚子裡有一個小孩。

還可以怎麼說 In Other Words

❶ As if!!
最好是啦！！

- You wish!!
  想得美喔！！

- Yeah… right.
  最好是這樣啦。

❷ Speak of the devil.
說曹操，曹操就到。

- Talk of the devil.
  說曹操，曹操就到。

- Here she comes when we are talking about her.
  我們正在聊她的時候，她人就來了。

❸ I asked Joycelyn if she's got pregnant.
我問 Joycelyn 她是不是懷孕了。

- I asked her when the due date is.
  我問她預產期是什麼時候。

- "Are you going to take any maternity leave right after you finish

the marriage leave?" I asked.
我問：妳是不是準備在休完婚假後再請產假啊？

 這句怎麼說？ How to Say That?

領導時尚的人 → Trend setter

英釋 someone who popularize the new fashion

中釋 帶領或是創造時尚新風潮的人。

A: Hey, look, here comes a metrosexual man. （嘿，你看，那裡走過來一個花美男。）

B: Oh, he's a fashion magazine editor. You know what, he's not only up-to-date the hottest fashion, he is a real trend setter. （喔，他是一本時尚雜誌的總編。你知道嗎，他不只是跟隨著流行腳步，他可是一個真真正正的帶動流行的人。）

 文化小盒子 Culture Box

　　不知道大家有沒有在韓劇中看過候選人選舉時的情景，他們會站在改裝過的發財車上，旁邊會站著輔選的人還有辣妹啦啦隊，除了向人群揮手，也會停下來發表政見。這樣子的改裝發財車，就類似我們這裡所談到的 band-wagon，而這一種用於選舉上的車輛最早的起源在 19 世紀中的美國，原本是用以宣傳，載有馬戲團樂隊的馬車，後來被用在參選人的造勢活動上，在活動遊行當中，會有支持者跳上馬車以表示支持，也有期許能在參選人選上後獲得好處的意味，所以 "jump on the bandwagon" 被用來形容表態對某一方（特別是指極有可能勝出的一方）的支持，贊成某人的意見，而後被延伸成為趕時髦，追隨流行之意。

218

阿倫碎碎念 Allen's Murmur

　　"Jump on the bandwagon" 最早是被用在政治上的表態，支持極有可能勝選的一方，而 bandwagon 除了指樂隊馬車之外，在政治新聞中也常能看到，例如 This was the moment when the Obama bandwagon started to roll. （從這個時候開始，歐巴馬的競選團隊便開始運作。）在這裡，bandwagon 可以做競選團隊、競選幕僚等解釋。

　　與 jump 相關的俚語有許多，在這裡要挑三個來介紹一下。第一個是 "jump the gun"，照字面上看起來跳過一把槍的感覺，但實際上是指田徑運動比賽項目中的賽跑，會以信號槍的槍聲來決定起跑的時間，但如果有人在槍聲未響之前就起跑，就會被視為犯規，而這種情況就叫做是 jump the gun，被延伸成形容一個人在時機未成熟之前所做下輕率的決定，可以說是「操之過急」或是「草率行事」。第二個是 "jump through hoops"，在看到這一句的時候，不知道大家會不會跟 Allen 我一樣心中會浮現一個馬戲團的畫面，馬戲團的表演中有一個訓練動物跳圈圈的表演，有些更危險的則會是用火圈，而 jump through hoops 指的就是這樣的表演，引伸成為形容做更多的事為的是要能夠達成目的，也就是「赴湯蹈火，在所不惜」。例如 "Janet has her boyfriend jump through hoops for her."（Janet 讓她的男友為了她赴湯蹈火在所不惜。）

　　而第三個則是我個人很喜歡的，每次看到這一句，我的腦海中都會跳出一個靈魂出竅的畫面，就是 "jump out of one's skin"，想一想，有什麼東西會從皮膚中跳出來呢？指的就是靈魂，用來形容某人被嚇得「魂不附體」的樣子，是不是很有趣呢？

Enragement Ring

惹毛女朋友之後，買來希望能讓女友息怒的贖罪戒指

Paul is sitting in his cubicle and looking at a ring. Allen sees it and he is now asking Paul about that ring.

Paul 正坐在他的辦公室隔間裡看著一只戒指。

Allen 看到後，現在正在問 Paul 有關戒指的事。

對話 Dialogue

Allen: What is that?

Paul: A ring.

Allen: <u>You tell me!</u> Of course I know it's a ring. A ring for **female**, but it doesn't look like an **engagement** ring. Don't tell me that you are going to **propose** with this ring.

Paul: No, it's not an engagement ring, it's an **enragement** ring.

Allen: Enragement ring? That's interesting. <u>What have you done?</u>

Paul: I went to a **sports bar** with Nick last night, and I was drunk and slept in Nick's **flat** without giving Vivian a call.

Allen: Oh, she must be very angry.

Paul: You are right. When I got home this morning, she didn't even want to talk to me. So I bought this ring for her to smooth things over.

單字 Vocabulary

1. **female** [ˋfimel] n 女人
   → She is a strong spirited female.
   她是一個堅強的女性。

2. **engagement** [ɪnˋgedʒmənt] n 訂婚、婚約
   → Tracy was showing off her engagement ring.
   Tracy 在炫耀她的訂婚戒指。

3. **propose** [prəˋpoz] v 求婚
   → How did you propose to her?
   你是怎樣跟她求婚的呢？

4. **enragement** [ɪnˋredʒmənt] n 激怒
   → What should I do to smooth things over in his enragement?
   在他被激怒的狀態下，我該怎麼做來緩和局面呢？

5. **sports bar** ph 運動酒吧
   → My girlfriend and I like to watch sports events in the sports bar.
   我的女朋友和我喜歡到運動酒吧觀看體育賽事。

6. **flat** [flæt] n 公寓
   → She has a large flat in New York.
   她在紐約有一間大公寓。

翻譯 Translation

Allen: 這是什麼？

Paul: 是戒指。

Allen: 這還用你說嘛！我當然知道這是一個戒指。給女生的戒指，但是看起來不太像是訂婚戒指啊。不要告訴我你要用這種戒指來求婚。

Paul: 不會啦，這不是訂婚戒指，是贖罪戒指。

Allen: 贖罪戒指？真有趣，你做了什麼啊？

Paul: 我昨天晚上跟 Nick 去運動酒吧，結果我喝醉了，睡在 Nick 家裡，忘了打電話告訴 Vivian。

Allen: 喔，她一定生氣。

Paul: 你說對了。我今天早上回家的時候，她一句話都不跟我說。所以我就買了這一個戒指要給她來平息她的怒火。

221

心情小日記 Dear Diary

January 8th

Dear Diary,

I mentioned the enragement ring that Paul bought for his girl-friend to Charlene tonight. Charlene said that she doesn't want the ring, if I made her angry; she wants me to buy her an "en-ragement bag." Then she handed me the magazine she was browsing, and pointed at a bag on it randomly. <u>I googled the price of that bag secretly</u> and found out it costs more than US$5,000. I vowed to myself then, no matter what, I would never make Charlene angry, because it might be costly.

1 月 8 日

親愛的日記，

我今天跟 Charlene 説了 Paul 買了一個贖罪戒指給她女朋友的事。Charlene 説如果我讓她生氣的話，她才不要戒指；她要我買一個「贖罪包包」給她。然後她就把她剛剛在看的雜誌遞給我，隨手指了一個包。我偷偷地在網路上查了一下那一個包包的價錢，發現它價值超過 5,000 元美金。我對我自己發誓無論如何都絕對不能惹 Charlene 生氣，因為要付出的代價實在是太昂貴了。

還可以怎麼說 In Other Words

❶ You tell me!
這還用你說嘛！

- Tell me about it!
  這還用得著你說嘛！

- It goes without saying.
  這還用說嘛。

❷ What have you done?
你做了什麼啊？

- What did you do to irritate her?
  你做了些什麼惹得她發火？

- What did you do to bring trouble on yourself?
  你做了什麼為自己帶來麻煩的事呢？

❸ I googled the price of that bag secretly.
我偷偷地在網路上查了一下那一個包包的價錢。

- I checked the bag price on the internet furtively.
  我偷偷地在網上查了一下這一個包的價錢。

- I surfed on net and got the detailed information of that bag.
  我在網路上搜尋了一下，得到了那一個包包的詳細資料。

 這句怎麼說? *How to Say That?*

和好如初 ➝ Make up

英釋 to resolve a quarrel

中釋 解決一個爭端,握手言和。

A: You shouldn't laugh at my sleeping face without makeup.（你不應該嘲笑我睡覺時沒化妝的臉。）

B: Baby, I know, it's all my fault. I shouldn't do that. It has been more than a week, don't you think it's time for you and me to make up now?（寶貝,我知道,都是我的錯。我不應該這樣做的。已經一個多星期了,你不認為我們也該是時候要和好了嗎?）

文化小盒子 *Culture Box*

　　"Enragement ring" 有人稱它為贖罪戒指,也有人稱其為消氣戒指。但其實就字面上的解釋應該是做「激怒戒指」來解釋。"Enragement ring" 這一個說法其實是由 "engagement ring"（訂婚戒指）所衍生出的,enragement 和 engagement 這兩個字其實只差了中間的第三個字母是不一樣的,但代表的含意卻有極大的不同,所以有人將眾所皆知的 engagement ring 改成 enragement ring 來表示在惹女友生氣後,買來要哄女友高興,和好的戒指。Enragement ring 所代表的不僅限於是指戒指（但大多是戒指）,也可以說是一件首飾,送花或是送巧克力等的就不能算是贖罪戒指。而贖罪戒指也專指是做了讓女友生氣的事的男友買來求和、讓女友消氣用的。那如果是女友買來給男友消氣用的禮物,就沒有這樣的說法。畢竟男人是要大度,而且女友是要用來呵護的,你說是吧?

阿倫碎碎念 *Allen's Murmur*

　　Ring 在中文裡，除了能當戒指解釋之外，還可以當作是鐘、或是圈圈、環狀物等來解釋。除了當作名詞使用之外，也可以當成動詞來用。

　　我要介紹的是跟上面說到的 enragement ring 相類似的俚語，叫做 "push ring"。在 2013 年底時，有一位英國作家在英國郵報上發表了一個英語新怪字名單，同年入榜的有 facekini（在沙灘做日光浴時所帶的防曬面罩）、phubbing（在社交場合只顧著低頭玩手機的行為）、bankster（從事非法運作活動的銀行家）等之外，push ring 也同時上榜，意思是指在太太生產之後，丈夫送的戒指，又稱做是生產戒指。這些入榜的怪字被認為極有可能會成為新的流行用語。而為什麼生產戒指要被稱為是 push ring 呢？不知道大家有沒有在影集或是電影當中看到生產的劇情，這個時候接生的醫生或是護士會在一旁安慰產婦，一邊叫著 "push"，要產婦用力將小孩擠出來，啊，是生出來啦！所以 push 代表的就是生產時的那個動作還有鼓勵的話，但是就不知道，丈夫在給 push ring 時，是否還有 push，要再接再厲再生下一個的意思呢？

　　不過，根據我所聽到的，我覺得台灣生孩子的婦女朋友們比較幸福，除了有一個月的坐月子習俗之外，還常聽到某某某生了女孩，夫家給了多少錢的現金，生了男孩給了多少錢，或是我還有聽說過是給一間房子的，相較之下，push ring 寒酸多了，不知道這種獎勵是不是可以稱做是 push cash 或是 push house 呢？

Achilles Heel

形容一個人的
致命傷。

Ray is talking to Allen in the Gents room, and shows

him where his Achilles heel is.

Ray 在男廁裡跟 Allen 講話，

還告訴 Allen 他的「阿基里斯之踵」在哪兒。

 對話 Dialogue

Ray: Allen, <u>could you give me a hand?</u>

Allen: Sure, no problem. I can give you my both hands.

Ray: It's interesting. Angelina told me her parents **invite** me to have the **annual reunion** dinner in their house on the Chinese New Year's Eve.

Allen: Oh, that's great. That means they **consider** you as a member of the family. What's bothering you?

Ray: Well, you know, speaking Mandarin is my Achilles heel. And Angelina's parents can't speak English at all.

Allen: Oh, I see. Okay, there're two more weeks before the Chinese New Year, and we have enough time for the **oral** practice. Besides, I'll teach you some Chinese Year's **greetings**.

226

Ray: Oh, Allen, I feel moved. I am so lucky to have a friend like you, you're the best.

Allen: Tell me about it!

單字 Vocabulary

1. **invite** [ɪnˈvaɪt] ⓥ 邀請
   → Whom did you invite for dinner?
   你晚餐邀請了誰？

2. **annual** [ˈænjuəl]
   adj 每年的，一年一次的
   → I want to enter myself for the annual contest.
   我要報名參加這次的年度競賽。

3. **reunion** [riˈjunjən]
   ⓝ 重聚，親友間的聚會
   → We have a happy reunion after many years.
   事隔多年之後，我們又快樂地相聚在一起了。

4. **consider** [kənˈsɪdər]
   ⓥ 認為；把...視為
   → We must consider all the possibilities.
   我們必須考慮到所有的可能性。

5. **oral** [ˈorəl]
   adj 口頭的，口述的
   → He made a short but clear oral report to us.
   他為我們做了一個簡短但十分清楚的口頭報告。

6. **greetings** [ˈgritɪŋs]
   ⓝ 祝賀、問候語
   → They had an exchange of greetings.
   他們彼此互相問候了一下。

翻譯 Translation

Ray: Allen，可以幫我一個忙嗎？

Allen: 當然，沒問題。我兩隻手都可以給你。

Ray: 呵呵。Angelina 告訴我她的父母邀請我除夕夜那一天到他們家吃團圓飯。

Allen: 喔，那很好啊。這樣表示他們當你是家中的一份子了。什麼讓你感到困擾呢？

Ray: 嗯，你知道的，說國語一直是我的致命傷。還有 Angelina 的父母並不會說英文。

Allen: 喔，我懂了。好吧，在農曆新年前還有 2 個多星期的時間，我們還

有足夠的時間來做口語練習。除此之外，我會教你一些中文的吉祥

話。

Ray: 喔，Allen，我太感動了。我有你這樣的朋友真是太幸運了，你是最

棒的。

Allen: 那還用得著你說嘛！

心情小日記 Dear Diary

January 10th

Dear Diary,

Ray came to my place to practice Mandarin speaking with me tonight, and he told me that Angie gave him a French kiss when she found out all effort he has done for her. After more than a week practicing, Ray did a great job. Now he can make a simple conversation with me fluently. I am very happy for him. However he dropped me with a bombshell before he leave. He said Angie's grandparents who can only speak Taiwanese, will also attend the dinner, and he wanted me to teach him some Taiwanese as well. Should I tell him that I actually speak Taiwanese in very poor pronunciation?

1 月 10 日

親愛的日記，

Ray 今天來我家跟我練習說中文，他告訴我在 Angie 發現他為她所做的努力

之後，她給了他一個法式熱吻。經過在一個多星期的練習之後，Ray 做得很

不錯。現在他已經可以跟我流利地說些簡單的對話了。我為他感到高興。然而他卻在離開前給我投了顆震撼彈。他說 Angie 只會說台語的祖父母也要一起吃年夜飯，他要我也教他說一些台語。我是否應該告訴他我的台語說得很爛嗎？

:: 還可以怎麼說 In Other Words

❶ Could you give me a hand?
可以幫我一個忙嗎？

- Can you do me a favor?
  可以幫我一下嗎？

- I was wondering that if you have time to help me?
  我在想你是否有空幫我一個忙？

❷ I feel moved.
我太感動了。

- I am truly touched.
  我真的被感動了。

- It really chokes me up.
  讓我感動到哽咽。

❸ He dropped me with a bombshell.
他給我投了顆震撼彈。

- He gave me the bad news.
  他給了我一個壞消息。

- He surprised me with his sudden words.
  他突然說了一些嚇壞我的話。

 這句怎麼說？ How to Say That?

致命傷、要害 → Vulnerable spot/area

英釋 a weak point, a place of especial vulnerability

中釋 缺點，尤其是非常容易被攻擊的地方。

A: He's handsome, and brave. I wonder if he has any weak point. （他人長得帥，又勇敢。我在想他是不是有什麼弱點呢。）

B: Yes, indeed. He's a very brave man, but henpecking is his vulnerable spot. （對啊，沒錯。他是一個很勇敢的人，但「妻管嚴」卻是他的要害。）

文化小盒子 Culture Box

　　Achilles heel 亦可寫做 Achilles' heel，照字面翻為阿基里斯的腳後跟，英文中的解釋為 a small, but fatal weakness（小，但致命的弱點）。中文為致命傷，或是罩門、要害的意思。在希臘神話當中，阿基里斯（Achilles）被稱為是「希臘第一勇士」，具有半人半神的身份。Thetis 從預言得知阿基里斯將會死於戰爭當中，為了破除這樣的命運及讓他得到與神一樣不死的能力，於是 Thetis 抓著小阿基里斯的腳後跟，將他倒浸在傳說中其河水可使人體免遭苦難及屠殺的冥河裡，於是阿基里斯獲得了刀槍不入的不死之軀，但唯一的弱點就在當初被母親抓住的腳後跟上。特洛伊王子 Paris 得到太陽神 Apollo 的指點，用箭射中阿基里斯的腳後跟，希臘第一勇士因此身亡。Achilles heel 便成為英文當中，用以形容堪稱完美的人或是事物中，極小但卻能造成巨大傷害的弱點。

阿倫碎碎念 *Allen's Murmur*

　　荷馬史詩 *Homeric Hymns* 是古希臘文學當中最早的史詩（epic poem）作品，其中包含兩個各 24 卷的長篇史詩「伊利亞特」及「奧德賽」，相傳是由古希臘的盲詩人荷馬所創作的。但根據德國考古學家亨利・謝利曼（Hein-rich Schliemann）在十九世紀的七十年代的實地考察及考古挖掘中發現了在荷馬筆下《伊利亞德》史詩中的特洛伊城（Troy）遺跡。而謝利曼當時所依據的便是在荷馬史詩當中對於其地理位置的描述，謝利曼的發現對荷馬史詩中故事的真實性增添了不少，也使其更具有歷史價值。

　　在荷馬筆下的阿基里斯是個半人半神的悲劇英雄，除了有神一般的力氣及勇氣，還有超凡的美貌之外，也具有凡人的性格。在伊利亞特的故事中，阿基里斯是一個願意為朋友付出一切的英雄，但他也有缺點（我可不是要提他那脆弱的腳後跟喔！），那就是愛記仇、易怒甚至是翻臉比翻書還快的程度，所以在英文中形容一位大人物在為了一件雞毛蒜皮大的事在生悶氣甚至是不願合作時，有時候會用 "Achilles in his tent" 來形容。至於為什麼要躲到帳棚呢？請恕阿倫我才疏學淺，沒看過完整的荷馬史詩，只看過電影和兒童版的希臘神話。我猜測應該是發生在戰爭中的情況，人在生悶氣時總是會找一個安靜的地方待著，而回到自己的帳棚應該是最好的選擇。這時候我們可以說 "Achilles went off to skulk in his tent."（阿基里斯回到帳棚裡生悶氣。）

My Salad Days

青澀的時光。

Allen sees Margot who is viewing photos in the café.

Allen goes to her with his coffee and a "salad."

Allen 在咖啡店裡遇見正在看照片的 Margot。

Allen 帶著他的咖啡和「沙拉」走向她。

對話 Dialogue

Allen: Hello, Margot. I haven't seen you for **yonks**, how are you?

Margot: I'm good, thank you for asking. I was sent to Europe for a business trip for around three months, and then I took my **annual leave** of twenty days and went back London.

Allen: Oh, I see. What are you looking at?

Margot: My family **photographs**, I brought them from my parents' house.

Allen: Wow, is that your daughter? She's sooooo pretty.

Margot: Thanks for your **compliment**, but it's not my daughter, it's me.

Allen: Oh, you looked so different in this photo. I could hardly **recognize** you!

Margot: Yes, and that was my salad days, when I was about eighteen years old. I was quite **boyish** with very short hair.

232

單字 Vocabulary

1. **yonks** [jɑŋks] n 【俚】
   很久；很長的一段時間
   → Hey, dude, I haven't spoken to you in yonks!
   嘿，老兄，好久沒跟你聊天了！

2. **annual leave**
   ph 年假
   → After a year, I'll get an annual leave of seven days.
   一年之後，我將會有 7 天的年假。

3. **photograph** [ˋfotəˌɡræf]
   n 照片
   → I took a photograph of my little daughter.
   我給我的小女兒拍了一張相片。

4. **compliment**
   [ˋkɑmpləmənt] n 讚美的
   話、恭維
   → Thank you for your criticism, and I'll take it as a compliment.
   謝謝您的批評，我會把它當成是一種讚美的。

5. **recognize** [ˋrɛkəɡˌnaɪz]
   v 認出、識別；認識
   → I didn't recognize you without your makeup.
   妳沒化妝，我沒認出妳來。

6. **boyish** [ˋbɔɪɪʃ]
   adj 男孩似的
   → She had her long hair cut into a boyish style.
   她將她的一頭長髮剪成像男生的髮型。

翻譯 Translation

Allen: 哈囉，Margot。我超久沒看到妳了，妳好嗎？

Margot: 我很好，謝謝你的關心。我被派往歐洲出差約 3 個月的時間，然後我休了 20 天的年假回倫敦一趟。

Allen: 喔，我知道了。妳在看什麼啊？

Margot: 我家人的照片，我從我父母家帶回來的。

Allen: 哇，這是妳的女兒嗎？她超漂亮的。

Margot: 謝謝稱讚，但這個不是我的女兒，這是我喔。

Allen: 喔，妳在照片裡看起來很不一樣，我都快認不出來了！

Margot: 對啊，這可是我的青春年少，那時候我大概只有 18 歲吧。我就像個小男生似的，頭髮超短的。

心情小日記 Dear Diary

January 11th

Dear Diary,

I met Margot accidently in the café around the corner which is nearby the office after work. <u>She brought loads of family photos with her, and introduced me her family members.</u> She said she's probably retiring this year, and her husband and she have come to a mutual agreement that they'll move back to London after retiring. She invited me to visit them in London after everything will settle down. It could be the next year, she said. And she wanted me to bring Charlene with me.

1月 11日

親愛的日記，

我下班後在公司附近街角的咖啡店偶然遇見了 Margot。她帶了好多的家庭照片，還為我一一介紹她的家庭成員。她說她可能今年會退休，而且她的先生和她已經達成共識，退休之後要搬回倫敦。她還邀請我在所有事情都弄好之後去倫敦辦訪她們。她說這大概會在明年吧。她還說她要我帶著 Charlene 一起去。

還可以怎麼說 In Other Words

❶ I haven't seen you for yonks.
我超久沒看到妳了。

- Long time no see!
  好久不見！

- Where have you been hiding yourself?
  妳躲到哪兒去了？

❷ Thanks for your compliment.
謝謝稱讚。

- It's very kind of you to say so.
  謝謝你的讚美。

- Oh, you are flattering me.
  喔，你過獎了。

❸ She brought loads of family photos with her, and introduced me her family members.
她帶了好多的家庭照片，還為我一一介紹她的家庭成員。

- She showed me her family photographs that she was viewing.
  她給我看了她剛剛在看的家庭照片。

- She showed me the pictures of her families, and told me their names.
  她給我看了她家人的照片，還告訴我他們的名字。

這句怎麼說？ How to Say That?

青春時期 ➔ Heyday of youth

英釋 the prime time of being young

中釋 年少時光的全盛時期。

A: Honey, look! It's our honeymoon photo. I looked stunning in this photo, just like a super model. （親愛的，你看！這是我們的蜜月照。我看起來漂亮極了，像是一個超級模特兒。）

B: Yes, and it's a different you in your heyday of youth. Now I remember why I married you. （對啊，這是年輕時完全不同的妳。現在我終於想起來我為什麼娶妳了。）

文化小盒子 Culture Box

　　在莎士比亞的劇本 *Anthony and Cleopatra*《安東尼與克麗奧特拉》中，其中有一幕描寫埃及豔后 Cleopatra 在感嘆她與 Julius Caesar（凱撒大帝）年少時一段逝去的曖昧情事，Cleopatra 說了一段話 "My salad days, when I was green in judgment: cold in blood, to say as I said then!"（我的青蔥年少，當時還缺少判斷力：冷血如我，才會說出那樣的話！）所以後人便引用莎翁劇中的這一句話裡的 "my salad days"，來形容青澀、缺少經驗的歲月時光，my 可以改為其它的所有格如 your, his, her 等等……。在英文當中，喜歡以 green（綠色）來形容青澀，例如 green hand（生手、菜鳥）。而一談起 salad，大家腦海中應該第一個浮現的是那綠油油的顏色，所以莎翁在這裡用 salad 來代替 green，用以比喻年少、缺乏經驗的時光。

阿倫碎碎念 Allen's Murmur

其實只要一說到 "My salad days"，我就不禁想到 Johnny 那一段每天午餐只能吃一小碟沒有淋沙拉醬的 salad，「慘絕人寰」的時光。他大約持續了快要一個月，我個人十分佩服他的毅力，但也覺得他那一段時間身上有散發出綠色的光芒。

說到 salad，會讓我想到美國，這一個號稱為 "a melting pot of nations"（民族的大熔爐）的國家，就在這近十幾年來，各族群都提倡要保有自己的文化傳統，於是有學者提出要將 a melting pot 的概念改為 "a salad bowl" 的說法，因為在沙拉中會加入各式各樣不同的蔬菜，除了主要的綠色之外，還有紅的、黃的、橘的等等，保有自己的色彩，也增加了沙拉本身的豐富性。這個觀念不僅僅是適用於美國，我覺得應該是在每個國家都適用。

除了 salad days 之外，大家應該都聽過 bad hair day 吧？每天早上睡醒之後，最害怕的就是頭髮亂翹，怎麼梳都梳不好。這時候，就可以說 "Today's my bad hair day!"。每天可能都是 bad hair day，但有一天則是固定在每週的星期五，稱做是 "casual day"，也可以說是 "casual Friday"，這個從字面上看來，大概能猜到意思，應該是與休閒及星期五有關，沒有錯，在美國及加拿大的上班族習慣會在星期五穿著較休閒的服裝上班，另外也有人稱為 "dress-down Friday"，and the order of the day is normally polo shirts or casual blouses with jeans.（通常在這一天會穿 polo 衫或是休閒衫搭配牛仔褲。）而在台灣，似乎沒有 casual day 這樣的習慣，我注意到的是很多人在星期五的時候反而會穿得比平時漂亮許多，應該為了下班後的聚會作準備吧。

Hair Migration

頭髮從髮際線開
始慢慢地向後腦
的移動，慢慢地
消失，也就是禿頭
的意思。

Allen and Paul are in the meeting room. Allen is telling
Paul that he's pulling his hair again.

Allen 和 Paul 在會議室。Allen 正在跟 Paul 說他又再拉他的
頭髮了。

對話 Dialogue

Allen: You've better break your bad habit of **pull**ing your hair when you feel **anxious**.

Paul: Did I pull my hair again? Oh, shoot, I really want to stop doing that. Can somebody **chop** my hands **off**, please?

Allen: Aha, I have a better idea, wanna know?

Paul: Of course, tell me, pleeeeeease!

Allen: All you need is a photo, Vince's **photograph**, I mean.

Paul: Yuk, your idea sucks. It really freaks me out.

Allen: Did you see Vince at the beach, last time we went to Thailand for **staff** trip? He's about in the middle of a **full-scale** hair migration! He's got more hair on his back and butt than on his head.

Paul: Say no more, that's the scariest story that I've ever heard, and I won't pull my hair any more.

238

單字 Vocabulary

1. **pull** [pʊl]
   Ⓥ 拉、拖、跩
   → Pull as hard as you can.
   用你的全力去拉。

2. **anxious** [ˋæŋkʃəs]
   adj 焦慮的
   → My roommate is a very anxious person.
   我的室友是一個非常焦慮的人。

3. **chop off**
   （用斧頭等）砍掉
   → Please call 911 for me before they chop my head off.
   在他們砍下我的頭之前，請幫我報警。

4. **photograph** [ˋfotəˏɡræf]
   Ⓝ 照片
   → The old man dug out a photograph under a pile of books.
   那個老人從一堆書的下面抽出一張照片。

5. **staff** [stæf]
   Ⓝ 員工、職員
   → He let on to the staff what our conversation was.
   他將我們的談話內容透露給員工。

6. **full-scale** [ˋfʊlˏskel]
   adj 完全的、徹底的
   → A full-scale dispute involving strikes would be illegal.
   牽扯到罷工之類的大規模糾紛是不合法的。

翻譯 Translation

Allen: 你最好改掉當你焦慮時就拉頭髮的壞習慣。

Paul: 我又在拉我的頭髮啦？喔，╳的，我真的想要改掉。有沒有人可以剁掉我的手？

Allen: 哈，我有一個更好的主意，要聽聽看嗎？

Paul: 當然，拜託請一定要告訴我。

Allen: 你只需要一張照片，我說的是 Vince 的照片。

Paul: 噁，你的主意爛透了。真是嚇死我了。

Allen: 上一次我們員工旅行去泰國的時候，你有沒有在海灘上看到 Vince 啊？他身上大概有約百分之五十的頭毛移民了，他的背和屁屁上的毛比他頭上的還要多。

Paul: 別再說了，這是我所聽過最可怕的故事了，我以後一定不會再拉我的頭髮了。

心情小日記 *Dear Diary*

January 29th

Dear Diary,

Talking about Vince's baldness, that reminds me my flat mate, Jason. He was a shaved head when I just met him, and he had that style for about one year. During that time, I had never seen him bareheaded, which made me mistake him as a baldheaded. Until we shared the flat, he decided to change his hairstyle. I found that he has a mass of hair (erm, of course on his head), and the growth speed of his hair was astonishing. It took around one month for him to have the hair length of the bob. Quite a phenomenal rate.

1月29日

親愛的日記，

說到Vince的禿頭，就讓我想到我的室友 Jason。在我剛認識他的時候他是個大光頭，而且他維持了那個髮型大約有一年的時間。在那段期間，我從來沒看過他沒戴帽子的樣子，所以我一直誤以為他是個禿頭。一直到我們一起住，他決定要變換一下髮型。我才發現他有一頭濃密的頭髮（嗯，當然是在頭上

啊），還有他頭髮的生長速度更是驚人。他大約只需要一個月的時間，頭髮
就能長到鮑伯頭的長度。相當驚人的速度。

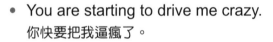 還可以怎麼說 In Other Words

❶ Can somebody chop my hands off, please?
有沒有人可以剁掉我的手？

- Please stop me from pulling my hair all the time.
  請隨時隨地阻止我拉頭髮。

- Can anyone bind my hands?
  有人可以捆住我的手嗎？

❷ It really freaks me out.
真是嚇死我了。

- You are starting to drive me crazy.
  你快要把我逼瘋了。

- You nearly scared me to death.
  你差一點就要嚇死我了。

❸ That reminds me my flat mate, Jason.
就讓我想到我的室友 Jason。

- It made me think about my flat mate, Jason.
  讓我想起我的室友 Jason。

- This put me in mind of Jason, who shares a flat with me.
  這令我想到了 Jason，就是那一個跟我合租一間公寓的。

這句怎麼說? How to Say That?

頭髮稀疏 ⟶ Thin on top

英釋 becoming bald

中釋 頭髮漸漸的稀少,正朝著禿頂方向前進。

A: Joseph is wearing a hat because he's getting thin on top. I guess he's trying to varnish over the truth.(Joseph戴著一頂帽子,是因為他的頭髮愈來愈少了。我猜想他是想要掩蓋真相。)

B: Then he should wear a wig not a hat.(那他應該戴的是假髮而不是帽子。)

 文化小盒子 Culture Box

　　台語裡有用「電火球」來形容禿頭,但在英文當中 "bulb" 則是用來形容聰明的人,而好主意則說成是 "bulbs",這個應該在英文的漫畫及電視或電影中常會看到在突然有個好主意時,會有電燈泡亮起的樣子出現。禿頭在英文當中,我們一般稱baldheaded、bald head或是baldie,而頭髮漸漸稀少,則會說是 "receding hairline"(逐漸後退的髮際線)或是 "thin on top",而一直退到後腦勺的,就稱為 "horseshoe baldness",因為只剩下頭的兩邊和後面有頭髮,就像是馬蹄鐵的形狀,這應該就是中文裡所說的「地中海」吧。而還有一種禿頭是從頭頂後方開始禿,稱為是 "big back bald",最後是全禿,稱為 "pilgarlic" 是 "peeled garlic" 衍生出來的,原意為剝了皮的蒜頭用來指禿頭或是禿頭的人。

阿倫碎碎念 Allen's Murmur

中文裡稱頭髮為「三千煩惱絲」，一般據信其由來起源自佛家的說法，而三千所代表的並不是數量，則與佛經中所說的「三千世界」有關。但其實現代人對於頭髮的煩惱並不是單單如連續劇中所演的，只要剪去那三千煩惱絲，所有的憂愁都會消散。而是到了一種有也煩、沒有更煩的境界。我指的是現代人因為壓力太大，而造成大量掉髮或是年紀輕輕就禿頭的事。

在英文當中，常常會用 hair 來形容情緒，例如 "let one's hair down"，是有「放鬆、不要拘束」的意思，因為在以前的西方國家，女子在出門之前會將頭髮盤起，回家後才會將頭髮放下，所以藉以比喻別拘束、也有開誠布公的含意在。當有人說 "It make my hair stand on end."（這讓我的頭髮都站起來了。）這時候的意思是讓我感到毛骨悚然，大家應該都有看過一些喜劇片或是卡通中，當劇中人物被極度驚嚇後，常會頂著一頭站立的頭髮吧，make one's hair stand on end 指的就是這樣的情景。另外如果聽到有人說 "You get in my hair."（你進到我的頭髮了。）這時候可不要白目的看他的頭髮裡有什麼，要不然對方可能會大叫 "Get out of my hair."（滾出我的頭髮。）因為 get in one's hair 代表的是打擾到某人，而 get out of one's hair 也跟滾有點關係，就是「別煩我！」滾遠點的意思。

還有一些跟動物「毛」有關的俚語，我想要簡單的介紹一下，像是 "finer than frog's hair"，其實指的是很好、再好不過了的意思。這是一個有點帶雙關語的回答，因為 fine 在英文裡，除了有安好之意外，還有細小的含意在，所以當人問你 "How are you?" 時，你可以回答 "Finer than frog hair."。最後 Allen 要講的是 "hair of the dog"（狗毛），意指解宿醉的酒，算是一種偏方，而其來源則是來自於以前在治療狂犬病時，有人相信只要從咬人的狗身上拔下一些毛，放在傷口上，就能治癒。"Hair of the dog" 如果要以中文來說的話，應該很像是「以毒攻毒」的意思吧！

Pig Out

像豬一樣地狼
吞虎嚥、大吃
大喝。

Charlene and Allen are talking on the phone. It sounds

like Charlene says she'll let the "pig" out tonight?!

Charlene 和 Allen 正在講電話。對話內容聽起來有點像是

Charlene 說她今天晚上要讓「豬」出來？！

 ## 對話 Dialogue

Charlene: Hi, baby. It's me, Char.

Allen: Yes, sweet heart, how's everything going?

Charlene: Not really good. So I phone you to let you know that I cannot go out with you tonight.

Allen: What's up? Are you okay?

Charlene: It's not me, it's Michelle. You know her, right? My best friend since my **childhood**.

Allen: Yes, I know.

Charlene: She just found out that her **fiancé cheated** on her this morning. And now she's in my place and **bawling**. Maybe we will pig out tonight. Michelle likes to **let off steam** by eating a lot.

Allen: Okay, I see. Take a good care of her. Call me after you finish eating, and I'll go and pick you up.

單字 Vocabulary

1. **childhood** [`tʃaɪldˌhʊd]
   n 童年、孩童時期

   → Except for her illness, she had had a fantastic childhood.
   除了體弱多病之外,她有一個很棒的童年。

2. **fiancé** [ˌfiənˈse] n 未婚夫

   → Kimmy's father regards her fiancé with approval.
   Kimmy 的父親對她的未婚夫非常的滿意。

3. **cheat** [tʃit] v 欺騙

   → He never cheated in exams.
   他考試從來都不作弊。

4. **bawl** [bɔl] v 放聲大哭;
   大吼大叫

   → Calm down, you know how he hates people who bawl all the time.
   冷靜一點,妳知道他有多討厭動不動就哭的人。

5. **let off steam** ph 宣洩情
   緒;發牢騷

   → I need a place to let off steam, or I'll go crazy.
   我需要一個地方來發洩一下情緒,要不然我就要瘋了。

6. **steam** [stim] n 情緒的緊
   張;精力;蒸汽

   → She picked the coffee cup up and blew off the steam.
   她拿起了咖啡杯並將熱氣吹走。

翻譯 Translation

Charlene: 嗨,寶貝。是我,Char。

Allen: 嗯,甜心,一切都還好嗎?

Charlene: 不太好。所以我打電話來告訴你今天晚上不能和你約會了。

Allen: 怎麼了?妳還好吧?

Charlene: 不是我啦,是 Michelle。你認識她,對吧?我小時候到現在最好的朋友。

Allen: 對啊,我知道。

Charlene: 她今天早上剛剛發現她的未婚夫劈腿。現在她正在我家大哭。也許我們今天晚上會出去大吃一頓。Michelle 喜歡用大吃大喝來發洩情緒。

Allen: OK，我知道了。好好照顧她。妳們吃完之後打電話給我，我去載妳們。

心情小日記 *Dear Diary*

January 31ˢᵗ

Dear Diary,

I went to pick up Charlene and her best friend Michelle tonight. They were in a buffet restaurant. Charlene said that she ate too much and could hardly move. And <u>Michelle vomited up in the lady's room for several times</u>, and she was still in the restroom when I arrived. After few minutes, Michelle came out and told us that <u>she's hungry</u> again, 'cause she already brought up all she eaten. Good thing Michelle felt much better after pigging out at the buffet. She said she even didn't remember that she had a fiancé.

1 月 31 日

親愛的日記，

我今天晚上去接 Charlene 和她最好的朋友 Michelle。她們是在一家吃到飽餐廳。Charlene 說她吃得太飽就快要不能動了。而 Michelle 則在女廁吐了好幾次，當我到的時候，她人還在洗手間裡。過了幾分鐘之後，Michelle 出來告訴我們她又餓了，因為她把吃下去的都吐出來了。幸好在瘋狂的大吃大喝之後，Michelle 感覺好多了。她說她甚至不記得她有過一個未婚夫。

還可以怎麼說 In Other Words

❶ She just found out that her fiancé cheated on her this morning.
她今天早上剛剛發現她的未婚夫劈腿。

- She caught her fiancé and the other woman were sleeping on her bed this morning.
  她抓到她的未婚夫和小三睡在她的床上。

- She perceived the truth that her fiancé was having an affair this morning.
  她今天早上得知她未婚夫有外遇的這個事實。

❷ Michelle vomited up in the lady's room for several times.
Michelle 在女廁吐了好幾次。

- Michelle made the round trip meal ticket in the restroom for many times.
  Michelle 在廁所裡製造食物回數票許多次。＝Michelle 在廁所裡吐了好多次。

- Michelle was throwing up in the lady's room for several times.
  Michelle 在洗手間裡吐了好幾回。

❸ She's hungry.
她餓了。

- She's starving.
  她快餓扁了。

- She's so hungry and probably could eat a hog.
  她快餓死了，大概可以吃下一頭豬。

 這句怎麼說？ How to Say That?

食量很大 → Eat like a horse

英釋 to eat a large amount of food; to be able to eat a lot

中釋 吃下大量的食物；能吃得很多。

A: She is very skinny, but she eats like a horse. （她很瘦，但卻跟馬一樣食量很大。）

B: Yes, and I bet she can eat a horse. （對啊，我猜她可以吃下一匹馬吧。）

 文化小盒子 Culture Box

　　"Pig out" 的英文解釋為 "to eat a lot; to make a pig of oneself"（吃太多的東西；把自己當作豬）。第二個解釋和中文裡的「豬上身」非常的類似。在中英文裡面，除了會用豬來形容吃得很多之外，還會用豬來形容愚蠢，例如「跟豬一樣笨」"stupid like a pig"。但事實上，根據研究顯示，豬的智商高過於人類最好的朋友狗，甚至是超過 3 歲的孩童，而且跟靈長類動物一樣在餵小豬喝奶時，豬媽媽會有類似哼歌的行為，與我們刻板印象中的豬是完全不同。我個人覺得之所以會醜化豬的形象，除了野豬會破壞農作物，及帶來很大的損傷之外，有可能是因為豬的食用價值遠遠大過於其成為寵物的價值，所以我們醜化豬，沒有感情的牽絆，在吃牠的時候也比較沒有罪惡感嘛！

阿倫碎碎念 Allen's Murmur

　　在 1995 年時有一部電影 *Babe–A little pig goes a long way*（中文名：我不笨，我有話要說），劇中的 Babe 是一頭可愛的小白豬，夢想著要成為一隻牧羊犬。在 2006 年時還被美國電影協會選為 AFI 百年百大勵志電影之一。因為劇中聰明又愛乾淨的 Babe 豬，完全地顛覆了豬在世人眼中的形象，但根據研究顯示，豬的智商為家畜之冠，而其也被證明是一種愛乾淨的動物。

　　在為可愛的小豬豬小小平反之後，我們就來談一談有關豬的英文俚語。跟 pig out 相似的說法還有一種 "make a pig of oneself"，也可以說是 "pig oneself"，用中文可以說是「豬上身」。而在英文裡的 "pig's ear" 指的可不是在吃麵的時候必備的滷味「豬耳朵」，在這裡，pig's ear 指的是啤酒，這是因為押韻的關係，而在英國特有的稱法。在美國跟豬耳朵有關的則是 "make a pig's ear"，指的是「將事情搞得一團亂」。而我在眾多有關 pig 的俚語當中，覺得最有趣的是 "pig in the middle"，猜猜看，是什麼意思呢？這個居然是中文裡所說的「夾心餅乾」，不過不是指可以吃的那一種，指的是在爭執的雙方之中，處在中間的人。這個讓我想到 Johnny 家的婆媳問題，Johnny always says that he's the pig in the middle of his wife and mom.（Johnny 總是說他是他老婆跟他老媽中間的夾心餅乾。）而如果要再說的可憐一點的話，可以將 pig 改成 piggy（小豬、豬仔），這樣是不是更能讓人感受到被夾在中間，那種委屈、可憐的樣子呢？

Love Handles

愛的把手，就
是指腰間的贅
肉，俗稱的
「游泳圈」。

Allen sees Johnny who just back from his vacation in front of the canteen.

While they are talking, Johnny asks Allen do not touch his "love handles."

Allen 在公司餐廳前看見剛休完假回來的 Johnny。當他們

在談話時，Johnny 要 Allen 不要亂摸他的「愛的韓兜魯」。

 對話 Dialogue

Allen: Hey, Johnny. How's the vacation?

Johnny: It's marvelous! Charlene and you should go there, oh maybe for your **honeymoon**. The sunshine, the beach, everything is beautiful, and the food is **superb**. Be sure to try the seafood there, trust me, you will not **regret**.

Allen: Yeh, I can see that from your fat **belly**. It's getting bigger than last time I saw it.

Johnny: Don't touch my love **handles**. That's for Laura only.

Allen: Okay. Johnny, seriously, how much weight did you gain recently?

Johnny: I dunno, maybe 10 pounds, I guess. Laura asks me to cut down on the big lunch.

Allen: Well, I **agree with** Laura, so you'll have salad only for lunch, right?

Johnny: Yes, I think so.

單字 Vocabulary

1. **honeymoon** [ˈhʌnɪˌmun] → Jessie's a honeymoon baby.
   n 蜜月
   Jessie 是個蜜月寶寶。（Jessie 是 Jessie 的父母在蜜月時懷上的孩子。）

2. **superb** [sʊˈpɝb] adj 一流 → She's a superb actress.
   的、極棒的
   她是一個一流的演員。

3. **regret** [rɪˈgrɛt] → We regret that not acting faster to sort things out.
   v 感到後悔
   我們感到遺憾因為沒能更快地將事情釐清。

4. **belly** [ˈbɛlɪ] → She is a professional belly dance teacher.
   n 腹部、肚子
   她是一個專業的肚皮舞老師。

5. **handle** [ˈhændl] → The handle is detachable from the box.
   n 把手
   箱子上的把手是可以取下的。

6. **agree with** → I see your point, but I'm afraid that I cannot agree with you.
   ph 同意、贊同
   我了解你的觀點，但我恐怕無法贊同你。

翻譯 Translation

Allen: 嗨，Johnny。假期好玩嗎？

Johnny: 棒極了！Charlene 和妳應該要去那裡，喔或許可以去度蜜月喔。陽光、沙灘，每個東西都漂亮極了，還有食物簡直是棒透了。一定要去嚐嚐那裡的海鮮，相信我，你一定不會後悔的。

Allen: 對，我從你大肚腩就看得出來了。跟我上一次見到它，它變大了許多。

Johnny: 別碰我「愛的把手」。這是 Laura 專屬的。

Allen: 好啦。Johnny，說真的，你最近到底胖了多少？

Johnny: 我不知道，大概 10 磅吧，我猜。Laura 叫我午餐要吃少一點。

Allen: 嗯，我同意 Laura 說的，所以你午餐要吃沙拉，對吧？

Johnny: 對，我想應該是吧。

心情小日記 Dear Diary

February 1st

Dear Diary,

Today, Johnny and I had our "smallest" lunches that we ever have since our babyhood. We both had a very tiny bowl of salad, and the worst thing was no dressing for the salad. Because he asked me to eat the same with him, or his determination might faltered. So I said yes to him, but I really didn't know he would have lunch in such a tiny portion. I swear that I'll never have lunch with Johnny again when he's on diet.

2月 1日

親愛的日記，

今天我和 Johnny 吃了自我們嬰兒期之後有史以來最少的午餐了。我們各吃了一碗非常小碗的沙拉，而且更糟糕的是不加沙拉醬。因為他要我跟他吃一樣的，要不然他的決心可能會動搖。所以我答應他了，但我真的不知道他午餐居然只吃那麼少。我發誓在他減肥的這段期間都不會再跟他一起吃午餐了。

:: 還可以怎麼說 In Other Words

❶ How's the vacation?
假期好玩嗎？

- Are you enjoying your holiday?
  你的假期過得愉快嗎？

- Did you have a perfect vacation as you planned?
  你有沒有過了一個跟你計畫中一樣完美的假期啊？

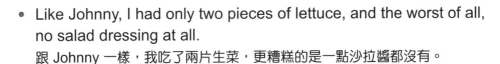

❷ We both had a very tiny bowl of salad, and the worst thing was no dressing for the salad.
我們各吃了一碗非常小碗的沙拉，而且更糟糕的是不加沙拉醬。

- Like Johnny, I had only two pieces of lettuce, and the worst of all, no salad dressing at all.
  跟 Johnny 一樣，我吃了兩片生菜，更糟糕的是一點沙拉醬都沒有。

- I felt like I ate nothing but air.
  我覺得什麼都沒吃到只吃了一堆空氣。

❸ I swear that I'll never have lunch with Johnny again when he's on diet.
我發誓在他減肥的這段期間都不會再跟他一起吃午餐了。

- I won't have lunch with Johnny any more before he's allowed to eat normally.
  在 Johnny 被允許可以正常的吃之前，我都不要跟他一起共進午餐了。

- Before Johnny gives up his diet plan, I'll try to avoid eating lunch

with him.

在 Johnny 放棄他的節食計畫之前，我會試著避開跟他一起吃中飯的。

 這句怎麼說？ *How to Say That?*

大肚腩 ➡ Potbelly

英釋 A protruding abdominal region

中釋 因為肥胖而造成突起的腹部區域

A: Hi, here's the seat for you, please have a seat. （嗨，這裡有個位子，請坐。）

B: No, thank you. I'm not pregnant, it's just my potbelly. （不用了，謝謝。我沒有懷孕，這只是我的「游泳圈」。）

文化小盒子 *Culture Box*

　　一定有許多人會好奇，腰間的那一圈贅肉為什麼要被稱做是 "love handles"「愛的韓兜魯」呢？如果有騎摩托車的男生應該會知道，在載心愛的女朋友的時候，是不是都會要女朋友緊緊地摟著你的腰，這樣的畫面一講出來，就讓我覺得很有愛，而腰間的那一圈肉肉是不是就很像是把手呢？再加上這有愛的畫面，被成為愛的把手是不是很貼切呢？好吧，阿兜仔其實沒這麼含蓄的，我聽過之所以被稱為 "love handles" 是因為腰間的肉是在「做愛做的事」時常會抓住的部位。而在英文中除了 "love handles" 之外，還可以說是 "bulging waistline"，或是 "potbelly" 等，但是相比之下 "love handles" 是不是好聽很多呢？

相信很多人都和 Allen 一樣有肥胖的煩惱。哈哈，要好好的維持身材可是需要極大的毅力及決心的，特別是我們這一種沈醉在幸福裡的人，這種幸福肥可是多少人羨慕不來的。

好的，不炫耀我個人成功的愛情了。這裡我想要跟大家談一談的是各式各樣的「肥胖」，沒錯，就是不同部位肥胖的說法。我們先從上面開始好了，臉很圓（胖），我們稱為 "chubby face"，有人常會問我那可不可以說是 "moon face" 呢？雖然 moon face 也是指臉部的圓胖，但是其造成的原因大多是因為藥物引起的，例如是長期服用類固醇所引起的副作用，所以是不能用來形容因為肥胖造成的圓臉。再來的話是 "flabby arms"，也就是俗稱的掰掰肉及蝴蝶袖，flabby 是不結實的意思，而手臂因為肌肉鬆弛，而在揮手掰掰的時候，感覺就像是一片寬大的袖子在揮舞。說實話，我個人覺得跟英文比起來，用中文罵人，毒舌多了。另外還有一種是專指女生的，叫做 "bra fat"，顧名思義就是穿胸罩時，有時候會因為太緊而造成有一截肥肉的突起。肚子的肥胖，除了 love handles 之外，還可以說是 "muffin top"（因為 muffin 的頂端會自然的膨起）或是 "spare tire"（備胎，跟中文裡的有游泳圈相似）。

最後就是千千萬萬女生最恨的，也是號稱史上最難減的部位，英文中叫做 "saddle bags"，中文呢？請恕我還沒學到，只能用描述的，這個部位就是指屁屁的兩側。如果有騎腳踏車或是重機的朋友就會知道「馬鞍袋」，就是橫跨兩側掛著的袋子，通常是掛在坐墊的後方，後輪的上面。用來指屁股兩側的肉像是自行車或是重型機車掛著兩個袋子一樣。好吧，我後悔了，用英文罵人也挺毒舌的！

255

Fecal Touch

帶衰運、掃把
星。事情都會
被搞砸。

After relieving himself, Allen now is talking to Bryan who's occupying the sink and washing his hands as if he just "touched feces."

在大解放之後，Allen 現在正在和佔據著洗手台洗手洗得像是

「摸到大便」的 Bryan 講話。

 對話 *Dialogue*

Allen: Hi, Bryan. And what are you doing now?

Bryan: Oh, Allen, it's you. I am just washing my hands.

Allen: But you have been washing your hands for ten minutes since I came in. For me, it's more like that you are trying to **peel** your hands.

Bryan: Have you ever heard of a story about our **CEO**?

Allen: You mean… he has the Midas touch?

Bryan: No, I mean he has the **fecal** touch. Everyone he touched would get **divorced** or breakup with girl or boy friend. Unfortunately, he **shook my hands** an hour ago.

Allen: That sounds **terrible**, and please don't touch me. How may I help you?

Bryan: Just bring me a brush.

單字 Vocabulary

1. **peel** [pil] Ⓥ 削去……的
皮，剝去……的殼；
替……剝／削……
→ Peel the potato and cut it in half.
削去馬鈴薯的皮，並將它切成兩半。

2. **CEO = chief execu-tive officer** 首席執行
官、執行長
→ He was soon advanced to the position of CEO.
他很快就被提升成為執行長。

3. **fecal** [`fikl]
[adj] 排泄物的；殘渣的
→ One of the ways that the parasite spreads is through the fecal matter.
經由糞便傳播是寄生蟲傳播的途徑之一。

4. **divorced** [də`vorst]
[adj] 離婚的
→ She is divorced, with a daughter and a son.
她離婚了，帶著一個女兒和一個兒子。

5. **shake hands**
[ph] 握手
→ Aren't you going to shake hands with me?
你難道打算不和我握手嗎？

6. **terrible** [`tɛrəbl]
[adj] 可怕的、嚇人的
→ It was a terrible blow to me.
對我來說這是一項可怕的打擊。

翻譯 Translation

Allen: 嗨，Bryan。你現在在做什麼？

Bryan: 喔，Allen，是你啊。我只是在洗手啊。

Allen: 但你從我進來到現在已經洗手洗了 10 分鐘了。在我看來，比較像
是你試著在把你手上的那層皮給剝掉。

Bryan: 你有沒有聽過執行長的故事？

Allen: 你是指……他有點石成金的能力嗎？

Bryan: 不是，我要說的是他的「帶賽」能力。他碰過的每一個人不是會離
婚，要不就是跟男/女朋友分手。

Allen: 聽起來真可怕，請不要碰我喔。那我可以幫上你什麼嗎？

Bryan: 幫我拿把刷子來。

心情小日記 Dear Diary

Feburary 7th

Dear Diary,

I asked Johnny about the CEO's fecal touch, and I got a full version of the story. It's just like a horror story. It is said that anyone who's in love and touched by our CEO, especially shaking hands with him, will gain the invincible power at work, but eventually break up with the one he/she loves. As a Chinese saying goes, "Unlucky in love, lucky at play." In this case, I'll say it's "Lucky at work and unlucky in love." I prefer not to get such luck because I will try my best to get the balance between my work and my love.

2月7日

親愛的日記，

我問了 Johnny 有關執行長的「帶賽」能力，我得到了一個完整版本的故事。就像是個恐怖故事一般。傳說中任何一個沉醉在愛河裡的人一旦被我們執行長碰到，特別是和他握手，就會得到工作上無敵的超能力，但是卻會與他/她所愛的人分手。就像是中國俗語中所說的「情場失意，賭場得意」。在這個情況，我會說是「職場得意，情場失意」。我寧可不要這樣的運氣。因為我會盡我所能在我的工作及我的愛情之間尋求一個平衡點。

還可以怎麼說 In Other Words

❶ Hi, Bryan. And what are you doing now?
嗨，Bryan。你現在在做什麼？

- Hey, mate! Are you doing okay?
  嘿，老兄！你還好吧？

- Hello, Bryan, how are you feeling today?
  哈囉，Bryan，你今天好嗎？

❷ It's just like a horror story.
就像是個恐怖故事一般。

- That is the creepiest story that I've ever heard.
  這是我所聽過最令人毛骨悚然的故事了。

- It sounds like the plot of the scary movie.
  聽起來像是恐怖電影中的情節。

❸ Unlucky in love, lucky at play.
情場失意，賭場得意。

- You cannot have the cake and eat it too. （英文中的說法）
  = You cannot have the fish and the bear's paw at the same time. （中文說法英譯）魚與熊掌不可兼得。

- You cannot make an omelet without breaking eggs.
  做蛋捲哪有不需要打蛋的。=有得必有失。

這句怎麼說? How to Say That?

飛來橫禍 → Sudden and unexpected disaster

英釋 Calamitous event, especially one occurring suddenly and unexpectedly and causing great loss of life, damage, or hardship.

中釋 不幸的、災難性的事件,特別是指出乎意料之外及突然發生的,會造成傷亡、損失或是困苦的情況。

A: Do you know that Jamie was hit by a flowerpot from the upstairs when he went home from the school? (你知道 Jamie 在從學校回家的路上被樓上掉下來的花盆給砸傷的事嗎?)

B: Yes, I know. What a sudden and unexpected disaster! I am going to pay him a visit, wanna go with me? (我知道。真是飛來橫禍!我打算要去探望他,要跟我一起去嗎?)

文化小盒子 Culture Box

　　"Fecal touch" 是由 "Midas touch"(點石成金)所衍生而來的一句新俚語。Midas touch 是用來形容某人的好運、好手氣,在做什麼事時都有如神助一般,必定成功,一般大多是指跟金錢相關的。而 fecal touch 則恰恰相反,是用來指只要是牽扯到某人的時候,這件事總是會失敗,或是被搞得一團亂,跟台語中的「帶賽」有異曲同工之妙。而如果以 bbs 鄉民的常用語來說的話,就是在討論政治議題時常會看到的「死亡之握」。

　　在使用 "Midas touch" 的時候要特別注意的是,Midas 是人名,所以 M 要大寫。"Fecal touch" 中的 fecal 是形容詞,意思為「糞便的」,其名詞為 feces 或寫作 faeces 跟一般口語中所說的 "shit" 相比較為正式的說法,常會在醫學檢驗報告中看到。

260

在英文當中，有許多常用的諺語是出自於希臘神話的故事情節當中，而 "Midas Touch" 也是其中之一。

在希臘神話故事中，Midas 是弗利吉亞（Phrygia）的國王，在還是嬰兒時期，就已被預示著將來會成為巨富。在他繼任成為國王之後，有一天他認出了被一群農民抓住的名為 Silenus 的 satyr（半人半羊的神/精靈，其地位類似於中國文化中的山神）是酒神 Dionysus 的老師，因此款待了這一個老 satyr 十天十夜，並將他送回酒神那。Dionysus 因此承諾給 Midas 一個願望，Midas 表示希望能有點石成金的本領，Dionysus 答應了，Midas 最後也因為他的貪婪而付出了一些代價。

然而在希臘神話中還有另一則與 Midas 有關的故事，相信大家都耳熟能詳，但卻不知道這個故事是與能點石成金的 Midas 有關，這就是驢耳朵的國王。這一個故事是在 Dionysus 收回 Midas 點石成金的能力之後發生的，洗心革面後的 Midas 不再貪戀財富，改為崇尚掌管鄉野及 satyrs 的牧神 Pan。有一天，太陽神 Apollo 和牧神 Pan 邀請 Midas 做他們音樂比賽的裁判。Midas 基於私心判 Pan 獲勝，Apollo 一氣之下將 Midas 的耳朵變成驢的耳朵，Midas 只好以頭巾遮掩，但他的理髮師卻挖了個洞，對著洞說出國王有對驢耳朵這一個秘密，在填平洞口之後，在這裡長出的蘆葦卻隨著風而洩漏了這一個秘密。因此後來有以 "King Midas' judge" 來形容外行人的評判，"King Midas' ears" 用來形容不管如何遮掩，都隱藏不了的膚淺，還有 "Midas' barber" 來指多嘴或是隱藏不了秘密的人。

John Doe

無名氏。

Allen meets Charlene at the gate of the company. Charlene is now

posturing in front of Allen to show how she likes the necklace.

Allen 和 Charlene 在公司門口碰面。Charlene 現在在

Allen 面前擺 pose，要讓他知道她有多喜歡這一條項鍊。

 對話 *Dialogue*

Allen: Char, you look **stunning** with that **necklace**.

Charlene: I know! And thank you, I really like this present. It must be very expensive. You shouldn't spend that much.

Allen: What?! I don't know what you are talking about?

Charlene: Come on, sweetie, I know you very well; and don't put on a show. Mr. John Doe!

Allen: John Who?

Charlene: Are you sure you are not the one who bought me this necklace? Isn't it a gift that you sent me for the **Valentine's Day**?

Allen: Nope. (Allen takes a gift box from the pocket of his **trousers**.) And here's the gift for you. I had planned to give you this after dinner with a **bunch** of red…

Charlene: Say no more about it. Don't **ruin** the surprise that you want to give me. Now please take off the necklace for me and put that gift box back in your pocket. I can't wait for the Valentine's Day dinner!

單字 Vocabulary

1. **stunning** [ˋstʌnɪŋ] adj
   【口】極漂亮的，絕色的
   → You look absolutely stunning tonight.
   妳今天晚上看起來漂亮極了。

2. **necklace** [ˋnɛklɪs] n 項鍊
   → My wife badgered me to buy a necklace for her.
   我的老婆纏著我要買一條項鍊給她。

3. **Valentine's Day** ph 情人節
   → The Chinese Valentine's Day is on the 7th day of July of the lunar calendar.
   中國情人節是在農曆的 7 月 7 日。

4. **trousers** [ˋtraʊzɚz] n 褲子、長褲
   → I was dressed in khaki trousers when I first met her.
   我第一次遇見她時，我穿著一件卡其色的褲子。

5. **bunch** [bʌntʃ] n 束；串
   → That indeed saved me a bunch of money.
   那確實省了我一大筆錢。

6. **ruin** [ˋrʊɪn] v 破壞、毀壞
   → You can't be with him, or he'll ruin your reputation.
   妳不能跟他在一起，要不然他會毀了妳的名聲的。

翻譯 Translation

Allen: Char，妳帶著那條項鍊看起來真是令人豔驚。

Charlene: 我知道！這都要謝謝你啊，我真的很喜歡這一個禮物。這一定很貴吧。你不應該花這麼多錢的。

Allen: 什麼？！我不知道你在說什麼？

Charlene: 拜託，親愛的，我非常了解你；別再裝了。無名氏先生！

Allen: 什麼先生？

Charlene: 你確定這一條項鍊不是你買來送我的？這不是你送我的情人節禮物嗎？

Allen: 不是。（Allen 從褲子的口袋中拿出一個禮物盒。）這個才是要給妳的禮物。我計畫要在晚餐後才要給妳這個，還有一大束的……

Charlene: 不要再說了。不要破壞你要給我的驚喜。現在請幫我將這一條項鍊拿下來，把禮物盒收回你的口袋。我等不及我們的情人節大餐了。

心情小日記 Dear Diary

February 14th

Dear Diary,

We finally knew who the John Doe is. Charlene's father called her at dinner time, and asked her if she likes that necklace. When Charlene told me this, I could feel my heart, which blocked my throat all night long, finally slide back into my chest. Actually, I was trying to find out who the secrete giver could be, but completely clueless about it. And I could probably tear my hair out of my head if Charlene didn't stop me at that time. Luckily Char's Dad called in no time and solved the mystery. And we had our first and the best Valentine's Day ever.

2月 14日

親愛的日記,

我們終於知道無名氏先生是誰了。Charlene 的爸爸在晚餐時間打電話給她,問她喜不喜歡那一條項鍊。當 Charlene 告訴我的時候,我可以感覺到我那一整晚堵在我喉嚨的心臟終於滑回我的胸腔。事實上,我一直試著要找出誰是那一個送禮物的神祕人,但一直都沒有線索。那時候,如果 Charlene 沒有阻止我的話,我有可能會把我的頭髮給扯掉。還好,Char 的爸爸沒過一會兒就打來了,解開了這個謎底。然後我們就度過了第一個也是最棒的情人節。

▦ 還可以怎麼說 In Other Words

❶ Don't put on a show.
別再裝了。

- **Stop pretending.**
  別裝蒜了。

- **As if you didn't know.**
  好像你不知情似的。

❷ Say no more about it.
不要再說了。

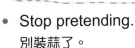

- **Don't tell me anymore.**
  別再跟我說了。

- **Don't rub it in.**
  不要再提了。

❸ I could feel my heart, which blocked my throat all night long, finally slide back into my chest.
我可以感覺到我那一整晚堵在我喉嚨的心臟終於滑回我的胸腔。

- My heart, which had been in my throat all night long, now fell back into place.
我一整個晚上都提心吊膽的，現在才放了下來，

- I was worried a full night and now finally can set my mind at rest.
我擔心了一整個晚上，現在終於可以放心了。

 這句怎麼說？ How to Say That?

匿名的；無名氏的 → Anonymous

英釋 having an unknown or unacknowledged name

中釋 身份不明或是不願意公開承認身份的。

A: Hi, new friend, would you like to introduce yourself?（嗨，新朋友，請介紹一下你自己。）

B: Hello, everyone. My name is Joe Gibson.（大家好，我的名字是 Joe Gibson。）

A: Erm, welcome to the Alcoholics Anonymous.（嗯，歡迎來到匿名戒酒會。）

文化小盒子 Culture Box

　　"John Doe" 的使用最早是出現在法律的相關領域，用以作為無名氏或是中文裡「張三李四」的代稱。"John Doe" 專指男性，而女性則會以 "Jane Doe" 來稱呼。最早的起源可以追溯至 15 世紀的英國，而一直到 19 世紀為

止，"John Doe" 都一直被專門的使用在有關土地所有權的訴訟上，代表的是原告（通常是被地主或是屋主趕走的承租人），而會以 "Richard Roe" 來代表被告（即地主或屋主）。英國國會在 1852 年時放寬了 "John Doe" 只能被使用在不動產所有權糾紛中的相關限制，因而約定俗成地被廣泛的應用在英國及美國的法律文件中。而以 John Doe 來表示匿名者是因為在 15 世紀的英國，John 是第二普遍的男子名（William 是第一名），而 Doe 根據有些學者的推測，應該是簡短易記，而且跟 Roe 押韻。也有人認為可能是與最早的訴訟案中的被告及原告的職業有關，因為 Doe 是鹿，Roe 是魚卵，有可能是獵人和漁夫，你覺得呢？

阿倫碎碎念 Allen's Murmur

在台灣，有名的「無名氏」除了常說的張三李四之外，還有好多位，例如信用卡填寫範例中的李大華，身分證範本上的陳筱玲，還有電視上的春嬌與志明以及總是車禍的小明。由此可知，在不同的文化之下，對於匿名者會有不同的代稱，而其代稱的方式無非就是從該文化中普遍的男女名字或是流行語中所衍生出來的。

現在再讓我們來回過頭討論一下 Doe 家族的成員。除了 John Doe 和 Jane Doe 之外，還有 Johnnie Doe 和 Janie Doe 分別代表著小男孩與小女孩，再更小的還有 Baby Doe。而在一些案例當中，特別是兇殺案或是兒童虐待案件中，會出現一些比較不同的名字，用以表示控方所感到的悲痛，例如是在密蘇里州堪薩斯市中的一宗謀殺案，控方便稱其中一名嬰兒受害者為 Precious Doe。而如果受害人數再多一點的話，除了有可能會以編號，例如 John Doe #1, John Doe #2…，或是會出現 James Doe 或是 Judy Doe。再更多時則會加入 Roe 家族，甚至是 Poe 家族。

Learn Smart! 039

B 咖日記：

Smart 俚語讓你英文 B 咖變 A 咖

Open Allen's Diary – The smart English slang to learn

作　　者　Chris H. Radford
封面構成　高鍾琪
內頁構成　菩薩蠻電腦排版有限公司

───────────────────────

發 行 人　周瑞德
企劃編輯　徐瑞璞
校　　對　陳欣慧、劉俞青
印　　製　世和印製企業有限公司
初　　版　2014 年 10 月
定　　價　新台幣 329 元
出　　版　倍斯特出版事業有限公司
電　　話　(02) 2351-2007
傳　　真　(02) 2351-0887
地　　址　100 台北市中正區福州街 1 號 10 樓之 2
E - m a i l　best.books.service@gmail.com

───────────────────────

港澳地區總經銷　泛華發行代理有限公司
地　　　　址　香港筲箕灣東旺道 3 號星島新聞集團大廈 3 樓
電　　　　話　(852) 2798-2323
傳　　　　真　(852) 2796-5471

國家圖書館出版品預行編目(CIP)資料

B 咖日記：Smart 俚語讓你英文 B 咖變 A 咖 /
Chris H. Radford 著. -- 初版. -- 臺北市：倍斯特,
2014.10
　　面；　公分
　ISBN 978-986-90883-2-9(平裝)

　1. 英語 2.俚語

805.123　　　　　　　　　　103018609

Simply Learning, Simply Best!

Simply Learning, Simply Best!